Andromeda 2

ANDROMEDA is a showcase for original science fiction
never previously published in any form. As Britain's premier
anthology series it presents here ten of the very finest stories,
both from well-known authors and up-and-coming newcomers,
that in their different ways reflect some of the directions
in which modern science fiction is going.
Peter Weston brings to bear the knowledge and discrimination
gained during more than 20 years as a science fiction
enthusiast. From 1963–74 his critical magazine *Speculation*
circulated internationally and was nominated five times for
the coveted Hugo Award. Now he lectures widely and
contributes regularly to various publications both within and
outside the SF field.

Also edited by Peter Weston

ANDROMEDA I

Edited by Peter Weston

Andromeda 2

An original SF anthology

London
DENNIS DOBSON

First published in Great Britain 1977
by Futura Publications Ltd
This edition first published in Great Britain 1977
by Dobson Books Ltd., 80 Kensington Church Street, London W8 4BZ

Printed in Great Britain by
Whitstable Litho Ltd., Whitstable, Kent
ISBN 0 234 72057 3

CONTENTS

INTRODUCTION

PETER WESTON

When I was very young I remember patiently calling into a newspaper shop every morning on the way to school for about three weeks. Finally my perseverance was rewarded, by publication of Arthur C. Clarke's THE SANDS OF MARS. It was almost the only science fiction title to appear that month, and you can imagine how thrilled and excited I was to bear off that slim volume triumphantly in my satchel!

I don't suppose I did very well at school that day.

When SF was scarce we aficionados treasured each precious find. Some of us became well-known faces at myriad second-hand bookshops in London, Birmingham and Leeds; others formed little circles whose main purpose was to allow members to read each others' acquisitions – and woe betide the one who should thoughtlessly bend back a cover or crease a spine.

Those were the great days for readers of science fiction, and oddly enough they appear to have been the Golden Age for writers too. Most of the SF titles on any current bookshop shelf were first written when science fiction was a sort of pariah in the world of letters; published in some obscure magazine which paid the author a mere pittance – if they paid at all.

Incredibly Isaac Asimov earned less than $8000 for his first *eleven* years of writing – during which time he produced his Robot stories, 'Nightfall', and the entire FOUNDATION series. Now a reasonably well-known SF author can earn more than that from one moderately successful book!

So when I look around at our field today, and at our fat and fêted practitioners, I sometimes wish they were once again starving in their garrets!

That's hardly a statement calculated to endear me to my

7

auctorial friends but it does point to a grain of truth, I believe. For science fiction has always been at its best during periods of unpopularity; standards have slipped at time of boom.

There's nothing any more mysterious in this than the Laws of Supply and Demand. The more publishers who enter a field, the greater the number of stories required, and average standards of quality are sure to drop.

Horace Gold, esteemed editor of *Galaxy* magazine for nearly twenty years made this comment after the conclusion of the last science fiction bonanza, back in 1959:

'Borderline stories which ordinarily would have been sent back for tuning-up and polishing had to be bought as they were because somebody else would have bought them without change. Routine ideas and treatments had to be "good enough" because magazines were buying wordage with which to fill pages and writers were harried into turning out material that was bought sight unseen. And new authors sold quickly, too quickly to learn anything but bad writing habits and were thus deprived of editorial guidance that would have taken them through their necessary apprenticeship.

And the bad drove out the good. Conscientious writers were demoralised into leaving the field.'

In my opinion the mid-seventies have seen a repetition of some of the mistakes of two decades before. Purely through its enormous popularity science fiction is being exploited as never before.

Let's think about this a little more carefully. There might perhaps be a discrepancy here, for it could be argued that some of the best SF stories ever produced have been written in the last few years. And I would go along with that conclusion.

What I am talking about is the hypothetical *average* level of quality in our field. For every book like THE DISPOSSESSED which I don't think could possibly have been written in the 1950's, there are ten, twenty or a hundred titles which are little if any better than the 'bug-eyed monster' nightmares which gave science fiction such a bad name in past decades.

All this has a direct bearing on the ANDROMEDA collections. For here is a genuine effort to transcend those impersonal market forces, a volume that sincerely sets out to bring you the best of current science fiction. Not just the best manuscripts which happen to be floating around in any particular month, or the best we can afford, but an idealistic sort of attempt to obtain the top work the field has to offer.

There are some practical difficulties of course, there always are. But ANDROMEDA is not bound to any arbitrary schedule, does not appear every month – or every six months, irrespective of quality. If sufficient material is not available on deadline day then the book waits that little longer. It is not the easiest policy to pursue for editor or for publisher, but we are convinced that in the long-term you, the reader, will come to recognise a good deal when you see it.

Or so I sincerely hope.

This time ANDROMEDA has a somewhat different flavour than before. The first book marked its debut with tales mostly by long-established writers; and already some of these stories have been selected for various 'Best of 1976' anthologies. This time we have no less than four 'first-time' stories by out-and-out newcomers. But each of them is completely professional, fully mature and in their different ways a pointer to the high peaks of achievement which protrude here and there through the plateaux of mediocrity.

Five of our other contributors have already made their names, or are already establishing their mark, leaving only the last item in the book, a true blockbuster, by Richard E. Geis – a man who claims never before to have written science fiction but paradoxically has managed to win more Hugo Awards than anyone else in the business.

Peter Weston, 1976

KING, DRAGON

BY TOM ALLEN

*Kings and dragons are classic elements of a fantasy tale, and so
who better than 'Tom Allen' to introduce both. For Allen, in
another incarnation, is well-known as the man who holds audiences
spell-bound while explaining the real meaning of THE LORD
OF THE RINGS; who discusses 'Beowulf' (with quotations
from the original Anglo-Saxon); and who writes some of the
best critical articles around.*

*Yet here we have a story which is very definitely science
fiction and no argument. A little reminiscent of Jack Vance,
perhaps, and that is surely praise enough. Traces of a dry sense
of humour and other nice touches. And 'King, Dragon' is Allen's
very first story. I look forward with relish to more from this
man in later volumes.*

The man ran down the long slope of Shunner Moor, head rolling, shoulders sagging with exhaustion, but never slowing,
never checking even for the moss-grown boulders that turned
under his feet. Far behind him – but not far enough– an olive-
coloured speck barrelled down the mountainside, half-running,
half-flying.

With a last effort the runner flung himself over the sharp lip
of Striding Edge. For a moment his eyes dazzled as he stared
down into its deep rift-valley: it seemed an age since he had
seen anything but the ground before his feet. Then he picked
out the shining snake of Oughtershaw Gill, twisting along
lazily a thousand feet below.

'It's too far,' he thought despairingly, 'I'll never make it. I'll
be half-way down when it reaches the top here, and then . . .
I'll dig down into the scree, that's what I'll do, I'll let the stone

slide over me, it's loose stuff and I'll be able to breathe till it's gone . . .'

No. That was his legs talking, not his brain. He knew his pursuer could sniff him out in a moment, under stone a metre thick. He had to get to the water in the valley. Deliberately, he turned and walked back the few paces to the rim, staring up the long swell that rose to Shunner Peak, searching for the shape he knew was there. A coldly calculating part of his mind whispered to him that only panic would loosen his muscles now. He saw it, he focused.

Then he was away, plunging down the ancient scars in the mountainside like a frost-loosened boulder, digging in his heels and sliding where the gravel was loose, leaping in long bounds where it turned again to broken slate. All the time in his mind was a picture of the terrible claws he had stepped round so carefully, a crawling in his back as he thought of the enormous weight landing on him from behind, scraping him down the rock like a bug smeared on a wall. For an instant his hands rose to the skin bag slung round his neck, as if to rip it off and throw it away. But it wouldn't give up now, he knew. And even at that moment, he thought of her face when the king's men came to take her away.

The water splashed under his feet, and still there was no bellow behind him. 'Upstream or down? No odds,' he thought, and turned up, splashing through the thigh-deep, swirling current. 'The moment its head comes over the edge,' he told himself, 'I'll drop and get between two stones. Maybe it'll miss me.' But the water was crystal-clear, straight from the mountains.

Round a bend and he was suddenly swimming. The stream had formed a deep pot. On the other side of it was a waterfall, springing down eight feet from one of the many clefts in the valley's shattered floor. Half-remembering the fairy-stories of boyhood he stroked clumsily across to the foot of the fall, paused to catch his breath, and then dived. For a few seconds the crashing torrent beat on his back, forcing him down, while he swam with all his strength. Then he was through. His head broke surface behind the fall. As he had hoped, there was a water-worn hollow in front of him; more than a hollow, a little cave. He got his knee over the edge and scrambled up into the darkness. As he did so there was a great roar and grinding of stone from the hillside behind him, a booming of immense wings. The dragon had come.

The man huddled in the cave, clutching his skin bag, watching the flickering curtain of water. Would it guess where he was? Was there a vent somewhere that would let his smell leak out? He imagined the great blunt head thrusting suddenly through to snatch him, or the armoured tail threshing the rock-face till it broke and sealed him in. 'No,' he thought, 'it wouldn't do that. It wants its cup back.'

After a while he heard the slow padding of enormous feet, pausing every now and then while stones shifted. A deep bass rumble filtered through the noise of the fall. 'Most provoking,' it said. 'Most provoking. Fellow could be anywhere.'

The sound passed. The man stayed unmoving. Suddenly the earth seemed to shake in a rhythmic pounding. The dragon was running down the streamside, gathering speed as it flailed its wings. Just by the waterfall it took off with a crack of beaten air, coasting away downslope towards Cotterdale and Stor Hall.

'He's gone,' the man said aloud. 'Old bastard.'

'We don't like him either,' whispered a dry voice behind him.

The man was too cold and stiff to start, but he turned round and backed away as quickly as he could. He could see nothing in the darkness, except maybe just a hint of reflection from the flashing water – a glint as of something hard and scaly.

'What are you?' he said.

' "Who are you?" would be politer,' said the voice. 'We just live here. We're the indigenous autochthones, you might say. Why was old Starkhort chasing you?'

The man pulled open the lashings of his bag, and held up the cup. There was an attentive silence.

'Yes. The wide-mouthed gold one set with balas-rubies. Some would have said it was of cruder workmanship than the engraved silver ones from the Settlement time. But for weight avoirdupois – yes, we can understand his annoyance.'

'What? You know everything in his treasure? Have you been in his den?'

13

'Oh!' said the voice, 'we get around. Now what are you going to do?'

The man hesitated. He'd never heard of creatures like these before. But they hadn't given him away. Certainly he needed help.

'I suppose he – Starkhort – will have headed for Stor Hall, for revenge. While he's there I'll break out, go up the gill to Thrang Rakes, and then over to Gunnerside Tarn. Then I'll go down to Gunnderdale. I'm from the Brighthall, you see.'

'We know,' said the voice. 'We can smell it. We wondered, if you're from the Brighthall, why you ran this way.'

'I thought if the dragon woke before the scent was cold, it would trail me to Stor Hall, not – not home.'

'Ah.' The voice seemed very slightly amused. 'You may find he's not so easily deceived. Forgive our pessimism, but "forewarned is forearmed", as you people say. Still, you should get to the Brighthall all right, on the path you propose. There's a cave on the north slope of Gunnerside Tarn. You could pass the night there if you liked. Don't light a fire, though.'

'Will some of you be there?'

'Probably. But we'll pass the word.'

The man shuffled slightly, unsure of the words for departure. 'Well, I'll be seeing you.'

Again there was a tendril of amusement. 'We doubt it. But the converse is probably true. We shall be seeing *you*. After all, we have an interest in you now.'

As soon as he came over Brockhole Bank the man knew his plan was ruined. A mile away in the bottom lay the Brighthall Garth. But from where he stood he could see the swathe of the dragon. A gap had been trampled through the palisade, not done cleanly, as if by axes, but with spiked posts still sticking up here and there, leaning sideways or snapped off short. For a moment he could imagine the claws ripping out posts, the head nosing through, the great body turning furiously round and round like a dog looking for fleas.

On the inner side of the garth the flimsy wattle huts had simply been laid flat by the sweeps of a gigantic tail. At the centre of the devastation was a long, blackened scar, with thin clouds of wood-ash lifting from it in the fitful wind. Out of the cinders rose a brickwork gable, the hall's hearth-end. It seemed to sway as he watched, and would plainly come down in the first gale.

'That's strange,' he thought. 'Dragons using fire ? But they're only animals!'

The real question was whether they would connect him with what had happened. His absence might not have been noticed. Of course he couldn't do what he had meant to with the cup, so the sensible thing would be to throw it away. But he knew he couldn't do that. If he could reach his own hut unobserved he would bury it under the floor, and wait for a better day. He lived on the far side of the garth, where things seemed untouched, and there was no one in the fields between. He could see a milling confusion around the flattened houses. Obviously everybody was building shelters. If he was still alive, King Kuno would be re-asserting his power.

He slipped away, keeping behind hedges and windbreaks and dry-stone walls, till he could creep up on the garth from behind the midden. No one would linger there, and there was a place where lazily-thrown rubbish had piled several feet up the side of the stockade. He jumped and rolled over, careless of splinters and stink. He was used to both.

His own hut was nearest to the midden, an accurate reflection of his social standing. He ran to it, seeing no one, stepped round the back wall and darted towards his doorway. As he came round the last corner hands grasped him.

Shock made him jerk for a moment, but then he stood passively. The hands shook him warningly and let go.

'What's this ?' growled one of his captors. He didn't wait for an answer, but pulled the bag from the dragon-thief's neck. He showed the cup silently to his mate: both thick-set burly men, dressed in stout wool, with iron-plated leather tunics – king's guards.

The thief considered running for a moment, but stood still. He knew one of the guards, Ansgar. They had been boys together, till Ansgar started on his military career. Two long iron-shod spears rested against the hut wall, and he knew Ansgar could hit an ox in the eye at thirty paces. He enjoyed doing it, as well.

'Right.' The elder guard pushed the cup back in the bag, not even trying to lever out one of the rubies and hide it. That more than anything proved it was no good arguing. The bag was thrust back into the thief's arms. He grabbed it hastily, and found himself sprawling on the ground in the same moment.

The guard rubbed his knuckles and jerked his chin at the burnt scar where the Brighthall had been. 'You did that. Trouble-stirrer, pig's get! Why couldn't you leave it alone!'

Half an hour later he was pushed forward towards the king. Several of the guards had shared their sergeant's opinion, so the thief was dizzily detached from his surroundings, seeing the world through one eye only. But he recognised his master, King Kuno, still unharmed, still enthroned on his high-seat, though they had set it up incongruously under a canopy made of hut-walls and skins. All around stood councillors and guards. Many of the commoners had stopped work, unrebuked, to watch.

The king held up the cup. 'See, all of you. This was the cause of the dragon's feud. It did not come unprovoked.' He had a high-pitched effeminate voice, which much belied his nature, if the stories were true. The man had heard women giggling and exclaiming, half in horror, half pleasure. The noise had sent him on his expedition – that, and the coyly eager expression on his wife's face.

'All right, you. You are Thorald, king's cowman. Why did a cowman turn dragonthief and bring all this upon us? What were you going to do with the cup? Drink your curds out of it?'

Nobody laughed more than politely. Thorald spoke up, resigned. 'King, I meant to give it to you.' There was a startled buzz. Even the king looked alarmed.

'Give it to me? And what was the cause of this – this loyalty?'

'I thought – if I gave you the cup, you might give her back. My wife, Inge. Or you might not take her.'

A councillor whispered in the king's ear. His puzzlement

cleared. 'Oh, *her*.' He smirked. 'You're a bit late there, I'm afraid. I had her yesterday. And the day before. She seemed quite happy about it. Had every reason to be, I guess.'

A familiar voice echoed him from the ruck of women behind the guards. '*Every* reason, king of men', it cooed.

'So. Your plan was foolish in all ways. *You* laid waste this town. *You* burnt my hall.' The king's voice rose to a squeak. 'But we know what to do with you.'

The cowman waited dumbly. Behind the king, in the dark window of one of the huts that still stood, he could see, he thought, a flicker, something glinting. Eyes ? The king went on.

'You see, when the dragon came, and all my noble guards ran away—'

'Catapults weren't manned,' said a sullen anonymous voice. 'You cut down on defence, you got to expect—'

The king turned round and the voice stopped. 'When my noble guards ran away, as I said, and my wise councillors scuttled round like a pack of girls offering advice a two-year-old would have thought foolish, and when I was obliged to seek in consequence a place of vantage: then, as it happened, one of my noble councillors stayed behind, and, I believe, had some speech with the dragon. Go on, Kettle!' He pointed to a councillor who sat on a stool, his splinted leg sticking out before him. The councillor began to speak, over the buzz of interested comment. 'So they *can* talk . . . I'd heard it said . . . they're still only animals, really.'

'When the dragon burst the hall-frame I was caught under a post. It saw me, and pulled the post off. Then it told me to crawl out of the way and watch and listen. After a bit it asked me for a light. I gave it my tinderbox. I had to—' he added quickly. 'It could have found a brand somewhere for itself.'

'They have little arms that grow from the sides, above the fore-claws. It was clumsy, but it knew what to do. It piled up timbers and started a blaze at the windward end. Then it spoke to me while the hall burnt down.

'It said it had been robbed, and demanded res – restitution, I think it said. I didn't know a lot of the words it kept using.

17

Anyway, it said this restitution didn't mean what it had done already. That was just to show us. It wanted its cup back, and it demanded the cup's weight in gold as an extra. If it doesn't get those it will come back and kill us all.

'But it said restitution really meant it had had bad feelings. And we could only pay for those by giving it good feelings. Now what would give it good feelings most, it said, was the man who had robbed it, alive.'

He stopped. The king nodded, sombrely. 'So that's what we'll do, cowman. A party will take you to within sight of Great Shunner Fell, and leave you, staked, for the dragon. All I hope is that you won't give it a taste for us.' He clapped his hands to show the session was over.

Then, of course, Thorald screamed and twisted and fought the guards till they knocked him down. But even while they were kicking him he thought he saw, through the feet, little scurrying movements in the shadows. The word was getting round.

He spat on his rag, and rubbed again at an obstinate patch of tarnish. He didn't know what he was polishing. The dragon had piles of stuff that came from old times and seemed to have no purpose. A lot of it was made of some stone you could see through, called glass. He had vaguely heard of it but had snapped one piece before he realised how brittle it was. Starkhort had fizzed with rage for a while, but then calmed down, muttering about savages and what could you expect.

Starkhort's head lay about six feet from Thorald's stool, where the light and wind came in at the entrance to the long shaft in the hillside that was the dragon's den. Once upon a time, Thorald thought, the closeness would have driven him mad. Now he was used to it. He even slept at nights. The dragon didn't sleep, of course, only about every twenty days when his belly was full. Thorald had guessed that years before, from the disappearance of oxen and the regular periods of inactivity. It had still been a bold step to test his guess. Bold and fruitless.

He had asked the dragon, shortly after he realised that it

didn't mean to eat him straight away, what would happen when it next slept. It had drawn back its lips in a kind of smirk. 'We shall have to see about that,' it had said. 'You polish away diligently, and who knows? I might find you indispensable. We may end with quite a friendly relationship, you and I.'

He didn't believe it. It talked to itself much of the time, and he had heard it reminiscing gluttonously about the taste of manflesh. He had about twelve days left, he reckoned. After that he would make a run for it: not for home, but for the Boggart's Holes in the hillside. A straight drop to an unknown depth. At the bottom his bones might lie ungnawed.

The dragon spoke, not troubling to lift its head from the bone-strewn floor. 'Thief, I can see from the way you polish that you have no eye for beauty. Why did you steal my cup?' It had not asked the question before.

He pondered for a moment, thinking what was best for him, or at least worst for others. 'I stole it for the king,' he said.

'The king *sent* you?'

'No. He didn't send me, but I stole it to please him. I hoped he would let me off a – punishment.'

The head lifted, suspicious. 'The punishments of kings must be heavy, to drive men like you into dragons' dens!'

'Heavy is the wrath of kings,' said Thorald sententiously, pretending to agree.

The tail slammed against the cave wall, and Starkhort half-rose, snarling. Thorald stared at it. Slowly the dragon fell back.

'King,' it said, 'that's a new word to me. Of course I haven't spoken to men since the old days. Tell me now, is "king" an elective office?'

'I don't know what you mean.' Thorald quite often didn't know the words the dragon used, and had learnt it was no good guessing at them.

'Ah. Never mind. You used to have them once. Set great store by them, I believe. When I was a dragonet – Why! Men even used to try and catch us, to teach us all about elections and planetary government and – what was it? – power sharing. They were the off-planet ones, of course, who dug these holes. Now they've stopped coming.

'Let's get back to business. What can kings do that makes them so frightening?'

Thorald pondered again. On the one hand he would like to give the dragon some ideas to vex King Kuno. On the other, its handiest human subject was himself. 'Well,' he temporised, 'you know about fires?'

'Of course, of course.' The dragon jerked to its feet again, swaying with excitement. 'I'm a pyromaniac, actually. Fire is the best of the things you brought us. But if you burn someone it spoils the taste. And it is *very* final, no stimulus at all to future respect.'

'Not if you burn them all up, it's true. But if you light a fire, you see, and then put metal in it – well, fire eats up wood, somehow, but metal seems to hold it. So you get the metal very hot, and then put it on a person. It's called branding. It leaves a mark.'

'Have you got a mark like that?' The dragon pushed its head almost to Thorald's chest. He peeled a rag, silently, off his shoulder. The king's KK stood out, an old but clear scar. The dragon peered at it, enormous slit eye only inches away.

It whisked round and started to rummage among its possessions. 'Oil – flint – steel – what am I going to use for a bland? Or was it brand he said? Heavy is the wrath of kings, eh? I'll show them. And there's some of my own sprats would be the better for a little lesson. One thing about these men, indigenous they aren't, but technologically innovative, now . . .'

Still muttering, it dragged its length out of the shaft entrance. Thorald watched it clumsily running down the slope. 'Four legs, two hands, two wings,' he thought. 'Most of its head must be busy controlling all those. A wonder it's got enough brains left to talk!'

'You did that very neatly,' said a familiar voice behind him. 'Jealousy, curiosity, sadism, injured pride: we aren't surprised he's so stirred up. We'll be glad if we can do anything like as well.'

Thorald peered into the shadows of the cave-roof, but saw nothing except a deeper blackness. 'What do you mean? What are you trying to do?'

'Oh, work on his counterparts, you know. Kings are nearly as curious about dragons as dragons are about kings. And they're much more greedy. Of course they're more frightened as well. Still, perfect greed casteth out fear, as your wise men say. And if the old fellow commits a few good solid outrages, even the kings will have to act.'

Thorald watched as a light plume of smoke began to rise from Mossdale Head.

'We didn't like his remark about sprats, though,' said the voice.

The dragon did not return for some days. Several times Thorald thought to make a bolt for it, but each time a feather of smoke or a distant shape on the fell-side showed him that Starkhort was not all that far away. When it did come back, late one evening, he cursed his own timidity. The dragon seemed pleased and affable, like King Kuno after a long and active night. It also seemed tired – a bad sign.

It crawled in and eyed Thorald with little interest. 'Still here? Very wise, very wise. Men and dragons ought to trust each other, that's what they used to say.'

It began to play mumblety-peg, left hand against right, with a knife it produced from somewhere. After a bit Thorald realised the knife was a pikehead, of the sort the men of Eller Garth used. 'They don't have kings,' he thought. Should he mention it? The metal was bent and discoloured by heat.

The rhythmic click-click-scrabble of pikehead hitting floor and dragon reaching after it sent Thorald nodding off to sleep. As his eyelids fell he could hear the dragon muttering.

'Primitive social structure,' it said. 'Like circumstances produce like results. Or is it cultural diffusion, I wonder?'

Thorald fell into an uneasy dream in which dragons on thrones sent kings to be branded, and cowmen lurked in caves polishing their women. He walked along a line of stockade posts and said, 'That one's getting too big, I'll have him for breakfast.' A whispery voice was talking to him . . .

There was a crack and a roar. Thorald sat up violently from his pile of rags, hitting his head on the table he slept under. He saw the dragon's eyes open too, and realised through his sleep that it had been silent for hours. 'It's morning,' he thought. 'I've slept the night through. It's started to sleep as well. I'll never make Boggart's Holes now. What was that noise? What *is* that noise?'

He and the dragon stared together at the wooden beam that framed the inner lintel of the cave. A black, diamond-shaped iron bolt had appeared in it, on a thick shaft with three wooden vanes. It had driven right through to the back of the beam. A catapult bolt! There was a roar outside, a bellow of horns.

Thorald stuck his head out of the entrance. A hundred yards below stood a line of men, metal glinting, pikes clumped. Over their heads waved banners: the Fighting Man for Woodhall, Gold Dragon for Stor Hall, red square for Eller Garth. The blue gridiron of the Brighthall stood slightly circumspectly to the rear. In gaps in the pike-wall stood the catapulteers. Gold circlets marked the kings, crowded together among their picked heroes at the centre of the line. 'It's an army!' he thought in consternation.

A redoubled roar from the men told him the dragon's head had appeared behind him. It seemed to whine deep down in its throat, and then scrape enormously at the floor. Thorald had just enough sense to dive into a corner as the dragon surged out, swiping at him with one claw as it went. Its scales rasped on the sides of the shaft. There was a simultaneous crash from the catapults, and a bellow of rage and pain from Starkhort.

Thorald got to his feet to watch it bounding downslope towards the pikes and the caltrops scattered in front of them. It reached flying speed just short of the line, soared into the air, and came down with a great snapping of wood and bone.

'What bad management!', said the voice. 'If they'd been thirty yards closer he wouldn't have been off the ground by the time he reached the caltrops. Then he'd have had sore feet! Or he might have stopped and given the catapults time for another volley. Still, why philosophise? If we were you, we'd collect a few of the choicer items and leave. This looks like a good clean fight with no survivors.'

'The voice was right again,' thought Thorald as he staggered out a few minutes later, sack on shoulder. The dragon had swept away the line of kings' carls in the centre, and the banners were down. But the gallant yeomen of Eller Garth were still forming a square of pikes, with two catapults in its centre, manned and shooting as the drilled ranks opened and closed order. The dragon seemed to be on fire, as well as abristle with bolts. Pitch arrows clustered thickly around its eyes and dorsal crest. As he watched, a halberdier rose from the pile of dead heroes and stalked up on it from behind, raising his six-foot axe for an armour-piercing blow to the tail.

'Strike hard, strike home,' thought Thorald, making off.

He came up to the Brighthall Garth with his arms aching from the weight of the sack. A corporal's guard of six men was on the gate: men too unreliable, or lucky, to be taken against the dragon. They stared at Thorald with uncertain awe.

'King Kuno's dead,' he said shortly. 'And all the other kings. And the dragon.' He let the sack drop open. 'This is mine.'

'Who says it's yours?' said the corporal. He was Thorald's acquaintance, Ansgar.

'I do. Do you know how I escaped from the dragon? Do you know how I came to be alive when all the rest are dead?' They didn't need to shake their heads, but eyed each other. 'What does a wise man do when he doesn't understand? He knuckles under. Isn't that right? Here—' he threw a bracelet to Ansgar, a silver cup to another guard, jewels and glinting coins to the rest. 'I shall deal my gold better than Kuno. This isn't all. But only I know where the rest is. Follow me.'

He shouldered his sack and marched through the huts, the sentries trailing behind, expostulating with each other in whispers. A crowd started to gather and follow, their voices babbling excitedly: 'He's back . . . it's a ghost . . . he killed the dragon.'

Most of the councillors were sitting round the long table in the makeshift hall, finishing an extremely prolonged breakfast. Thorald strode past them, the soldiers he had bribed closing up automatically behind him. They had had time to weigh up the situation.

One of Kuno's innumerable bastards sat in the high-seat.

He rose as Thorald came up and began to shout 'Guards . . .'

Thorald clicked his fingers. 'Ansgar, old friend . . .'

A spear sprouted from between the bastard's eyes. Thorald pushed the tottering body sideways and sat down in the high-seat. He spilled his sack's contents on to the floor.

'Now listen to this, everybody. I shall only say it once. Kuno is dead. All the kings are dead. The dragon is dead. I don't want to hear any more talk about them. We shall now have a new order, returning to the spirit of the men of old times who settled this planet.' The word raised a buzz.

'There are no kings now. I shall be the Elective Officer. There is no dragon either, but I shall have certain – advisors.' He lifted his head to stare into the dark behind the hall's smokehole. The crowd buzzed again: 'the voices . . . he's in with *them* . . . little scaly things, my son *saw* one.'

'I lived many days with the dragon, I learned its secrets, I know where its wealth now lies. Without me it would not be dead. I can punish traitors, can repay loyalty.' He stopped and looked round.

A councillor stepped forward and shouted 'Long live Elective Officer Thorald!' Thorald threw him a ring as the rest joined in and the guards clashed their shields. The crowd, relieved to see a decision, cheered and waved.

A woman broke from the circle and ran to throw herself at his feet, crying, 'My husband!' The shouting stopped. Thorald patted her blonde hair absently.

'You have reason to greet me now, Inge dear. But not *every* reason, as I recall.'

He crooked a finger at Ansgar. 'Take Inge out and impale her.'

'Impale, king – er – elective officer, sir ?'

'Mount her on a stick. One of the palisade logs will do, if it's sharp enough. I don't mind which way round you put her.'

They tore her away, screaming. Thorald watched her through the door and then turned to the councillors. 'Now, what I think we need first is a list of names and duties . . .'

Elective Officer Thorald lay alone in the dark. There had been several volunteers to take Inge's place, but he thought that had better wait till the situation was clearer. Besides, as so recent a widower he ought to show a little respect.

There was a faint grating noise somewhere up in the beams. 'They were getting careless,' he thought. 'Would it be possible to catch one? Or advisable? Maybe they were getting bigger.' He had his suspicions, anyway, about what they were.

The voice spoke. It sounded a little different from the previous one – or ones. A bit deeper perhaps. 'Starkhort's dead now,' it said. 'His heart's still beating, but the brain's gone. He won't recover. This changes matters, now. I thought you ought to know.'

Thorald started to speak, then stopped. 'Don't you mean, "*we* thought you ought to know"? I never heard you say "I" before.'

'That's one of the ways the situation has changed, you see. Just as long as Starkhort was alive we were all agreed about one thing, and that was the most important one. Now he isn't – well, we're of different minds, or we very soon will be. That's the way things are with us, you see.'

Thorald considered that slowly. 'Are you – the one I'm speaking to – are you one of the ones I spoke to before. Because if you are, and there's some sort of – contest coming, then I owe you something and would want to give you my support rather than someone else. I don't know what my support is worth. But I think I ought to pay.'

'Right,' said the voice. 'The way we do things means that your support isn't worth anything at all, but we do agree on the last thing. We think you ought to pay.'

The voice seemed to be getting nearer. Thorald sat up. He thought about calling for a light. But how long would it take to come? The voice went on.

'We've got rid of the kings for you, you see, and you helped us to get rid of the dragon. That's fine. But you taught the dragon to *brand*, as well. We heard you. That wasn't necessary.'

'Yes it was,' Thorald replied. His weight was on his feet now, ready to jump for the door. 'He wouldn't have gone down the valleys otherwise, and roused the kings.'

'But he didn't just go down the valleys. He looked in caves and holes as well. He caught Starta, and Fugla, and little Windle. He *branded* them. He branded me.'

'And me.' Another identical voice came from the door.

'And me.' A third, from the foot of the bed.

'Tomorrow we start to hunt each other, to see who will be king dragon, but while Starkhort's heart beats we keep our compact with each other. We're dragonets, you see. He was our father.'

Thorald ran without warning or sound for the door. Something raked his cheek, and his arm batted a half-seen dimness aside. Then pain caught his ankle. He turned and tried to kick the shape off, but the fangs dug in further, injecting a stream of fire into his veins. The leg seemed to rise swelling from the floor, and his cheek crashed into the planking. As the darkness swirled in finally he saw a little winged shape rise from the floor beside him.

'Why co-exist if you don't have to ?' it said.

Outside the soldiers were whispering. 'I ain't got nothing against him, you know, I ain't no traitor, what he did to his wife, that was right. But he's no king, Grimma, no more than me – or you, I mean, or any of us.'

'Yeah. And them little scaly things, they aren't natural, not animals with voices.'

'No.' There was a silence. Ansgar muttered thoughtfully, 'I wonder what they *taste* like.'

AGORAPHOBIA, A.D. 2000

BY IAN WATSON

JAPAN – the world's leading economy by 1985, if you believe the futurologists. A juggernaut of growth, investment, ever-increasing GNP, yet at what cost?

Here's a man who found out. Ian Watson read English at Oxford then in 1965 left to lecture overseas, first to Tanzania and then in Japan. The futuristic environment he found was sufficient to inspire his first SF stories, for NEW WORLDS, and his contribution here to ANDROMEDA was written as a late response to the experience of crossing a park in Tokyo after several solid months spent submerged in megalopolis.

Ian's first novel, The Embedding, *was nominated for the John W. Campbell Memorial Award, while its French translation won the Prix Apollo as Best SF Novel of the Year. His short stories have appeared in many magazines and collections, including* Best SF : 1974.

The Japanese astronaut, Yamaguchi, waited while the masked officials unsealed the 130-acre Shinjuku Gyoen Park, the sole remaining open space in the Tokyo megalopolis. They lifted the warning barriers aside, broke the seal on the padlock, inserted the ceremonial iron key. The corroded wicket swung open. The analogue of Mars lay before him.

Almost, but not quite.

For the main gate opened into the European-style court designed by a Frenchman, Henri Martinet. This gravel court, flanked by the tall knobbled skeletons of dead trees, sloped uphill at an angle of ten degrees before leading out on to the open tableland of the park proper, effectively blocking this off from view.

'Remember, the first hundred meters are the easiest, Yamaguchi,' the familiar voice of the Mission Director warned him over his helmet radio, stiff and formal with the seriousness of the occasion, the tipsy camaraderie of the farewell party forgotten, as it should be. 'Don't be deceived. It looks just like a road. But it's a road to nowhere . . .'

A road? Yamaguchi looked around him. Yes, the stretch of scattered gravel certainly did resemble a torn-up road or underroad somewhere in the City. And the tall knobbly trees, they would be utility poles branching with insulators, surge diverters, cross arms . . . or perhaps the fifty-meter tall steel screws which scooped out the ground before piles could be driven for new buildings. The rows of dead trees stood ready to rip holes in the earth, to hammer in the pins for buildings, and more buildings – cancelling the absurdity of empty space with objects, with meaning.

The Space Agency officials stood back, keeping their eyes fixed on Yamaguchi to avoid looking at the expanse of the European Court sliding uphill at an angle of ten degrees towards – nowhere.

He stepped through the wicket and his boots crunched the gravel as he started uphill.

And a voice whispered in his mind, as he remembered the Code of Behaviour.

'*This is the day for you to commit hara-kiri. The weather is fine and the day is auspicious. May you be able to commit hara-kiri without any difficulty . . .*'

At the top of the slope he paused and gazed ahead. The dead trees here formed a wide arc surrounding the final zone of gravel. Beyond this lay a desert of dry white crab-grass, smooth and uniform, opening out in all directions away from him, pushing the massed buildings of the City absurdly far away, creating an impossible bubble of space in the very midst of the City. The sheer pressure of this space! It could hold back all those millions of tons of steel and concrete without faltering! Yamaguchi walked out across the final zone of gravel, and thought he heard it vibrate like a tight-stretched drum. But it was only his own blood drumming, pounding. Telemetry would be recording his leaping pulse on a graph outside the park for the benefit of Space Science.

Then he stepped off gravel on to the desert of grass itself and the crunch-crunch sound of his boots vanished, leaving only the booming of his blood, and the distant booming of the City, coming from far away, yet meshing with his own blood and comforting him, for he was a man of the City. He walked on over the springy turf, sending no radio messages now and receiving none. The Code said: *'Whenever any conversation is attempted by the hara-kiri performer, "Put your mind at rest" is the stereotyped response usually given; indulgence in conversation might only serve to disquieten the mind . . .'* Telemetry alone would monitor his progress and his physical and mental state.

The sun shone down weakly through the smog out of the blue of outer space, transforming the desert's surface of white grass into a vast gently-curving convex mirror . . .

He wasn't conscious of having climbed any significant incline since leaving the shelter of the European Court, yet suddenly he seemed to be above the world, perched on this convex mirror which began to turn beneath him. Now the City seemed equidistant from him on all sides, though he had only penetrated a short distance into the park. He seemed not to have moved any nearer to his goal – that far horizon of buildings with red and white checked balloons floating over them – yet the European Court, when he glanced back, had shifted into the remote distance. His eyes were not playing tricks on him, he knew. It was just that judging such great distances as these was outside the present experience of Man. His hours in the simulator did not help him much, though they doubtless staved off nausea.

The background boom of the City was the grinding of the globe as it turned beneath him like a giant's clockwork toy. He felt dizzy. Then perspective did begin to play tricks on him.

The scene leapt in at him, then bounced away. He was a giant perched on a tiny globe, terrified of falling off into endless space. He was a mouse scurrying across an immense plain while overhead an invisible hand groped for him from the sky. He felt a desperate need to take cover in the tunnels of the City. A moment later he was a giant again, dwarfing the City at the end of the plain, terrified that gravity might be *turned off*. In free fall he would float up into the endless sky. Every human being in the City was close enough to something to hold on to, but not him. There were only a few dead saplings a hundred meters away. Or was it a thousand meters?

The Code of Behaviour said: '*Hara-kiri is not a mere suicidal process; it is a refinement of self-destruction and none can perform it without the utmost coolness of temper and composure . . .*'

Why then was Yamaguchi running, stumbling along in his thick rubber boots and bulky suit, panting like a dog on a hot day while they witnessed his humiliation through their remotely controlled telescopes slung from those distant balloons?

He ran to the nearest tree. Like a dog he felt compelled to urinate against it. Of course, the urine flowed into a special bag strapped to his thigh. There was no risk of it running down his leg. Still, he imagined that it was running down his leg, and felt ashamed.

'*A hara-kiri performer should tuck his sleeves beneath his knees to prevent himself from falling backwards . . .*'

Without the weight of his spacesuit he would float up into the sky; without his spacesuit's all-enveloping life-support systems he would fly apart explosively.

The small white sun beat down through the haze on to this dead bent tree, casting a shadow that could be used to tell the time if he stayed here long enough. The silence was a huge blob of clear jelly that conducted only a faint throb from the distant City, the fading rhythm, of his own existence . . .

At last, torn between shame and fear, Yamaguchi trudged off in a direction chosen at random, perhaps retracing his steps, but most likely not. He had lost touch with the horizon now. It mocked him with its faintness, equidistance, similarity.

Soon the sun was sinking and the smog haze closing in. The neon signs that had sprung to life all over the City only made the desert seem darker and more hideous. Yamaguchi almost walked past the flat disc set in the grass without noticing it.

It was a tree stump sawn off flush with the ground, with a wire handle fixed to it.

But, of course! There had to be something underneath the Park! Subterranean passages, underground factories, transit tubes. If the Park was just something laid on top of part of the City's body, like a mat, then there was nothing to be afraid of. The City was *here* as well as *there*. He could raise this lid. Discover a ladder leading down to safety. How many lids there must be, concealed about the park. He would never have seen one had he marched in a straight line from gate to gate. But he had wandered off course. It was just an illusion that he was *outside* the City trapped in some obscene bubble of unnatural force!

The bulky spacesuit prevented him from bending over or kneeling down. However, he had a telescopic probe in his instrument pocket for taking soil samples, which he now took out, extended, and hooked through the wire handle.

The tree-stump wasn't heavy, it was only a few centimeters thick.

Underneath was a small pit with cement walls, leading nowhere. At the bottom of the pit sat a steel globe with knives and shears and clippers sticking out of it like arms. As the fading light struck its sensors, it appeared to move slightly. Shears to snip tentatively. A knife to rotate. He had stumbled on one of the robot-gardeners in its nest.

The shock of encountering life – or what appeared to be life – in this wilderness, made him drop the telescopic probe, and run, anywhere . . .

And now the desert spread around him desolate and absurd, becoming a black void as the sun disappeared.

Before exhaustion overwhelmed him he located another tree, took the umbilical tether from his instrument pocket, and, fumbling with his clumsy gloves, fastened one end of the cord to his waist and the other to the tree trunk. Carefully, so as not to damage his suit, he lowered himself to the ground, paying the cord out slowly.

Later, as Yamaguchi slept fitfully, the Moon rose, and the robot-gardener, fully alert now, climbed out of its cement pit and rolled towards the astronaut, tracking him by his body-heat.

When it reached him, it extruded its sharpest knife, plunged the blade through his suit and into his abdomen. Without a moment's delay it dragged the blade across his belly from left to right, then, turning the knife in the wound, made a brief upward cut.

As Yamaguchi thrashed about in hideous pain, fastened within the cumbersome spacesuit, the robot raked him over on to his belly and extruded a long curved sword with a shining blade. Swiftly the sword slashed through his neck, a little below the plexiglass helmet.

The Code said: '*It is considered expert not to cut the head completely off in one stroke, but to leave a portion of uncut skin at the throat . . .*'

Yamaguchi had failed, nonetheless he met an honourable death.

Back at the Space Agency Center outside the Park, beyond the court designed by Henri Martinet, now locked and sealed again, the telemetry officials noted the termination of life functions, as well as the sudden surge of readings just before the end.

CROSSING THE LINE

BY BOB SHAW

Bob Shaw's story in the first ANDROMEDA volume has already drawn considerable praise. That one was a near-classic fusion of science fiction with detective mystery; now Bob turns to something completely different with a novel – and warmly human – treatment of the 'matter transmitter' theme. And you know, in his future world just as in ours you can't take things with you when you go; but just the same there's no reason to throw them away!

When Hewitt picked the dog up he got the impression it was slightly heavier than a real animal, but that might have been because it was still inert, a dead weight in his hands. He ran his fingers through the wiry hair, noting as he did so that the markings of a Lakeland terrier had been perfectly simulated. There was no doubt that the dog was very well made, but there was a lingering question in his mind as to whether it was worth a month's salary. He turned the compact body upside down and gave it a tentative shake.

'It won't rattle,' Burt Pacer said, from behind the commissary counter. 'Fluid solenoid construction throughout. Just like real muscles.'

'I can tell it's a good machine, Burt.' Hewitt frowned into the dog's immobile face. 'It's just the money.'

Pacer smiled sympathetically. 'We're a long way from Earth.'

Hewitt nodded, wondering if the comment was meant to explain the cost of the little robot or to justify the extravagance of buying it. There were other things he and Liz could do with the money, and for weeks he had been stoutly rejecting the idea of getting a dog for Billy. The trouble with domestic budgets, however, was that they were sometimes required to accommodate items whose true value could not be reckoned in cash. Yesterday evening, for instance, Hewitt had stood at the rear window of his house and had watched his eight-year-old son scamper to the far end of the mowed plot which was their back garden. There had been nothing to stop Billy running on through the longer grass of the plain beyond, but the boy had come to a halt and had stood there, reluctant to advance into alien territories. The sight of the small figure – utterly alone, upright, probably thinking of friends he had left behind on Earth – had filled Hewitt with sadness. With the emotion had come uncertainty about the ambitions which had led him to subject his family to the rigours of the Ferrari Transfer, and he had reacted by deciding to enquire about a dog first thing in the morning. The memory of how he had felt at that moment resolved the conflict in Hewitt's mind.

'Okay,' he said. 'You talked me into it.'

'Right.' Pacer took Hewitt's citizenship card and showed it to the computer terminal along with the dog's specification tag. He worked with an airy casualness which was intended to remind people that he was a qualified electronics man and only helped out at the commissary on a voluntary basis, for the good of the colony.

His official ownership of the dog, now confirmed, prompted Hewitt to start activating it. He probed at the back of its skull with his finger-tips, searching for the subcutaneous push-button which was mentioned in the instruction leaflet.

'What are you doing?' Pacer said with some show of concern.

'Trying to turn it on.'

'I thought it was for your boy.'

Hewitt was mildly surprised. 'What's that got to do with it?'

'It's best if the prime owner is the one who activates the dog,' Pacer said. 'His should be the first face it sees.'

'Is this a joke?'

'No joke, Sam. All our dogs are the same. We programme in

a canine personality which causes each dog to fixate on one special owner.'

'I don't know if I like the sound of that,' Hewitt said slowly.

'Oh, it'll be friendly to everyone else in the family, but it's important to have that one special relationship with the owner – that's what the whole boy-and-his-dog thing is all about.' Pacer had forgotten to be nonchalant, and a note of evangelical zeal was creeping into his voice.

'I just wanted to make sure it works,' Hewitt said defensively. 'I was going to switch it off again.'

'You can't do that, Sam.'

'What? Why not?'

'The brain is too sensitive and complex for that sort of treatment. It *can* be wiped clean, of course, but it has to be done progressively, using special equipment.'

'What have I bought here?' Hewitt set the rodog down in a swath of sunlight which lay across the counter. The individual hairs of its coat gleamed brown and black and white. 'It sounds like it's going to be as much trouble as a real dog.'

'A piece of clockwork wouldn't be much use to your boy,' Pacer commented, folding his thin freckled arms. 'Besides, there's the security aspect – the way the dog is made, no stranger can come along and steal it and blank out its memory of the proper owners.'

'I must be mad,' Hewitt said as Pacer fitted the dog into its carrying case. 'I can't afford to pay eight hundred monits for a supertoy.'

'You can always bring it back.' Pacer closed up the plastic case and slid it across the counter. 'If young Billy gets tired of it, or maybe you get another transfer, bring it in and I'll give you a fifty percent refund.'

'Can you do that?'

'No trouble. We can wipe the brain clean and sell the dog to somebody else. There's a big demand for this sort of product on Mesonia.'

'I may take you up on that,' Hewitt said. He lifted the case and went out into the bright mid-morning ambience of the street. This part of the colony had been in existence for eight

35

years and the maturing shrubs and ornamental trees outside the buildings created a sense of homeliness and permanence. Feeling the warmth of the Spring air, Hewitt was glad he had decided to walk to the commissary building. He was tall for a colonist and he enjoyed the exercise of striding along the busy street in the direction of the southern residential development where he lived.

His route home took him past the arrivals and induction centre, which was a pyramidical structure whose architecture reinforced the dual-space properties of the pyramid-shaped receiving chamber at its heart. The number of vehicles parked outside it suggested to Hewitt that the null-space transmission conditions were favourable and that new colonists were being brought through. He could imagine them stepping out of the chamber, naked and hungry, stunned with the realisation that they – in one instant – had left Earth and all its ways forty light years behind them. The Ferrari Transfer was psychologically brutal, as well as being fantastically expensive, but it was the only practicable form of interstellar travel that mankind had ever devised.

At least, Hewitt thought, inhaling the scented air, *the newcomers are getting a good day for it.*

As he walked up the long slope his views of the surrounding terrain became more extensive and he could see, stretching away to the west, the manufacturing areas which were supplied from the mineral-rich hills beyond. He was always impressed and stirred by the visible evidence of how the original cadre of pioneers, equipped with only a few basic machines, had managed to create a viable settlement on an alien planet. That was where the real challenge and excitement of colonisation lay – in being in the first hundred, stepping out of the chamber onto virgin soil, living rough and working hard to pave the way for others. It was also where the big money lay. Tax-free quadruple pay for the first four years, with nothing much to spend it on, and – at the end of that time – prestige and a plushy engineering consultancy. As an expert on extraterrestrial soil mechanics, Hewitt was doing well on Mesonia – on a raw planet it was vital to know how much or how little in the way of foundations each costly new structure required. But he had arrived seven years behind the trail-blazers, when the bloom was off the cosmic grape, and his only chance for rapid advancement lay in the possibility that he might be selected for a later outward thrust.

Hewitt neared the end of the main road and turned into the side avenue in which his single-storey house was the last one before the sea of grass began. Billy was sitting on the front step, alone as usual. The Company encouraged settlers with young families, for the simple reason that a child's body had less mass than an adult's and therefore could be transmitted far more cheaply. It was an economical way of getting future colonists into space. Few people who underwent the Ferrari Transfer liked bringing children with them, however, and the colony tended to be a lonely place for a boy of eight. Billy, ever watchful, saw Hewitt as he turned the corner and came running to meet him.

'Hi, Dad!' Billy fell into step beside Hewitt and took his hand. 'What's in the case?'

'Guess.' Hewitt had not said anything about going to look at a dog because his common sense might have reasserted itself in time to prevent the purchase.

'Well,' Billy said soberly, taking measured paces, 'it can't be a dog.'

'Can't it?'

'*Dad!*' Billy looked up at him, his round face an absurd caricature of delight, and Hewitt experienced a pang of pure happiness. He handed the case to his son and almost laughed aloud with pleasure as Billy darted ahead and disappeared around the corner of the white-painted house. Hewitt followed at an unhurried pace and was met at the kitchen door by Liz, who was wearing a silver spark-suit which emphasised the blackness of her hair. The Saturday-morning aroma of fresh coffee wafted around her through the open door.

'Thanks, Sam,' Liz said, pressing her cheek against his lips. 'I know we can't really afford it, but it'll be so good for Billy.'

'It's all right.' He drew her against him. 'We'll just economise on toothpicks and string and things like that for a while.'

37

'You're crazy,' she said warmly. 'Come in and have some coffee.'

'Okay, but I'll show Billy how to get the dog going first.' Hewitt paused as he heard his son talking to someone in the living room. 'Who's in there ?'

Liz looked apologetic. 'Carl's here.'

'Aw, *Christ*! This is supposed to be my day off.'

'I know, darling, but I can't very well send him away when he calls at the door.'

Hewitt closed his eyes for a moment, then went through to the living room, suppressing his resentment over a family occasion having been invaded and spoiled. Carl Mendip was slightly older than Hewitt and was his immediate senior in the constructional engineering section. He boasted a lot about being able to bank most of his salary, and spent much of his off-duty time sitting in Hewitt's favourite chair extolling the pleasures of bachelorhood. When Hewitt entered the room Mendip already had the dog out of its case and was handing it to Billy.

'Morning, Sammy boy,' Mendip said. 'These things aren't worth the money, you know.'

'It was worth it to me.'

Mendip shrugged. 'I wouldn't have paid it.'

'Did anybody ask you to ?'

'In a bad mood, are we ?' Mendip examined Hewitt with calm amusement.

Hewitt stared back at him, trying to be impassive, wishing he had controlled his tongue. One man in their engineering section was likely to be transferred to Nimrod, a world which had been broached only recently. As the senior and most experienced man, Mendip had the best chance, but Company policy had dictated that he should also nominate a member of his section for consideration, and – with an unsubtle display of magnanimity – he had put Hewitt's name forward. Ever since then the dominating factor in their relationship was that Mendip's recommendation could be withdrawn by him at any moment. It was a yoke which Hewitt wore with increasing irritation even though he knew the situation was fairly temporary.

'Sorry, Carl,' he said, and turned his attention to Billy, who was sitting cross-legged on the floor with the rigid-limbed dog in his lap. 'What are you going to call it, son ?'

'I think I'll call him Bramble,' Billy replied.

'What a name!' Mendip gave a hoot of derision. 'You can't call it that!'

Billy looked puzzled. 'Can't I, Dad ?'

'Bramble suits him very well and that's what we'll call him.' Hewitt moved in between the other man and his son and knelt down. He guided Billy's finger on to the activating button and explained what he had to do. Liz came into the room at that moment and watched as Billy held the dog with its face towards him and depressed the button. There was no sound, but the rodog yawned as though wakening from a sleep, its eyes brightened into life, the short legs stirred slightly as they adjusted to distribute the weight, and the ribcage began to pulsate in a simulation of breathing.

'Bramble!' Billy spoke in a rapt voice. 'Bramble!'

Bramble began to wag his tail.

In spite of himself, adult though he was, Hewitt felt a thrill of awe at the achievement of the robotics engineers. 'Set him down and go into the kitchen and see if he'll come to you,' he said.

Billy put the dog on the floor, backed away from it until he was out of sight in the kitchen and called its name. Bramble wagged his tail, then bounded across the room and skidded into the kitchen with the exuberant clumsiness of a real pup. Billy reappeared with the dog clutched to his chest and a beatific expression on his face.

'Can I take him outside, Dad ?'

'All right, but don't go far – he still has to learn his way around.' Hewitt was unable to repress a fond grin as the boy ran out into the sunlight at the back of the house. He would have liked to complete the indulgent parent act by standing with an arm around Liz and watching Billy at play, but Mendip's presence ruled that out.

'I hope you get your money's worth out of it,' Mendip said, lowering himself into an armchair. His pale oval face turned this way and that as he surveyed the room.

'Perhaps I already have,' Hewit answered.

Mendip nodded. 'I guess I'd feel guilty about bringing a kid out here.'

'I don't feel guilty,' Hewitt said quickly.

'Well, maybe I used the wrong word, but you know what I mean – when a kid can't even have a real dog . . .'

'Bramble is programmed to be as good as a real dog. Better.'

'It ought to be better if you're laying out a month's salary for it. Hell's fire!' Mendip shifted to make himself more comfortable. 'I suppose you and Liz will have to tighten the old belts for a while.'

Hewitt shook his head. 'We don't go out much anyway.'

'That's right – you don't. A place like Mesonia is okay for somebody like me who can get around and enjoy the social life. You'd be surprised at what goes on at some of the parties over on the East Hill, Sammy boy.' Mendip gave a ruminative laugh. 'You know Marie Duchamp, the systems analyst in Structures One? Well, she and another girl . . .'

'Carl,' Hewitt put in evenly, 'what are your plans for today?'

Mendip blinked. 'Plans? I thought I'd just visit with you and Liz. Keep you company.'

'You've no plans to get around a few wild parties?'

Mendip smiled his thin-lipped smile. 'Sammy! You almost sound as if you didn't want . . .'

'Coffee's ready,' Liz announced, coming into the room with a tray.

'I don't know if I should have one,' Mendip said to her. 'I have a feeling Sammy wants me to clear out.'

'Nonsense! You have to stay for a meal now that you've come out this far.' Liz distributed beakers of synthetic coffee, giving Hewitt a reproachful frown as she did so. Hewitt slumped into another chair, sipped the hot liquid and tried to calculate how much he had contributed to his boss's bank balance in the form of free meals in the past year.

'Sam's always grouchy in the mornings,' Liz said. 'Will you try one of these biscuits, Carl?'

'No, thanks.' Mendip patted his stomach. 'I'm keeping my weight down – just in case.'

Liz smiled understandingly. 'When will you hear about the transfer ?'

'Not for another four or five weeks, but I'd rather keep myself light. I don't like crash diets.'

Hewitt was tempted to cut in and reprove Mendip, a senior engineer, for talking about weight when he meant mass, but he decided against being petty in the hope that the day could be rescued from disaster. He knew what Mendip meant, anyway. The Ferrari Transfer System – instantaneous travel from one location to another which had similar spatial properties – was technologically superb, but from the practical viewpoint it had a major drawback in that its cost/weight graph took the form of a steeply ascending straight line. No matter how much mass the engineers transferred, no matter how many times they did it, no matter how many refinements or improvements they tried to introduce to the system – the expense of transmitting each and every gram of matter remained at the same astronomical figure.

The harsh economics of the Ferrari Transfer ruled out any prospect of easing Earth's population problems, but by the 22nd Century the world political situation had stabilised enough to permit international funding of a project to seed other planets with the nuclei of human colonies. In philosophical terms, the project was grandiose and far-seeing; in operational terms, it was a matter of paring every cargo down to the absolute miserly limit. The prime qualification for colonists was that they should be slightly built. Even then, they were subjected to rigorous reduction dieting before the outward journey, and were dispatched naked and with all hair removed from heads and bodies. The second qualification for interstellar settlers was, of course, dedication.

Not in utter nakedness, but trailing clouds of glory do we come, Hewitt had often quoted to himself. But on this Saturday morning – with suburban placidity on one hand, and Company politics personnified by Carl Mendip on the other – the clouds of glory were not in evidence. He felt that he might as well be incarcerated in some hopeless prairie town back on Earth, that the sacrifices he and Liz and Billy had made were going to achieve little unless he got the transfer to Nimrod . . .

'What are you dreaming about now, Sammy boy?' Mendip said comfortably.

'Dreaming?' Hewitt queried the word, sensitive to his boss's habit of slipping professional criticism into casual conversation. 'I was wondering why they have to take so long to decide who's going and who's staying.'

'The mills of the Company grind slow, but if it'll ease your mind I can let you know your chances aren't too good, Sammy.'

'Why's that? I thought you put in a good assessment for me.'

'Oh, I did.' Mendip looked benign. 'But there's an economy drive on – and there are three of you.'

'Three *people*,' Hewitt said. 'That's the whole point of the operation, isn't it? The idea is to populate planets – not plant flags on them.'

'I know, but it's cheaper to produce the people after you get there.' Mendip looked appraisingly at Liz. 'I reckon that all women in the colonies should be made available to all men who could impregnate them.'

'That let's you out,' Hewitt said, in an automatic response.

Mendip's ice-blue gaze fastened on him in the instant. 'What do you mean, Sammy boy?'

'Nothing.' Hewitt laughed, wondering if his annoyance had driven him too far.

'Your plan wouldn't work,' Liz said diplomatically, smiling at Carl. 'When the word got back to the girls on Earth that you were waiting for them they'd rush the transfer terminal. The system wouldn't be able to cope.'

'You'd still have first claim,' Mendip said, mollified. 'I'm good to my friends.'

Hewitt stood up, went to the rear window and watched his son playing with the dog on the rectangle of mowed grass. The little robot animal was running, leaping, twisting, barking, scampering around Billy in a manner which made it difficult to believe that it was a machine which had been designed by robotics engineers and built in a factory only a few kilometres away. Billy was totally absorbed in his new companion, rolling

42

on the ground and laughing while it clambered over him in a mock attack.

Late that evening when Mendip had left, after consuming two expensive high-protein meals, Liz spent a few minutes tidying the living room. The dog lay quietly on a rug and watched her moving about, its attention directed to one of its secondary owners now that Billy had gone to bed, its brain establishing pathways of familiarity and memory.

'Why don't you leave the place the way it is, and I'll tidy up in the morning?' Hewitt said. 'I'm too tired to do it now.'

'It's tension that's making you tired,' Liz told him. 'You shouldn't let Carl get under your skin.'

'I can't help it. If he's such a hell-raiser why doesn't he go out and do it instead of spending all his time around here?'

'I should have thought that was obvious. Anywhere else he'd have to meet people on equal terms, and he doesn't feel adequate for that. With us, he knows his seniority in the Company gives him the edge he needs, especially with a transfer coming up. He can say anything he wants in our house.'

'It doesn't seem to bother you,' Hewitt retorted.

Liz gave him a level stare. 'It bothers me, but we're dealing with your career, aren't we? After giving up everything we had on Earth, and travelling forty light years, are we going to risk your getting a bad assessment because I couldn't jolly your boss along? It's up to you, Sam – if you want, I'll pour a pot of coffee into his lap the next time he comes near me.'

'I'm sorry, Liz.'

'It's all right.' Liz, graceful in her natural generosity, came to him and kissed his forehead. She knelt down beside his chair and began stroking the dog. It licked her hand.

'Why are you doing that?' Hewitt said in genuine bafflement.

'Dogs like to be stroked.'

'But he's only a machine.'

Liz looked at him with womanly scorn. 'He doesn't know he's only a machine.'

The following four weeks passed more quickly than Hewitt had anticipated. Mesonia was still in an early stage of its development, and therefore was using a nine-day week in which there was only one rest day. The long stints of concentrated effort usually made Hewitt very tired, but Carl Mendip had taken to remaining in the office as much as possible – waiting for a decision about the transfer to Nimrod – and this freed Hewitt to do a number of field trips to outlying communities. He enjoyed the long silent drives through the Earth-like but unspoiled landscapes.

These pleasures were a bonus posthumously conferred on him by Eugenio Ferrari, whose transfer system enable men to travel forty light years in exactly the same time that it would take to cover four or four hundred. The near-magic of Ferrari's physics meant that mankind could be highly selective about the location of colonies, only establishing them on green and friendly worlds. The colonists were faced with hard work, but little danger or discomfort.

Liz's job as a dental assistant meant she was unable to accompany him on the field trips, but Billy was able to go on days when he was free from classes. He always insisted on bringing the dog, which sat upright on the seat beside him, its brown eyes shining in a semblance of life. Hewitt found himself wishing he understood more about the molecular-circuit electronics of its brain so that he could appreciate what was going on inside the neat, sharp-eared head. All he knew was that the robotics engineers had done their work well, because Bramble had a canine personality all of his own, an individuality which – to Hewitt's surprise – was not entirely tailored to the convenience of his owners. The little rodog liked chewing shoes, for example, and objected noisily when they were forcibly removed from its jaws. It did not eat, but every day lapped some water which was used to keep its eyes, nose and tongue moist, and it frequently overturned its dish, necessitating mopping-up jobs. When accidentally locked in a room it would whine continuously and scratch at the door until permitted to rejoin its owners.

On one occasion, when the dog had been with them about two weeks, it caused a minor commotion in the Hewitt household by disappearing for several hours. Hewitt thought it was stolen and was angry about the loss of a valuable piece of

44

property, but he was even more concerned about Billy's reaction. The boy wept inconsolably and ran around the house, pulling open cupboard doors and calling the dog's name. Later that evening, when Billy was reduced to an occasional exhausted sob, Bramble had been spotted trotting down the avenue towards the house with his head held high, like an animal character in one of the historic Walt Disney cartoons. It transpired that the dog had wandered beyond the area which was properly imprinted on its memory and had spent a long time carrying out a random search for a landmark it knew. Liz had scolded it and slapped its flanks exactly as she would have done with a real pet, and it had responded by scuttling off into Billy's room with its stubby tail between its legs. Billy had been overjoyed at the reunion with Bramble, and it was then that Hewitt felt the first stirrings of unease at the extent of his son's preoccupation with what was, after all, only an assemblage of electronic and mechanical components.

In general, however, Hewitt did not pay much attention to the dog. It was providing companionship for his son in a satisfactory manner, and to that extent it had been a worthwhile investment.

And he forgot about it entirely when the news came through that he – and not Carl Mendip – had been selected for transfer to Nimrod.

Mendip came to Hewitt's desk and watched him for a while with pale, reproachful eyes. 'I expect you're feeling proud of yourself, Sammy boy,' he said eventually.

Hewitt looked up from a site plan he had been pretending to study. 'Not especially. It was all in the luck of the draw – and your recommendation must have helped.'

'Don't you forget it.' Mendip brooded for a moment, unsatisfied. 'You've put on some weight, you know. You're going to have a hard time getting rid of it.'

'Only a couple of standard kilos – I can shed that in a week, easily.'

'Liz has put it on, too.'

'Liz is good at dieting.' Hewitt grew wary, sensing that his

45

boss wanted to mar the occasion for him by whipping up antagonism. 'She can trim down in time for the medical.'

'That's going to spoil things a bit for you – women always lose it in the wrong place.' Mendip cupped his hands in front of his own chest, holding imaginary breasts.

'Secondary sexual characteristics aren't too important to me,' Hewitt said easily, his defences intact. He could swap banter of the most bawdy kind with other men in the office and think nothing of it, but Mendip had a way of particularising every sexual reference to make it offensive.

'The Company ought to relax the weight rules a little for women,' Mendip continued. 'After all, if they're placing so much emphasis on their role as breeding animals that they're handing out transfers on the strength of it, they should let them keep their tits. What do you say, Sammy?'

'It's a point of view.' Hewitt toyed with a heavy scale rule. One part of his mind admired the craftsmanship with which – in one sentence – Mendip had degraded Liz and denigrated Hewitt's professional standing. Another part of his mind weighed the consequences of flicking the scale rule sideways and shattering Mendip's front teeth. Such an action would result in his transfer orders being cancelled, which was too great a price to pay, but the temptation was considerable.

'Two points of view,' Mendip said.

'If you don't mind, Carl, I'd better get on with this.' Hewitt tapped the site plan. 'I want to leave a clear desk.'

He lowered his head and stared determinedly at the plastic sheet until the other man had moved away and the moment of danger had passed. The tachygram from Earth had come in only ten minutes earlier, and there had been no time to contact Liz with the news. Hewitt decided against calling her from the office because, with Carl Mendip near, it would have been impossible for him to speak in a natural manner. He worked until the middle of the afternoon before acknowledging that his lack of concentration was rendering the exercise meaningless, then he left the office and walked home, pacing himself to arrive at the house soon after the time when Liz would bring Billy home from school. It was a warm day, and he found Billy sitting on the back lawn with a glass of yeastmilk in one hand and a book in the other, while contriving to have one arm around the rodog. Bramble came running to meet Hewitt, wagging his tail in the hope of being stroked. Hewitt, as always, was unable to bring himself to show affection for a machine – regardless of how life-like it might be – and Bramble, looking mildly dejected, returned to his prime owner.

'Hi, Dad,' Billy called contentedly.

'Hello, son,' Hewitt replied. He went into the house and found Liz examining that week's menu display on their meal dispenser. Her short black hair was combed to the smoothness of an enamelled helmet and she was still wearing the traditional white of the dentist's surgery.

'Oh, you're home early,' she said, with a note of disappointment. 'Why are you home early?'

'What a greeting!' Hewitt slung his jacket over a chair. 'Do you want me to go back to the office?'

'Of course not. It's just that the menu isn't too interesting this week and I thought I might prepare the meal myself.' Liz gave him a lingering kiss.

'There's no need to go to all that trouble – I'll find something I like in the machine.'

'But I'll soon have forgotten how to cook,' Liz protested.

'That's what you think,' Hewitt said triumphantly. 'It'll be quite a while before they have meal dispensers on Nimrod.'

Liz stepped back from him at once. 'Do you mean . . . ?'

Hewitt nodded. 'I've got the Nimrod posting.'

'I'm glad for you,' Liz said slowly. She walked to the window and stood with her back to him, looking out to where Billy was sitting on the grass. 'I know it's what you wanted.'

'What *I* wanted? It's a big thing for all of us, isn't it?' Hewitt was disturbed by his wife's reaction. 'It's equivalent to my getting about six promotions all at once.'

'That's why I'm glad about it. I really am glad about it, Sam.' Liz walked to the meal dispenser. 'I guess we'd better forget about a special meal for tonight – we'll have to start cutting down right away.'

47

'What is this, Liz?' Hewitt caught her arm and turned her to face him. 'Are you afraid of the Ferrari chamber?'

'I'm not afraid. I'll go anywhere with you.'

'But you don't seem . . . Don't you want to see a brand-new world?'

'This one is still pretty fresh after only eight years.' Liz gave him a wise, patient smile. 'Let's be honest about that side of it, Sam – the only reason Nimrod has been chosen is that it's exactly like this world, and exactly like all the others we're colonising. There'll be no difference.'

'Except that I'll be going in with the rank of Project Leader,' Hewitt said heatedly. 'Or doesn't that count for anything?'

'It counts for a great deal. That's why I'm glad for you.'

Hewitt began to feel desperate. 'Don't keep saying that. Liz, if you didn't want to leave here, why didn't you let me know earlier?'

'Who said I don't want to leave?'

'You don't need to say it. It's obvious, for God's sake.'

She looked up at him and spoke with the honesty he had always treasured. 'I didn't say anything because everybody was so certain you wouldn't be picked. And the reason I don't want to go is that I believe it would be better for Billy to grow up in one place. The last move upset him, and I think it's too soon for another.'

Hewitt shook his head. 'The Company psychologists advise on that sort of thing.'

'I know. The *Company* psychologists.'

'They wouldn't . . .'

'I'm his mother, Sam, and I know what I'm talking about – but I'm not going to fight you on this thing, because I know Billy will come through it, and I know you'll do everything you can to help him come through it.'

'Of course I will,' Hewitt said, relieved. 'The three of us . . .'

'There's just one condition.'

'Anything you say, Liz. What is it?'

'You have to tell him about Bramble.'

'What is there to tell?' Hewitt gave an uncertain laugh. 'Do you mean you want me to tell him the dog can't go?'

'Yes.'

'Well, I don't mind doing that. Billy's old enough to understand the position.'

Liz went to the door and opened it. 'Go out and tell him now.'

'What's the hurry?' Hewitt said reasonably.

'Sam go out and tell him now.' Liz spoke in a faint, cold voice.

'All right! All right!' Hewitt went out to the back of the house, approached his son and knelt in the short grass beside him. 'I've got a big new job, Billy – so we're all moving to Nimrod.'

Billy looked all around – taking in the now-familiar view of white-painted dwellings among trees, grasslands sloping down to the river, the valley's palisade of slate-blue mountains – then lowered his head without speaking. The dog stared up at Hewitt from its nest in Billy's lap.

'Did you hear me, Billy? I said we're all going to Nimrod.'

Billy met Hewitt's gaze directly and his round face was momentarily overprinted with an image of the adult he would one day become. 'Dad, I'll do without pocket money for the rest of my life if you don't kill Bramble.'

Hewitt's jaw almost sagged. 'What's all this about killing him? You can't kill a machine, Billy.'

'Don't take him back to the store when we go.'

'But we couldn't leave him running around here. It would be . . .' Hewitt stopped abruptly, having almost defeated his own case by speaking of cruelty. If one could not kill a machine, it was equally impossible to be cruel to it.

'Why shouldn't I take him . . . *it* back to the store.'

'Because they would do something to his head and he wouldn't know us anymore. He'd be in a box.'

'It's all for the . . .'

'Dad, let me leave Bramble with somebody, somebody from school, and then someday I could come back and get him. He's got a good memory. He's got the best memory you ever saw! He wouldn't forget . . .'

'Billy!' Hewitt was surprised by the force of his anger. 'There's a four hundred monit trade-in on that machine, and we're not going to walk off and leave it. Now try to grow up!'

49

He jumped to his feet and was striding back to the house when Bramble came scampering and growling around his ankles. Hewitt gave an irritated flick of his right foot which caught Bramble squarely on the ribcage. The little rodog yelped as it rolled over, then dashed back to Billy. Hewitt slammed the kitchen door behind him and stood there, breathing unevenly, staring at his wife.

'Don't forget,' she said, turning away from him, 'you've still to decide what we're having for dinner.'

Prior to their departure, Hewitt and his wife were awarded three full days of leave from work. The break was officially supposed to give them the chance to make final arrangements, but in fact it was a time of mental preparation for a little death. People who underwent the Ferrari Transfer simply walked away from all their material possessions, leaving one life as naked as they had entered it, being born into another in exactly the same condition. The only assets they took with them were their personal attributes and skills, plus – by the grace of the Company – their credit ratings.

Hewitt had originally intended to let Billy keep the rodog until the last day, but the boy had stopped eating and spent most of his time in his room with Bramble in his arms. Sometimes when Hewitt was passing the bedroom door he heard Billy whispering to the pet, at others there was a silence broken by painful sobs, and he decided it would be better not to prolong an unhealthy situation.

Accordingly, immediately after breakfast on his first day's leave, he picked the rodog up while it was lapping at its water dish and – without any announcement – took it out to his car. It was not until he saw Billy's shocked face staring at him through a window that Hewitt admitted to himself that he had been hoping to get away from the house unseen. He dropped the warm sentient bundle on to the car's rear seat and drove away with the maximum acceleration the magnetic engine could produce. At the corner of the main road he glanced back once and saw that Billy had run halfway along the avenue behind the car before giving up. He was standing there, helpless. Bramble had raised himself on his hind legs to look out through the rear window, and he gave one low bark as Billy was lost to view.

Hewitt swore savagely, cursing the dog's designers and manufacturers for sins they were unaware of having committed. He slowed the car down and drove into the central area, past the gleaming pyramid of the transfer building, and stopped outside the commissary. When he picked up the rodog it squirmed in his grasp, but in a playful manner, its main objective apparently being to lick his face. Hewitt tucked it firmly under his arm and pushed his way through a transparent door to the domestic electronics department. Burt Pacer, who had sold him the rodog, was again on duty behind the counter.

'Morning, Sam,' Pacer said cheerfully. 'And congratulations – I heard about your transfer.'

'Thanks.' Hewitt set Bramble on the counter, keeping a tight grip of the studded collar as the dog's feet skidded about on the slick plastic. 'I wish I'd known it was coming. I could have saved myself a lot of money and trouble.'

'Didn't it work out ?' Pacer lifted the dog in his thin freckled arms and examined it critically while it strove to lick his face.

'Too well – that was the trouble.'

'I might be able to let you have five hundred on it, seeing as how you only had it a few weeks.'

'That would be good,' Hewitt said. 'What'll you do with it now ?'

'We'll blank out the brain . . . wipe it, you know . . . and de-activate the mutt and put him back into inventory.'

'Does it take long ?' Hewitt was not sure why he was asking.

'About ten minutes should take care of it,' Pacer replied. 'Malcolm Harris does these things because he knows more about molecular logic circuits than I do, but he's out having his coffee right now. Do you want to talk to him about it ?'

'No – I just wondered.' Hewitt walked to the door, then turned to look back at the dog which was scrabbling frantically on the counter in an effort to follow him. 'It's a hell of a thing when they have to build robot bloody dogs.'

Pacer shrugged. 'We're a long way from Earth.'

Hewitt nodded and went back to his car. Before moving off

he sat and watched the struggling rodog being carried away into the rear of the store. He drove homewards slowly, taking detours and spinning the journey out to fifteen minutes so that Bramble would have been returned to inventory, and the episode finally closed, before he had to speak to Billy again. The first thing he saw when he reached the house was a blue Company car often used by Carl Mendip parked in the driveway. For once, the sight was quite welcome because the presence of an outsider could be useful in keeping emotional pressures down. Hewitt went in through the back door and found Liz alone in the kitchen. Her eyes had a slightly pinkish look, as if she had been crying, but her face was composed.

'Where's Billy?' he said.

'Where do you think? In his room.' Liz's voice was completely neutral. 'Would you like some coffee?'

'No – I have to watch my fluid intake.' Hewitt went through to the living room to where Mendip was prowling around, sipping coffee and examining various small ornaments with critical interest.

'How's it going?' Mendip said with a rare joviality.

'Okay.' Hewitt sat down in his favourite chair.

'I took an hour off to come out and see how you and Liz were getting on.'

'Thanks, Carl.' Hewitt watched as Mendip continued his course around the room, picking up recently-acquired trinkets and setting them down again. The principal items of furniture belonged to the Company and would be renovated for use by another colonist, but Hewitt and Liz had tried to personalise the place to some extent by buying extra pieces, such as flower vases, since their arrival on Mesonia. None of their purchases had been expensive – because of the ever-looming possibility of being transferred – but they helped make a standard Company house into the Hewitt home, and Hewitt disliked the casual way in which Mendip was handling them.

'It's a weird business, being transferred,' Mendip said. 'It would be better if you had a lot of packing to do.'

'Why's that?'

'Keep you busy, keep your mind off it.'

52

'I'm not bothered,' Hewitt said.

Mendip sniffed disbelievingly. 'Young Billy was crying when I came in.'

'He's upset about the dog.'

'I told you that was a bum investment, Sammy boy. How much did you drop on the deal?'

'Three hundred.'

Mendip hissed his breath inwards. 'Some people shouldn't be allowed out alone.' He picked up a small ceramic glow-clock and dropped it into his pocket.

'Carl?' Hewitt sat upright. 'What are you doing?'

'It's all right – I checked with Liz.' Mendip gave a frosty smile. 'You can't take it with you, you know.'

Hewitt felt himself nearing a dangerous edge. 'Put the clock back,' he said.

'I told you Liz said it was all right for me to take a few things. There's no point in letting the Company have them.'

Hewitt stood up. 'Put the clock back where it was.'

'But what will you do with it?' Mendip made no move to return the clock.

Hewitt considered for a moment. 'On the morning we leave I'll put it in a pile with our other things and smash them up with a hammer. Just to keep the buzzards off.'

'I don't like that remark.' Some of the scanty colour had left Mendip's face. 'I could put in a report about your attitude.'

'And I could put in a counter-report about you being a looter.'

Mendip slowly took the ceramic piece from his pocket and weighed it in his hand. 'Is this your idea of gratitude, Sammy boy? Is this the way you treat a friend?'

Hewitt put on a look of surprise. 'No. I wouldn't dream of treating a friend this way.'

'I see.' Mendip turned to Liz, who was just entering the room. 'Did you hear that, Liz?'

'I heard.' Liz looked at Hewitt with an impersonal gaze. 'I paid for that clock – so I'm entitled to give it away.'

'What *is* this?' Hewitt said. 'We don't go in for separate ownership.'

'That's what I used to think. Until this morning.' Liz turned to Mendip and closed his fingers around the clock. 'Put it away in your pocket, Carl.'

'Thanks, Liz.' Mendip smiled serenely at Hewitt.

'If you try to leave here with that clock,' Hewitt said in a shaky voice, aghast at what he was doing and yet unable to draw back, 'I . . . I'll . . .'

'It wouldn't be a good idea to hit me, Sammy.' Mendip put the clock in his pocket. 'That way, you'd lose the transfer.'

The words went through Hewitt like a chill wind, enfolding his mind in an icy stasis, bringing time itself to a standstill. He stared helplessly at his wife, and at Mendip, and it seemed to him that they would all be there for ever because he was being required to make decisions of which he was incapable . . .

'Bramble!' Billy burst into the room with a shout and ran to the front window in a blur of bare arms and legs. 'Bramble's come back!'

Hewitt turned disbelievingly and peered out of the window. He experienced a curious blending of relief, affection and pride as he saw the little rodog, compact and jaunty, trotting along the avenue towards the house. Its head and tail were held high and it looked absurdly pleased with itself, again like an animal character in one of the historic Walt Disney cartoons. Billy jumped down from the window seat, was out through the front door in a second and they saw him running across the front lawn. Bramble abruptly gathered speed, and boy and dog met in mid-air, then rolled in an excited tangle into a flower bed.

'Well, I'll be . . .' Hewitt whispered reverently. 'He must have got away from the store.'

Liz moved close to the window. 'But how did he find his way back?'

'Damned if I know. Billy said he had a good memory, but I didn't think this was possible,' Hewitt said. An instinct made him follow Liz to the window and slip his arm around her. She leaned back against him.

'Better not let the kid get too worked up over it,' Mendip said in an oddly taut voice. 'I'm going back to the office now – I'll drop the dog off at the commissary on my way. Save you the

54

extra trip.' He hurried out of the room. Hewitt ran after him and caught up just as Mendip was grasping Bramble by the collar and pulling him out of Billy's arms.

'Leave the dog alone,' Hewitt snapped.

'What are you talking about ?' Mendip faced him on the sunlit grass. 'This isn't a real dog.'

'He's more real than you are, Carl. Put him down.'

'You're not thinking straight,' Mendip said.

'Perhaps not.' Hewitt was dimly aware of neighbours beginning to take an interest in the confrontation. 'But if you don't put him down, I'll put you down.'

'You wouldn't be that stupid,' Mendip said, brushing past Hewitt towards his car.

Hewitt threw a punch which was meant to land on Mendip's chin, but which – because he had not tried to hit anyone since he was a boy – connected squarely with the other man's forehead. Mendip gave a startled moan and dropped Bramble. Hewitt's right hand was aching from the effects of the blow, he knew he was making a fool of himself in front of the entire neighbourhood, and he also knew he was ruining his chances of fast promotion – but he was filled with a sudden gratitude towards Mendip. It was a deep thankfulness for having made him understand what was important in his own life, and it was a thankfulness which could be expressed only by raining blows on Mendip's head and upflung arms. The wild punches, often meeting with sharp elbows, threatened to break Hewitt's own knuckles, but he succeeded in driving Mendip to his knees while Billy backed away holding the dog. Suddenly Liz was beside him, restraining his arms.

'That's enough, Sam,' she said gently. 'I think you've made your point.'

Mendip scrambled to his feet, dishevelled but virtually unhurt. 'You've done it now, Sammy boy,' he panted. 'This has to go on report. You're never going to see Nimrod.'

'You can send me a viewcard,' Hewitt said, through his own gasps. 'Go away, Carl.'

Mendip turned to Liz. 'Of course, it's you I'm most sorry for.'

She held out her hand and smiled. 'We want our clock back, please.'

Mendip took the clock from his pocket, dropped it into her hand and walked to his car without saying another word. They watched him drive away, then Hewitt went into his house, walking slowly and with as much dignity as possible. As soon as he was screened from the view of his neighbours, he held up his skinned and bleeding knuckles, blowing on them to ease the pain.

'Look what I've done to myself,' he said. 'If I'd hit him once more, he'd have won.'

'I'll soon fix those,' Liz replied. 'Wait till I get the medikit.'

A few minutes later, while Hewitt was having his battle wounds dressed, he heard his son laughing outside. He looked out of the rear window and saw Billy and Bramble running down the garden away from the house. They were still gathering speed as they reached the far end of the mowed plot and plunged, unafraid, into the long grass where the rest of the world began.

FIDEI DEFENSOR

BY MIKE SCOTT ROHAN

I like 'Fidei Defensor' for several reasons. For its skilful story-telling, for one, but also for the fresh new angle taken by Mike Scott Rohan in what is the nearest thing yet to a conventional 'space' story in the ANDROMEDA series to date.

Yet Rohan realises that mid-20th century American culture is unlikely to last forever, and even now accounts for the way of life of no more than 5 per cent of the human race. What customs and habits shape the lives of that other 95 per cent? The only comparable treatment that springs to mind is Greg Benford's famous 'Deeper than the Darkness', where again Oriental philosophies play a dominant role.

This is an uncommonly solid piece of work for a first profes-sional sale. Mike Scott Rohan edits reference books, encyclo-pedias, and so forth as an occupation but is working on other stories which I hope will be equally successful.

The *Uma*, for many years the *Way of the World* but rechristened for this run, was three months out of New Benares and braking down in normal space. It was necessary to remove surplus velocity, leaving enough to take a wide curve into the solar system, chasing the blindly fugitive Earth. When it was caught a second braking would match velocities to enter orbit.

'And after that, Ram,' said Captain Rad'krishnan, 'the rest is up to you. I assume it will not take long to find the Ganges?'

'I have the old maps. Provided enough natural landmarks remain unchanged I will have no trouble, if not – we will be able to find it. It was very large, had many cities on its banks.'

The navigator returned to his book, not prolonging the conversation. Bringing the ship about would not become his business unless bungled, which it would not be. In the meantime he had nothing further to say to the captain.

No offence was intended or taken. Two people caught in the lifesystem of a cargo starship – not exactly cramped but painfully economical – had two alternatives. They could become the closest of friends, or lovers for that matter, or they could become artificially distant, substituting personal separation for physical. Absolute reserve developed, and selfish self-sufficiency. The process was seldom sudden, or even conscious. If you objected to the way your navigator kept his quarters you ceased to go into them. If you objected to the captain's old-time religion you didn't mention religion or anything which called it to mind, which of course meant almost everything eventually. It was a natural separation made almost frictionless by the self-discipline essential to starship crewmen, but it did not allow any degree of friendship. Curtness in such a relationship amounted to courtesy. Ram didn't even look up at the main window as turn-over began, impressive sight though it was. Attitude jets spat gently on the main hull, then others on the motor pod a mile away, making the centre of the thin boom joining them the axis of a circle traced on space by their extremities. Hull and motor slowly swung until the ship was reversed; still it plunged headlong into the solar system, only now the motor led the way, mouth gaping as if to suck at the planets in its path.

'Turnover complete,' said the captain. The brain traced NO COURSE CORRECTION REQUIRED in pale white letters on the window. Again Ram's failure to reply or even react was a polite tribute to his faith in the captain's skill. They had tried sleeping together at the beginning of the voyage, but proclivities had jarred. Ram had been irritated when the captain invoked Ambika, Parvati's aspect as fertility goddess, when she took her contraceptive. She had found him sexually immature and inclined to treat foreplay as a mathematical process akin to plane navigation, a fault she would have found too tiring to correct.

BRAKING SEQUENCE BEGUN traced the brain as it

took over. The captain leaned back in the control chair and bit down on a betel pill. 'Music?' she inquired.

'If it's western – and twentieth century . . .'

'*Mathis der Mahler*,' she decided, and tabbed the controls in the chair-arm. The first movement began, the angel chorus. Slow strings and woodwind, brass tracing a measured theme over their vaulting rise until they met in a bright triumph. The strings shimmered, cold as the stars, in a celestial vision. With dark woodwind behind they glittered with a life no star ever had in space. A cold night, perhaps, with the clarity of mountain air – in the Himalayas, perhaps, the legendary peaks. New Benares had few mountains and, being further out on the spiral arm, fewer stars in the night sky. She would see India's sky, thought the captain, see it soon. She smoothed the magnifying patches out of the window and stared at the bleak stillness of space.

The second movement, the Entombment of Christ. The music took a rapt graveness, still as the stars ahead. Flute and clarinet shone out from sombre strings. Only the pale tracings of the brain flitted aimlessly across the window, over the stars. The firing sequence – the captain stared at them absently. The *Uma* was old and not well maintained. No spacecraft could ever become an old tub, but age always brought problems. FIRING – 10 drifted across the screen as the Temptation of St. Anthony, the third movement, began. A blare of brass, flame licking from hellmouth; monsters leapt and trampled throughout the music. There was little the captain could do except watch and worry; it was best left to the brain's lightning reactions.

She had no real reason to be apprehensive, but she couldn't help flicking on a patch over the distant image of the motor, bringing it closer, larger until she could see the cones of the attitude jets along its flanks. The left bank of jets – she increased the magnification of that area, half in shadow. FIRING – 2 rose out of the shadow, but beneath it there was a definite glow, dull and red as the music, in the cluster of attitude jets. She peered past the letters to be blinded by a sudden swelling ball of light that enveloped the side of the motor pod. The window lost magnification and dimmed as the glow grew to a pulsing fireball, but too slowly. Ram dropped his book as he saw the captain in ghastly silhouette clutch her eyes and fall forward like a broken shadow puppet. The brain sounded a maddeningly unnecessary alarm.

'Yes, yes,' growled Ram and tabbed it off. The sudden silence was broken by a furious tattoo on the hull. It was as if the stars were falling on the window, glowing dots slamming into the transparency and the hull about them. Great scars and gashes streaked the window, but the transparent ceramic was as strong as the hull, and thicker. Damaged, it held. Ram bent over the captain, curled into a tight ball with her hands over her eyes. A patch of the wall by some monitors was smudged black suddenly; wisps of smoke, and a sickly smell trailed into the antiseptic air of the cabin. As he uncurled her he heard the swish of the extinguishers behind him. The glow had faded sufficiently for the pale letters written over space to be easily visible. PREMATURE FIRING, they spelled out, ATTITUDE JET MALFUNCTION EXTENSIVE DAMAGE.

'I'd never have believed it,' said Ram sarcastically as he dumped the captain in the control chair. She was moaning to herself. 'I'm blind, I'm blind, what was it, I'm blind.'

'At least your eyes aren't too badly damaged,' he told her dully, as he swung the medical probe over her face. 'No, you'll be all right – okay – in a few hours. The window was meant to react to suns, not explosions. They don't happen – they *didn't* – damn the owners! And their maintenance crew.'

He read off the window: MOTOR DESTROYED * EXTENSIVE HULL PUNCTURES * LIFESYSTEM INTACT * LANDING BOATS – it paused – BAY DAMAGED* ALL BOATS DAMAGED * HOLD PIERCED * UNABLE TO PRESSURIZE – 'which won't hurt the passengers, at least,' he said with a grim smile. 'It never was pressurized this trip. We don't have to worry about *them* . . .'

The captain glared toward the sound of his voice.

'We most certainly do!'

'Eh? Well how? I mean we can't deliver them now, whatever happens; they're dead weight – if you see what I mean. Best ditch them now!'

The captain choked on moral outrage. 'You'd do a thing like *that* to innocent—'

'—people considerably deader than I want to be just yet. Ashes, dust, no more. The attitude jets are still working, you know, the ones on the main hull. They might just help us yet. Why clutter things up with surplus mass ? Jettison them – with full honours, if you like – but let's jettison them.'

The medical unit swung back and the captain sat up, blinking traces of yellowish cream out of the corners of her eyes. She peered owlishly at the parade of damage reports that shuffled across the window.

'Ram, I can't see much, but I can tell you here and now that we haven't a chance. The best thing we can do is hit Earth head-on. That way our cargo will reach its destination eventually. We've no hope—' She waved her hand, as if tossing something aside; he caught the hand, turning her towards him.

'Now don't go all despondent on me! Lots of ideas – lots already. Don't dampen them, will you ?'

'Do they all involve – ditching – our poor passengers into space, like so much burnt cow-dung ?' she inquired, in a tone of Brahmin authority. He snorted.

Hinduism had been all but dead for centuries when Earth was abandoned, but its impress still lay on Indian culture. The same was true of Christianity and Islam, and of religious Judaism. In the Centuries of Settlement now ending, however, religion had gathered strength again as embattled pioneer societies clung ferociously to their spiritual values. Their religion became their expression of future and past, their link with roots and with destiny; it became a symbol of progress towards the ideal and of the memory of their Golden Age, the dead past of Earth whose glories grew in legend as memory faded. Christians looked toward Jerusalem, Jews toward Israel as their Zion lost once more. The Black Stone of the Kaa'ba had been taken with all ceremony to the Place of Remembering Mecca, but the Moslem at prayer raised his hands to the stars that held the Shrine of the Birthplace. For them, the object of devotion had become more celestial and remote as memories faded and were filtered by time, until its desecration was forgotten –

as, perhaps, was Eden's. And as with Eden, none had returned –
until now.

The new Hinduism was born of the old, but the parent
would not have known the child. It had made what was merely
a desirable end in the old faith into the absolute tenet of the
new, the culmination and reward of faith. It was at once the
attainment of *samara*, the heavenly rebirth, and the attainment
of the higher good, the merging with creation that was *nirvana*.

'To die is to return home,' sang the holy men, over and over.
'Returning home to one's father's house,
The drop that regains the stream,
The great stream that flows on for ever.'
Thousands had lived and died in this faith, that one day, when
a ship could at last be spared to make the long return journey,
their ashes would be scattered on the waters of the River, the
sacred Ganges, to be carried down to the Sea which held the
ashes of their ancestors, from which all life had come. As the
ashes dispersed and mingled in the waters, so the soul would
be dispersed in the Universal Ocean to attain *nirvana*. That
long-awaited day had come.

'You can't betray your ancestors!' the captain snapped. They
had been arguing for hours. 'No matter what you believe yourself. What would you gain?'

'Life!' growled Ram, looking up from readouts which projected themselves across his sweat-streaked face. 'Listen, you,
we still have a chance. Only one good one, though; our speed's
the problem, but this will make use of it. We have one usable
boat left – well, it will hold together long enough to land us,
won't it? So we send back a distress call by robot courier and
wait on Earth for a rescue ship. Six months at the most, I think,
and we could salvage the food units, maybe even grow something. Isn't that enough of a hope?'

'Not to make it worth abandoning souls, Ram. And the plan is
half-witted. We have to get into orbit to use the boat. And it's
hardly usable – one side is full of holes, it can't be pressurized
and it would fall to bits when it hit the atmosphere.'

'It won't have to,' said Ram smugly. 'We'll use the *Uma* herself.'

She looked at him bleakly.

'Bad taste,' she said after a while, thickly. 'Very bad taste, such a joke. Or – Ram, you *child*—' speaking through teeth on edge, 'have you really forgotten that THIS SHIP CAN'T EVEN ENTER THE ATMOSPHERE – let alone land, which is what you seem to have in mind. So—' Gathering hysteria only turned the captain's face stonier, as smoothly inhuman as a temple carving. Its only possible outlet would be a hysterical shriek, something Ram found himself dreading as a disturbance of calm. Calm, the cool water he lived in, being made muddy and opaque.

'We don't *have* to land,' he said hurriedly but in a soothing tone, as to an enraged idiot. 'Of course not. Just – well, let me show you . . .' He tapped controls, then waved his hand in a circle at the window. A pale and shaky circle of light flowed in its path over the stars.

'Earth, right ?'

His hand cut a line in the air, which the window echoed.

'Our course—' He extended the line, curving it towards the circle till it struck the rim and bounced off at a tangent. He froze the design there. 'We aim the ship just *so* – we eject in the boat as the ship strikes the atmosphere. We'll have used the power we have left in the attitude jets to slow us down a bit, and we'll strike the atmosphere at a shallow angle. At that speed the air will deflect the ship out into space again – meanwhile we've ejected in the boat; our suits will keep us safe for longer than we need, so it doesn't matter if we can't pressurize it. Damaged or not, it won't have any re-entry stresses and the ship won't come down on our heads. The brain can do it—' she had not seen him touch the controls, but suddenly the design vanished and rows of figures paraded arrogantly across the stars. 'That's a chance, then, isn't it ?' said the navigator kindly, for the captain was looking blankly in front of her, blinking away tears.

'Y-yes,' she admitted at last, 'that might work. I'd never have thought of it myself – but Ram, no, we can't! We'd be leaving the passengers to go sailing off into space, they'd never be picked up – we can't do *that*!'

'When the rescue ship came—'

'It wouldn't be able to find them. Not if they'd been careering off on an unknown course for months – space is too big. And they might be deflected into the sun. . . . Ram, think of what their relatives back home would say, think of it! I won't stand for it!' she said, imperious again. 'I'm still in command.'

'Your eyes—'

'They're recovering. I've said my last word, Ram. Our heading will be for Earth. I'll programme the brain to aim us appropriately. In the meantime I suggest you go and sort out something to believe in and prepare for a more dignified end.'

His door slammed as punctuation. The captain immediately regretted her last remark. The temptation to save yourself at the expense of others is strong. . . . She had hated the tempter for a while, but she would apologise before the end. When they were both calmer. Now, however, they were on the edge of the solar system; the brain had to be programmed. Ram's figures still marched back and forth across the window. She faded them out of it and began her own calculations.

They took her too long because her eyes kept failing her as she strained them; finished at last, she was peering through a dim brown haze as she set the controls, as if at the bottom of muddy water. She slumped down in the control chair and allowed the heavy eyelids to slide down at last. They felt strangely cool. Her head fell back and a slack relaxation spread from the shoulders down. Her knees sagged apart, her arms flopped on the comfortable chair-arms, then she hunched painfully into herself in an agony of fighting off sleep. It did her no good. Emotional stress is the most wearing of all, and the cool neutral light pained her eyes even through closed lids.

She really must dim it, but by now sleep held her like quicksand. Struggling to fight her way up, she stirred one arm, but it did not move. All at once she was awake and flailing the other arm. Ram grabbed it also and taped it to the chair-arm on the other side, then clutched her feet together – at the cost of a kick on the cheek – and taped them to the pedestal of the chair. All without a single word, and he kept his eyes away from hers.

Religion grows in a society that feels a need to believe, usually

64

because it has something to fight. When the dragon is dead, the barbarians routed and a coddling utopia is brought about man no longer needs the sustenance of religion. The gods languish. Ram saw his cargo simply as a load of carbon that had once been superstitious enough to pay for this last voyage; most of his generation would have agreed with him, not as atheists exactly but as sophisticates. What could such a crude ritual as cremation and ash-scattering have to do with the essence of religion – how could the disposition of the body affect the soul? If it existed. And what made the Ganges so special? Better to give your body to your *new* world, become a part of it. Ram was ready to pander to his ancestors' whims as a matter of good pay and professional skill, but quite unready to let them stand between him and his life.

'It's for your own good,' he told the captain, and believed it. She made a low snarling noise at him through her nose. He had been forced to tape her mouth because of screams and bites every time he went near the controls. 'It *is*,' he insisted, 'and if you won't see reason, Brahmin or no, I'll bundle you into the boat trussed up in a pressure bag. If I have to. But I'll do one thing for you – I won't jettison the ashes. They're not actually in the way. Look,' he protested to a stony face, 'there's always a chance that the ship will encounter the Earth again one day, if it stays in the system. And if it does the ashes will all end up in the Ganges sooner or later. And meanwhile the ship will have taken the atmosphere shock and we'll have ridden down light as a falling leaf—'

He made a fluttering motion with his hand, from under her long straight nose down to her lap. His hand rested lightly on her knee; she slammed her other knee hard against it, making him yelp and wave his hand about. This petty triumph was eclipsed by a sudden flurry of activity from the read-outs. Necessary course changes and angles of approach scuttled palely across the window, pausing a second for approval before vanishing as they were keyed into the helm. Ram watched with the air of a general at a march-past, head thrown back and arms crossed across his chest.

'So there you are, Paroo,' he said as the display at last faded, giving ground to the impassive stars. 'A more than fair chance of survival, wouldn't you say?' The impudent diminutive of her name was making the captain squall behind her gag. Ram, unheeding, poured himself cold fruit juice.

'A toast to our joint survival. Sorry you can't return it – well, look, no reason you shouldn't have a drink. Promise not to scream or bite and I'll take off the gag. ...' She stared impassively at him, and he peeled off the tape. She spat in his face and he hurriedly replaced the tape.

'Damn it, you'll thank me for this – once we're safe on Old Earth. You'll see!' He tried to slump in a chair, turning his back on her, but immediately felt an animal vulnerability, as if a predator's eyes bored into his back.

'Got to repair boat,' he muttered, and drained his juice. Maybe a door, an airlock, a vacuum suit would shut out the eyes. 'You'll thank me for this,' he repeated as he stamped out, 'once we're there I'll take you to India, if you like. But anywhere on Earth will suit me. I want to see greenery again – plants, trees, flowers, birds and animals. ...' His wistful voice trailed off down the corridor. A door shut on it.

Ram was patching up the boat as best he could. The boat bay in which he was working was riddled with large and small holes, and it was easier to work in a suit than patch them all. Only half the lighting still worked, and he was glad of this; the other boats were mere hulks, disturbingly skeletal. They made him think of what might happen if the brain was wrong. That was simply not possible if it was working properly, and its fail-safes in case of damage were excellent.

It was lucid enough now; he peered at a flayed-open section of the ship's hull and pale glowing lines appeared in the faceplate of his suit, superimposed on the circuitry he saw. They traced out paths and patterns, labelled and mapped them, pointed out damage and necessary modifications. When he asked questions the answers came in pleasingly impersonal detail. He actually preferred the isolation of the suit, insulating him not only from vacuum but from the brooding presence in the control room. The suit was a little womb-like world in which problems of survival had little meaning. With that thought it suddenly became uninhabitable and mild claustrophobia set in.

Hurriedly he finished his work. He had cannibalised part of the ship's food system. All he needed to do now was repair the damaged launch cradle that must lift him clear of the ship. It would be a long job, but not hard; the cradle was run out on a simple linear motor of which it itself was the only major moving part. The massive coils, fractured in a dozen places. . . . He had the time but must sacrifice some of it. The suit felt leaden, the flickering patterns in its faceplate hurt his eyes. Even before the airlock had fully pressurised he was fumbling with seals and catches.

The control room seemed like a cool fresh garden as he came up the companionway, even with scorched walls and slight smell of smoke. His eyes suddenly met those of the bound captain, no longer dim but gleaming, unblinking, a jewelled cobra stare.

'She is beautiful,' he thought, 'agelessly beautiful. And both gentle and savage like – like one of her gods.' He remembered his schoolboy religion, another aspect of Parvati, the she-principle of Siva. . . . Durga, perhaps, and Kali. She-destroyers, even of themselves ? Strange, that a goddess should seek to lay down her life for men, dead men at that. He shuddered suddenly. It was entirely consistent with the nature of a goddess that she should want to lay down not only her own life but his as well, without consent. This avatar of whoever was a danger to him. Emphatically he did not want to die, not so young, and disappear from the universe. If he had had children, now, a continuity of life, he might have been more willing to die, or if it was somehow to give life to others. That is satisfying. But to die in the service of the dead – he shook off the spell of the cobra. The captain was a slender woman, bound, once more.

'We'll make it!' he smiled at her, 'but first we have to know where we're going. The brain can time this nicely, so we can choose the area we hit by adjusting to the planet's rotation. Boat's loaded, not much more to do. Those big holds they put in for the ashes are very useful. . . . Pity they didn't spend the money on a motor overhaul instead. . . . There are lots of fresh provisions aboard too, and betel pills for you . . . I think we'll have a good time.' He paused in his prattling, though silence fought on her side, and stared out at the stars. 'You know,' he remarked, 'if it's only half as good as it's made out to be, Earth, then I'm really amazed at the pioneering spirit of Man. It's a miracle anyone ever left the place. . . .'

He instructed the brain to develop a braking sequence that would allow it to impact on a suitable area to keep them alive for a few months. He hoped the shock-wave wouldn't do too much damage below, or knock the boat too far off target; better choose somewhere with lots of nice open land, preferably fertile. The country life would do them good after months in this airtight hearse.

All the time he had been working the brain had been scanning the distant planet; he hoped it would choose India. That might shut the captain up; they could even take some token ash along . . . But he would settle for anywhere decent.

AVAILABLE LANDING AREAS ? he asked the brain.

The window glowed. NONE it said.

The captain heard a choking sound as if something tore in Ram's throat. She was turned away from the screen but could follow what he was demanding of the brain from the scuttling dance of his fingers on its inputs, small creatures dashing madly about their cage. Atmosphere scan data; cloud pattern data; he called them up like a damned magician calling up successive familiars. And, as familiars do, they betrayed him further.

The captain could not see the answers except in his face, but she saw them clearly. They bent his stiff shoulders down. His head sagged for a second, then he spun her round to face the window across which data filed aimlessly, repeating itself. He almost tore the tape from her mouth, but caught himself and removed it gently. She did not speak.

'Well,' he said at last. 'Now I know why they left – eh ? Pioneering spirit,' he muttered, making the words a curse. 'Blind terror, more like. That – *place* – it's dead, it's decayed, rotten. The ground is chemical-ridden, radioactive. Just dust,

68

mined and farmed to death, I suppose. The sea—' he choked as though tasting its bitter waters, '—it's the same, poisoned, ravaged. What rivers are left - oh yes, I found the Ganges all right. Half slime, what there is of it. The air's not breathable. The only traces of life are a few half-starved micro-organisms in the rivers. But it's dead, all of it. We're taking ashes to ashes—'

He giggled slightly, then control slammed into face and body like a blow. 'We couldn't live a week down there. Not without as much survival gear as we'd need in space.'

'It must have been so bad,' said the captain softly, 'that they ruined it altogether in the effort to leave.' Ram tore away tapes.

'They have destroyed me,' he said thickly. 'But there is still a chance. Mars and Venus were colonised, were they not? I might reach Mars in the ship's boat when we cross its orbit. There might be something left there that will keep us alive - you are welcome to join me, of course. It's a chance.' The captain looked at him a minute, massaging cramped muscles.

'You must not get angry, Ram,' she said, 'if I tell you that it's no chance at all.' She blocked off a snarl with a gentle gesture. 'You must not, because you know it yourself. Why wear yourself out in the effort?'

'I - You're right, damn you, there's no chance really. But why should I sit back, eh, and wait for death, a death that won't mean anything?' He wiped the hopeless data from the window, leaving the stars pure.

'Beautiful—' sighed the captain.

'But cold!' snapped Ram. He sighed. 'The stars around the solar system. As beautiful as legend made them, but cold like the system - it's cold, it's dead. We're the only life in it now, you and I. I can't just throw life away, if Earth is dead. Do you see, woman, do you understand?'

The captain swung violently away from the window. 'Yes,' she said, more calmly than she'd acted, 'I begin to. Survival unto death - that's a paradox, but it makes sense. In a way it is inescapable logic. I should not have argued, Ram; you have principles to justify also, and at a similar cost. I will not come with you, my principles are not yours, but I will help you all

I can.' The navigator had turned away, was bent over the input board. She put a hand on his shoulder. 'I'm sorry we ever disagreed.'

'At any rate,' he said, 'our paths do not conflict. A plunge towards Earth – it will suit me as well as any course we can take. We lack the power in the attitude jets to improve it materially.' He smiled quite effortlessly. 'Which makes us friends, doesn't it ?'

They had arced deep into the system by now, passing the outer planets without a glance. Such distant glory was beyond human concern, and human concern was what they were finally discovering, replacing a sterile politeness. They laboured together in the boat bay, welding the cracks in the cradle motor's stator coils, coils that must hurl the boat well away from the ship. Against the crushingly great backdrop of Jupiter their activity, motion, any affirmation of life became significant. Each the other's mirror, they reflected humanity in a desert worse than dead, for never having been alive.

'And even death is human, eh ?' grinned the navigator. The grin showed even through the cocooning spacesuit and couch, even on the small monitor the captain watched in the control room. 'You know,' Ram chuckled, 'it's not too late to come with me, Paroo. It'd make a lonely ride more pleasant . . .'

'My name,' she said coolly, 'is Parvati . . .' But the smile in her voice broke through. 'No, Ram. You are tempting, very tempting. But I have a responsibility to my passengers.'

'Captain goes down with her tradition, eh ? Well, it's time. Take care of them, eh ?' The monitor cut out, changed to a view of the bay interior. It was easier, reflected the captain, easier rather than harder to part. She watched the outer door open, the cradle clamps release. Easier because each understood the other's reasons. 'I wish you every good, Ram,' she said over the voice link. 'Including luck if there is such a thing. And you've a responsibility too. Initiating launch sequence.' As power came on the cradle lifted gently on the growing magnetic field of the stator and began to slide forward as it did so, to gain speed. Then a blue spark leapt in its path, another, a shower, a flame—

70

'Ram!' shrieked the captain. The cradle lurched down into the sparks, tilting the boat off to one side; a sizzling arc leapt from the coil to meet it. A weak join—

'Ram! Get out of there!' she called again, but the cradle smashed with sickening slowness into the wall ahead. A great beam wrenched loose and struck like Kalkin's sword down the centre of the paralysed landing boat. A white flash made the arc look dull. The hull rang thunderously; again came the swish of the extinguishers, distant now. The monitor was dead. The captain did not look at it.

'So you are coming with me, indeed,' she said to the suddenly empty room. 'I'm glad.'

The dead Earth fled, but, mindless, did not know it.

The brain easily located the barrenness that was India, thanks to Ram's excellent programming, and braked the ship at the exact moment. With no life below to worry about it could impact as near the Ganges as it could get. The captain had abdicated control to it. She had other things to do, collecting everything inflammable into the centre of the control-room floor.

She cut open the gutted recycling plants until she found alcohols. She disconnected the extinguishers and began flushing the air with the pure oxygen reserve. The procedure was unorthodox, but had a satisfying ritualistic quality. When all was ready she sat and listened to music. She did not speak to Ram, because he understood well enough.

From the speeding arrow the planet fled, but could not turn from its path. Spinning helplessly, it exposed the brown scar on its flank that was India. The distance scale on the window flickered down into uselessness. The captain swung herself on to the alcohol-doused pile. Her head swam from the oxygenated air; she whispered, but not only because it burnt her throat.

'Kali the Terrible,' she breathed, 'Durga the Invincible, Uma the Mystic, you are all of these and more. But in the Beginning and End you are Parvati who sits by the side of Siva. . . .' A mile ahead the fused point of the boom struck a white flare from the outer atmosphere. "Accept a sacrifice!' Her laser touched off the pile, the room filled with a flash-fire.

A white light slashed the murky clouds apart, a booming shockwave blasted the dead, dusty soil from the plains of India, blew the tainted snow from the Himalayan peaks and burnished them bright with the dust. The ocean was struck back, licked with heat, then it gathered, rose and fell in wrath upon the stained beach. Hurricanes whirled the dusty air and broke in thunder and lightning into the first rain there for centuries, huge droplets stirring the few microscopic plants and animals that clung feebly to life in the poisoned slime of what had been rivers.

Ablation slowed the ship as it flayed open the hull, and the *Uma* struck a hundred miles south of the Ganges. Its crater opened a broad chasm in the land, cracks radiating from it; lava boiled out and cooled in the rain. The precious ashes were blasted back into the air, to be caught and borne down again by the torrential rain to lie with the vapourised remains of the ship.

And as the rain grew it swelled the Ganges, which sought and found a new path, a crack leading to the great chasm. Slowly, tentatively, like a child taking its first steps, the Ganges edged down its clean new channel, bearing a precious burden of life over a plain covered with fertile volcanic mud and wholesome ashes such as had been sprinkled on its waters once before, long ago.

HERITAGE

BY SCOTT EDELSTEIN

*Here is a very human, immediate story which brings the reali-
sation that stock science fictional characters are almost invari-
ably 'loners' – male, bachelor, ageless, without obvious ties or
commitments. Not at all real people like you and I, enmeshed
as we are in a web of social obligations and responsibilities.*

*Is Scott, in the story, really free to do his own thing ? Does
he make the right decision? I can't think of another story which
has gone down this road since Ward Moore's clasic 'Lot'.*

*As for the real Scott Edelstein he is not talking about him-
self, at least not in print. 'Am I indeed Scottie, the protagonist
in "Heritage"?' he asks. 'Would it make any difference if I
were a house painter or a Buddhist monk? I submit that it simply
does not matter.'*

*Certainly Scott is rapidly making a name for himself in
science fiction, having sold to almost all of the magazines and
anthology series and now editing several volumes himself.*

I awoke. It was late morning; bright summer sunlight shone
through the window. Living in the woods had changed us in
many ways, but one habit of the effortless suburban life we used
to lead still remained, we were all late sleepers.

My awakening had been abrupt; I had deliberately struggled
out of unconsciousness to deal with something that was not in
order. I looked to my left. Donna was sleeping peacefully on a
pile of blankets beside me, snoring softly. Mark was curled up

73

beside her in a foetal position. His hands were wedged between his knees to keep them warm.

My own paranoia, I thought. I had always been the most wary of the three of us, perhaps because I wanted the most to survive. Or perhaps because I was the most afraid of death; to me, they have always amounted to the same thing.

Then I heard soft voices coming from outside. Whoever the people were, they were making no attempt to surprise us.

No trespassing signs were posted all around the area, along with notices announcing that we were fully armed, could shoot with accuracy, and were not afraid to use our weapons.

The people outside were either very confident – which meant there might be dozens of armed men and women waiting outside to attack us – or very stupid.

I shook Donna. She stirred immediately, opened her eyes, sat up. 'People outside,' I said quickly. 'They're pretty loud; they may be a distraction for a mass attack.'

She stood up quickly, let the quilt that had been covering her drop to the floor. Our nakedness suddenly struck me; we had not seen other people in weeks and had forgotten that nudity was unusual for most of the world. I immediately forced the thought out of my mind; there was no time to dress. *Dress for battle*, I thought.

Together, we awakened Mark. He was sleeping very soundly, as usual, and we had to slap him several times before he opened his eyes. Donna explained to him what was happening while I took three rifles and ammunition from the rack. I checked the guns; they were already loaded.

The voices outside had become much louder; the trespassers could not have been more than a hundred steps from the cabin.

'Cover us through the window,' Mark said to Donna. She nodded slowly and looked at both of us with eyes that radiated energy. In another time, she would have been burned as a witch. Mark smiled back at her; I was already at the door, ready to open it.

Mark joined me in a moment. 'Ready?' he said softly.

I nodded.

'Now.'

I pulled open the door. Mark ran through it, hoisted his rifle to his shoulder, shouted, 'Stop right there!' I was outside barely one second later, raising my own gun, ready to fire.

A middle-aged couple stood at the edge of the clearing that was our yard, their hands held straight up. They were dressed in expensive, colourful clothing. The man wore a suit jacket with matching slacks; the women wore a pantsuit outfit.

I heard Donna mumble 'holy shit' from inside the cabin.

I looked around the clearing, saw no other people. I looked at Mark, who was squinting at the people standing in the clearing.

'I can't see anyone else anywhere,' I said to Mark.

'Can you see their faces?' he asked, still looking down the barrel of the rifle.

'No.' Even with glasses, my eyesight has always been poor. 'But by their posture they look about fifty. Maybe fifty-five.'

Mark's long, straight yellow hair stirred in the late morning breeze. 'I think they're your parents.'

A rush of memories entered my mind. I shook them off. 'God, I hope not.' ..

'It's just the thing they'd do.'

I know.

'Scott-ie?' the woman said. Her voice was almost a whine; it always had been. She spoke my name slowly, plaintively, her voice shaking even more than I remembered it to. For twenty-five years she had addressed me in the same tone of voice. I remembered growing up, in the suburbs. Neighbours and relatives knew me as a frightened, neurotic mama's boy; that was the impression my mother tried so urgently to put across. Her voice was one of her most effective tools.

'What do you want?' I said.

'Look, at least let us come closer, okay?' my father said, fear showing through his annoyance. He was the sensible one of the family; he had no patience for anything that challenged his sensibilities.

'All right,' I said. They began to move forward. Neither Mark nor I lowered our rifles. 'Stay inside,' I said to Donna, who mumbled an affirmative.

75

'You're going to have to handle this yourself,' Mark said. 'I've got a gun, but it doesn't mean anything. They're going to go at you with guilt.'

I nodded. 'I know.'

'If you let them talk to you, you'll be playing their game. You'll have to beat them at it, or else send them away right now.' The wind grew stronger, pressing gently against my skin. The scent of greenery filled the air.

'Stop there,' I said to my parents when they were about twenty paces from the cabin. 'You can hear me from there.' I could see them in detail now; my father's face had aged almost ten years since I had last seen him three years before. His jowls sagged and his eyes were very tired. My mother's face was covered with quite a bit of make-up, obscuring her age. Her hair was dyed yellow; I had never in my life seen it gray. She was crying.

'You know your mother doesn't hear very well,' my father said. I knew; she had used that both as a weapon and a defence for years. I thought, *why was life with them always a battle?*

'That's too bad,' I said. 'Stay where you are.' *Watch it, buddy; don't get sucked into their way of thinking. There's no purpose to being nasty.*

Mark lowered his rifle, strode towards them. 'Don't worry,' I said. 'He's going to check you for weapons. You'll get them back when you leave.'

My father was wearing a shoulder-holster, in which he carried a pistol. My mother carried no weapons.

'Did you need to use the gun at all?' I asked.

'What?' my mother said. She turned to my father. 'Joey, what did he say?' She never asked the speaker to repeat his words; she always depended on someone else.

I waited.

My father turned to her. 'He asked me if I had to use the gun.'

'What? Gun? He's using a gun? What did he say?' Her speech grated on me. Her words were senseless. As always. My mother was never a stupid woman, merely deluded, ignorant, and scared.

76

My father explained it to her once again. She feigned understanding. My mother never understood anything she didn't want to understand, yet she pretended and lied to make things easier on herself. I recalled confronting her with words: 'Haven't you been listening to what I was saying?' I would ask her. Her reply was always, 'Of *course*. But tell me again; I want to hear it one more time.'

Feelings, thoughts, perspectives, and lifestyles may change; memories remain.

'No,' my father said to me. 'Things were pretty quiet.'

'Be careful on your way back. Even around here there are bad shortages. People will kill you for your money.'

Mark walked back to where I stood, handed me the pistol. He looked at me; his eyes were bright, with no single emotion. 'I'm going back inside; I'm going to sleep, okay?'

'Okay.' He walked into the cabin.

'Why did you come here?' I said.

'Your mother and I' – that was always how he started his spiel when he wanted something from me – 'can't keep on living in Beechwood anymore, it's getting much too rough. You've been reading the papers, you know what it's like.'

I hadn't read a newspaper since I had moved into the cabin. 'I know,' I said.

'The riots are spreading out of Cleveland. Our money's hardly worth anything anymore. Even the markets won't take it. And most of them closed down. Your mother and I haven't had a piece of meat in two weeks.'

Poor babies. No juicy sirloins laced with hormones and chemicals. For years they had ridiculed me about my eating habits: for eating 'that organic stuff' and for eating when I was hungry rather than on a schedule.

'There's not even any kind of work I can really do, anymore.' He had been a salesman all his life; with money practically worthless, and with half the population starving, what good was a salesman? And there were plenty of younger men to fill all the jobs involving manual labour.

I didn't need to hear the rest of the story. 'You want to come and live with us, is that it?'

'Scottie,' my mother said. 'Put that gun away.' With almost a hint of authority in her voice. 'It scares me.'

'We have to,' my father said. 'There's no other place we can go back to. Believe me—' He said this with half a sneer. '—if we didn't have to, we wouldn't.'

I held my rifle down at my side, but did not put it down on the ground. I tried to choose my words carefully, then gave up and let the words flow freely. Semantics was their game, not mine.

'I'm sorry, but there's no way you can stay here. There's just no way we can feed five people. We're barely feeding three as it is.' I surprised myself with my directness and conciseness.

'Scott,' my mother said, 'what else do you expect us to do? We were wrong. We didn't know. You told us the cities would collapse and you were right. Now we have to stay with you.' She had dropped the child's label from my name, but only as bargaining propaganda. She was using the logic she had been using all her life; admit you are wrong and give in, and everything will be fine. The fact that we could only grow enough crops and raise enough small animals to feed three people did not concern her.

'I told you – we just can't feed you. If you moved in here with us, we'd all starve.'

'Look,' my father said, obviously annoyed, and frightened. 'Have a little sympathy for once, will you? We brought you up and supported you for eighteen years. We would have supported you longer if you hadn't left home when you did.' They had promised never to use that argument against me. *Promises are only words.*

There was no point in talking; there never had been. 'You can't stay here. I've told you why. We don't have anything else to say to each other. Please leave.'

'Jesus Christ!' my father burst out. 'Can't you, for once in your life, stop thinking about yourself? Just this once stop being selfish and think about us, for a change.' The guilt trip. I ignored it.

'Scottie,' my mother said, on the verge of tears, 'we saw your vegetable garden, and your animals.' She managed a false

78

smile. 'They're nice. You can feed us, I know you can.' The smile faded.

I had been a farmer for three years; she had never been on a farm in her life. Years before, when I would mention the slaughtering of cows over a steak dinner, she would say, '*Scottie not at the dinner table, for God's sake.*'

'Look, you stupid bitch,' I heard myself say. 'You've believed all your life that any lie you could think up could be turned into reality. Well, it can't now, do you understand me? We've got some vegetables and some rabbits and chickens. That's not going to feed five people – for once in your god damned life, do you hear what I'm saying?'

She responded only by bursting into tears. Though she had occasionally sworn at me, it was the first time I had ever sworn at her, to her face.

'Scottie,' my father said. 'Let me ask you a question. Answer it for me and we'll go, and never come back.' He still thought I was being motivated by hatred and spite; does anybody *ever* listen to what other people say? 'Okay?'

'Okay, ask it.'

'If there had been enough food, would you have taken us in?'

I had commited myself to answering it. If I answered no, he could push the guilt trip hard, perhaps even believe I was lying about the amount of food. People will believe anything that benefits them.

If I answered yes, I would be lying.

Lie to him; it's only words.

'I don't know,' I said, foolishly opting for compromise. 'I'd have to ask the others.'

'Ask them,' my father said. Thirty years as a salesman had made him a master at manipulating people. In the past he had rarely tried to manipulate me. 'Ask them if there's enough food to feed us, while you're at it.'

I raised the gun and pointed it at them once again. I was trembling. 'Go away. If we can support ourselves, so can you.' That, we both knew, was untrue.

My father looked at me. I met his gaze; I had to. I meditated while looking at him, keeping my eyes locked with his but not seeing the terrible emotions in them.

My mother screamed, her voice catching, '*You bastard !*' She ran toward me, and I automatically sighted down the barrel at her. She tripped, fell to her knees, sobbing. My father knelt beside her. She made fists and hit him several times, then collapsed at his feet.

She wailed, long and mournfully: '*Scott-ie.*'

I pointed the rifle at my father. To distract myself from my feelings, I chanted a mantra, very softly.

My father looked at me.

'We walked about ten miles from the road to get here,' he said.

'It's only three miles,' I said.

'I had a tank of gas in the car for an emergency. There's less than a quarter tank of it left. We'll have to stay here or we'll die. Maybe other people can live picking berries off bushes, but we can't.' He paused. 'We can be just as stubborn as you if we have to. We're staying, and that's that. You're not going to get us to move.'

He helped my mother to her feet. She leaned on him. Together, they began walking slowly toward me.

You're going to have to handle this yourself, Mark had said.

I tightened my grip on the rifle, chanting more loudly. I heard a gunshot. A bullet hit the ground just in front of my father's feet, ricocheted across the clearing. They stopped walking.

Donna had fired the shot. I turned my head. 'Thanks,' I said into the cabin.

'Everything is the way it has to be,' I said, knowing my mother would not hear, my father would not understand. 'We're all on our own.'

'Wait until you turn fifty-five,' my father said, almost spitting the words. 'When you can't be so damned independent anymore. There won't be anyone around to take care of you.'

There would be a day, someday, when one of us would no longer be able to do his or her share of the work. Mark, Donna, and I had agreed that whomever reached that point first would be killed by the other two. We all knew that when the time came, we would see things differently.

We did not think about it. We dreaded that moment and even more dreaded its inevitability. We ignored both.

'You had better go now,' I said. I played the card I should have played in the beginning, had hoped I never would have had to play at all. 'I probably wouldn't shoot you, but Donna would. We're both excellent shots.'

I aimed to one side of my father's head and pulled the trigger A bullet whined past him. My mother gasped and began sobbing once again. 'The next bullet will be in the forehead. Donna will shoot if she has to.' I lowered the rifle to my side, placed it gently on the ground.

I picked up my father's pistol, opened it, poured the ammunition out into my hand. I strode to within about six feet of my father, then threw the pistol and bullets at his feet. 'Don't load the gun again until you're out of the clearing,' I said.

'Forget it,' he said. 'We won't take it. We'll die either way.'

'*Joey!*' my mother cried. He shook her into silence.

'You're foolish not to take them,' I said mildly.

'Not so foolish as you.'

I looked into his face. 'Goodbye, Dad,' I said. I looked at my mother but she looked away; she wouldn't even give me a straight goodbye. 'Goodbye, Mom.'

I turned, walked back to where I had left my rifle. I went inside the cabin, without looking back.

I said to Donna, 'Tell me when they're out of sight.'

Mark was sitting on the blankets in the lotus position, hands together in front of his chest, eyes closed. I put the rifle away and sat down beside him.

In a few minutes Donna turned away from the window. She placed her rifle on the rack. 'They took the pistol.' She squatted and took my hands. Her dark red hair fell over her cheeks. 'They'll be back,' she said.

'I know. We'll have to be ready.'

A few minutes later we made love. When I climaxed I imagined we were in my bedroom in my parents' suburban apartment, hearing my mother walking toward the room to check on my behaviour.

Two weeks later, my father, visibly thinner and almost certainly insane, attacked the cabin without a weapon. Mark shot him. We buried him next to the garden and let his body enrich the soil. We never learned what happened to my mother.

A SMALL EVENT

BY ROBERT HOLDSTOCK

Let me say straight out that 'A Small Event' is my own personal favourite among the numerous stories Rob Holdstock has now seen into print. Like his highly successful 'Travellers' in the first ANDROMEDA this one deals with time; but in an oblique sort of way that's not really what the story is about at all. You may in fact find 'A Small Event' to be about a number of things, for Rob has built a considerable amount of speculative thought into his piece. Yet in the last act he masterfully draws together the threads – even the very title itself – to produce a movingly human tale.

Rob Holdstock is rapidly becoming one of the most successful of the current wave of new British SF authors, with one novel available in both hardcover and paperback and further books well advanced in the pipeline. I'm pleased to welcome this second contribution to ANDROMEDA.

There was a great gathering by the banks of the Taim, and we were among the last to arrive.

We had left the gyro spinning silently and happily on the side of a hill, and indulged ourselves in a physical walk across the last few miles of naked moorlands. One of my great pleasures is to feel unfiltered wind on my face, the soft springiness of water-sodden turf beneath my feet; there is no sound quite as mournful and musical as the low moan of wind between hills; no colours can quite match the subtle shades of grey that streak a stormy sky.

And so I had insisted on walking although Harmony, the

83

female of my current triad, soon tiring of this extravagant spending of energy had strapped on her warm-field and gravity belt; she whisked high into the dusk sky, where she bobbed and blew, a small yellow shape, hair and gown streaming in her wake.

I plodded across the low foothills around the Taim valley, examining every brand (no, species! They were natural) of hardy plant I saw.

By early evening we were within sight of the gathering of aesthetes; the MECH's huge machine towered into the sky, breaking the natural skyline with its sharp angles, sparkling with inner light. I too, then, strapped on my gravity belt and rose beside Harmony. She came close and smiled and we held hands so that her power pack was recharged from my own by way of our skin. I tingled when I touched her, and we laughed and flew swiftly down to the river.

We dropped to the ground a short way from the first of the glowing camp-fires, a small red box from which simulated flames cast light and heat in a circle twenty yards across. The noise of laughter and conversation was inviting and confusing; I imagined I could recognise the voices of old friends, but in the season of alteration it was impossible to say. The nicest, richest voices were never long with a single individual; bought at high prices they passed between two or three persons a year. My own voice had belonged to an actor now seven hundred years dead.

Walking into the area of the gathering I was greeted at once by several acquaintances. By the nearest fire was Helios Ice-Shaper of Polar South who greeted us in that most revolting of south polar ways; he spat in his hand and slapped the palm to my face. I recoiled and he grinned, turning to Harmony, waiting the return of the compliment. Harmony touched a finger to her nose and ran around the man, who turned back to me, surprise and anger in his face.

'Animal!' shouted Harmony. 'Beast!'

I pushed past IceShaper myself, a dramatic gesture received with dramatic silence.

84

I recognised others, notably Aragos from Isreel and Collector from Old Nor. With both of them we spent long minutes talking and exchanging news. Eventually I found Silver, seated more or less alone by the very edge of the river, his gaze fixed on the moonlit, firelit waves of water. Harmony saw him and ran to him, kissing and fondling the reticent youth while I, the 'older' man, waited my turn with patience.

Silver had lately been the moody member of the triad, and he had left our home some fifteen days before the announcement of the coming event. Harmony had been hysterical at first; myself, approaching the problem practically, I could see no reason why, wherever our silver youth had hidden himself, he would not hear of the forthcoming excitement. And he was bound, I had reasoned, to make his way to the site and meet us there.

The accuracy of my prediction earned me much hugging and love from Harmony, who was suddenly as happy and excitable as the mental child she was. I put my arm around her and smiled at Silver, whose face broke into a wide and knowing grin; in the fragmentary moonlight, by the bright light of the fires, his silver skin was alive with glitter and the very act of blinking sent flashes of radiance from his face.

'Why did you flit off like that?' I asked him.

'We were worried,' said Harmony severely. 'You really should tell us when you plan to throw your moods.'

'Yes, I'm sorry,' said Silver, glancing at me with an indefinable expression on his smooth face. 'I was thoughtless.'

'So why go?' needled Harmony, stroking his white hair back from his forehead.

'Oh . . . pressure, I suppose . . . I don't know . . .'

'Love pressure?' I asked. 'Me pressure? Harmony pressure? City pressure? Art pressure? Pressure on its own doesn't tell us anything.'

'Nothing at all,' agreed Harmony. 'What made you go? What *really* made you go?'

Silver shook his head, looked out across the flowing waters of the Taim. 'I don't know. Just . . . just a feeling, a depressed feeling. I can't explain it.'

We didn't push him further. We were both too glad to be a threesome again. We erected our tent and consummated the camp site for an hour or so, and if there was something troubling Silver deep down he certainly didn't show it.

Outside, then, for an evening investigation of the MECH.

I recognised the human component of the MECH immediately. He was a man in miniature, standing less than half my own height and further testimony to his complete eccentricity was the sparkle of wires across his close-cut hair – a vault-network worn *outside* the cranium. His dwarfdom, however, was a post-nat-tank choice on his part – somewhere in his home city the excess flesh remained, preserved, in case he should decide to return to normal size.

I had last met him seventeen years ago, at the site known locally as Stonehang, a primitive place of worship which had been long since swallowed into the earth leaving only one or two rounded, weathered boulders as evidence of the site's importance. The MECH, new to me then, with a very small machine component, had impressed us all with his prediction that the site – a focus of time every seventeen hundred years – would give us a five-minute view of the distant past, a shimmering image in the air of sacrifice and seduction, of warring brothers and the bestial feasting of our ancient ancestors. For the Midget's speciality was *time*, and the distortions in time that could be caused by physical effects. I felt an immediate anticipation, a twinge of excitement – time, that most fascinating of dimensions. We would soon witness its disruption, I was sure.

But what purpose was served by the huge bank of machinery?

And huge is no exaggeration. The bank of green- and red-faced screens towered high over the camp site, stretching up for at least twenty feet and lying along the ground fifty feet to the flowing waters themselves. The Midget operated controls along this entire length, concentrating frantically and using the information to send his thoughts racing back along the face of the machine to somewhere else, changing readings, settings, standing back and watching the vector plottings on the great screens above his head – we all looked up to see the glowing white lines, angles, moving dots, pulses, spinning and twisting shapes.

It was all quite unaesthetic, probably substantially meaningless, and yet because of its involvement with time and the consequences of time disruption the MECH probably had to work harder than others to predict the cosmic events that we, the elitist aesthetes, might find amusing. For this reason we were, as we approached, respectful of the man's light show – more than a little of it would be of real importance, and more than a little could go wrong in the event of hostile personal fields tampering with the delicately-tuned interior workings of the machine-man complex.

'Hi, MECH!' I shouted at a moment when the little man relaxed from his involvement with the battery of signals.

He turned, stared through huge blue eyes at his three visitors, looked from one to the other of us, recognised me, smiled, frowned, shouted: 'I'm busy as *sky* and you come *chitterchattering*! Can't you see how delicate everything is, how precise it all has to be? Go away, don't bother me for the moment . . .'

Harmony giggled at the little man's strange antics. Silver watched him expressionlessly, failing to observe any humour in the situation. I said, 'But Midget . . . what are we to see? What are you predicting?'

The Midget was furious. He shouted something incomprehensible and busied himself with the nearest console of the gigantic machine component. We all watched as certain of the displays went through ugly contortions.

Finally, with an audible screech of frustration, the little man pressed a hand-shaped plate at the very bottom of the machine and came across to us. He had put the whole thing on automatic.

'A human *is* necessary,' he snapped, perhaps detecting my unvoiced thought. 'Imagination for one thing. Check on the machine. Keep a positive life field interlinked with the *son of a bitch*.'

'What sort of language is that?' asked Silver in irritation.

His depression was showing at a bad time; it was important to keep the Midget favourably inclined towards us or we might never find ourselves invited by this MECH again.

But the Midget puffed up with pride and began to lecture us on the old languages of earth. That particular expression, he told us, was called *slang*, and it had been spoken by a mighty race who had once lived on a land mass west of Ireland.

It all sounded very improbable, and gently I returned the little man's interest and enthusiasm to the prediction at hand.

'It will hit the Earth at precisely eleven forty-three point three three seven tomorrow morning – we won't notice *that* of course, because it will have already sped through the atmosphere with noticeable and spectacular effect. It will hit the Earth seven feet from the northern shore of the Taim – you can see where the point has been marked with a light focus. I shall, of course, turn that off before the event.'

Still a little confused as to what exactly we were about to see, I tried to keep him in conversation. He grew impatient.

'Look, there are the vectors, you can follow them all night if you wish, just don't bother me. By the time it reaches point 221, that's marked on screen five, I have to exert traction through the machine to alter its course very slightly so that it doesn't miss the earth. The precise effort on my part will cause it to strike at the co-ordinates I've already given you. Do you see? Will you go now? Will you stop annoying me?'

He bounded away. Silver left our group and went to sit by a camp fire near to our tent. I stood in the chill night, Harmony standing close by and projecting her sympathy for the depressive. She seemed less childish than usual, as if some deeper maturity within her was pushing through the mask she had adopted.

I turned back to the MECH and tried one last time. 'Exactly *what* are we going to see colliding with the Earth?'

His voice, high with anger and excitement, sounded across the campsite, caused heads and bodies to turn. 'A quantum black hole, you fool, a quantum black hole of course!'

What *is* a black hole?

Why, simply (it was explained to us by Robeard of Tunis) a point in time and space where matter has collapsed in upon itself until it is no longer there. A universal node which sucks light from the nether regions thus appearing black since the reverse of light is, of course, dark. A cosmic inaccessibility, a place where the power of a Galaxy is directed, a negative attraction into which whole worlds might easily vanish if the hole had not been properly screened.

At least (added Robeard) that's what I think it is.

Thus enlightened we waited out the night.

Entertainment by the banks of the river Taim:

Silver drew third in the lottery for entertainment during the long night. Harmony drew fourth, but lay just outside the circle around our campfire since her particular artform required some work beforehand. Myself, I drew nothing, which was as well since I had nothing to offer.

The Moon was a pleasant disc, low over the eastern horizon, watching our antics with something less than its full face. The zenith was cloudy, but a sprinkling of stars testified to the ever-present heavens. How, I wondered, as we waited for the entertainment to begin, would one spot a black hole against the black night sky? It seemed to me to be useless to try and distinguish the hole from where we sat, most of us gazing idly heavenwards.

For thirty minutes we watched Jarrol, from the southern land of Isreel, digesting a variety of living creatures; his stomach and belly walls were made of transparent bio-silicone, a closely knit sheet of living connective tissue and silica. He illuminated the proceedings internally, and had treated the animals with special dyes that were released with bizarre effects as Jarrol's ultra-powerful digestive juices stripped layer after layer from the struggling but swiftly motionless, beasts.

I had never been convinced of the artistic value of Jarrol's creativity, but my companions applauded wildly. There was a market for anything, I supposed.

More to my taste were the death memories of a strange solitary man called Diabla, from the ancient fortress city of the eastern steppelands that had no name. Diabla had extended his very real telepathic abilities to the watching of the dead as they struggled out of the mortal sphere. We shared what he had seen, a series of edited clips from forty or fifty dying-dead. In the few minutes after life there were voices, shapes, colours, feelings – but they made no sense, and when some sort of familiar pattern did begin to emerge, that was the end of the clip – to have remained linked with a fleeing soul any longer would have been death for Diabla as well.

Then Silver was called into the circle. He was in no mood to be entertaining but he recognised the importance of etiquette at occasions such as this. As I urged him to the centre of the ring he shook me off, roughly, almost angrily, then turned and looked at me with an unvoiced apology in his eyes. He walked away from me to take up his position by the fire; I felt a great sadness, almost despair. Silver was growing away from me, and had been doing so for some weeks. Why he was distancing himself I didn't know, but it made me angry, and the anger was because of my unhappiness. I watched him by the fire, moody, solemn, and I knew that he was thinking of me, and of nothing else, and that I would hate to know what was in his mind.

Silver stripped off his clothes and pushed his silver cells to their full brilliance so that his body gleamed in the firelight like polished alloy. To attune his mind he stared at the nearest visitor to him, and gradually her shape was etched in black and silver upon his torso, the detail becoming sharp after a few seconds.

'How does he do it?' whispered a woman close to me. Her partners had no idea, and after a moment I felt the gentle tingle in my scalp that told of the mind probe she was directing, not only to me but probably to everyone else about the circle (with the exception of Silver, naturally). I allowed my knowledge of Silver's genetic peculiarity to filter three levels toward my conscious mind and felt each fact snipped away by the curious mind that sought enlightenment.

Silver's skin colour was the result of surface melanophores that could, at his will, expand to cover him completely and allow their silver or black pigments to give him his particular colouring. At will he could selectively depigment his body in lines and etchings to show whatever image he wished. Thus: a girl, her hair in artistically portrayed folds, her eyes, large, sparkling in the firelight, her lips moist, parted, ready to engage the sensitive skin of her lovers as soon as the night's enjoyment had become . . . tiresome.

Silver, excelling himself, was the focus of attention for nearly half an hour, depicting many of those in the circle engaged in erotic or hilarious activities. His *tour de force*, was a scene from history, stretching across his torso from side to side, up to the lower part of his face and down his legs almost as far as his calves. The Great War of antiquity, a war fought between millions of men, with gunpowder and knife, with plane and ship. And what a spectacle Silver made of those events. In the frozen instant of war, in the depiction of a battle as it might have been seen from the air, there were literally thousands of individual shapes, figures, soldiers, engaged in their bloody exchange. Each figure was the controlled expansion of just a few cells!

Silver's final and most dramatic touch was the suffusion of his subcutaneous tissue with blood; through his translucent skin the deeper flesh shone brightly, redly, and the entire montage became awash with rivers of crimson – and there, beneath that wave of gore, those million men died, faded and were lost.

Silver sat quiet, and we were awed. What mental power had been required for that particular feat! What fantastic microcontrol! Pride coursed through my body, pride at being the lover of so magnificent an artist. Harmony was almost crying, perhaps for the same reason. We hugged each other while Silver breathed hard, and listened to the resounding applause of his audience. True genius was measured not by the collision of asteroids but in the capability of handling a million body cells all at once.

And yet we all sensed that Harmony's aesthetic display would outshine even Silver's, and as she finally came into the circle, into the firelight, there was an almost tangible sense of anticipation. She kissed Silver, who walked to the edge of the circle and sat solemnly regarding the young woman. Harmony waved quiet the greeting round of chest-slapping and sat down upon the warm turf. She signalled that we should all remain silent for a few minutes, and we fell still. The aura of expectation in the air grew stronger.

Harmony sat with her eyes closed, cross legged and motionless, concentrating; she had told me, in the past, of the sensations she experienced whilst pushing the biological process in her womb forward at an unnaturally fast rate some pain, to begin with, then dizziness which had to be controlled (this was the result of wild hormone changes, in her blood stream). Then a feeling of peace and a sense of communication – mind filling with the sound of the foetal heart beat, the surge of foetal blood, the multi-levelled waves of foetal awareness.unbesmirched by the pollution of sensory input.

After a few minutes Harmony was ready. Distantly, from other fires, came the sound of cheering, of laughter, of singing – the entertainment of the elite took many forms, but our own circle had provided an evening of mainly anatomical amusement.

It was warm in the red light of the fire, with the waters of the Taim splashing gently a few yards away; behind Harmony the slopes of a hill rose to sombre heights, penetrating the lower of the scudding clouds. All was very relaxed.

She disrobed, to the accompaniment of whistles of appreciation; Harmony was slender and graceful, every womanly feature dainty and precise. No angle was too sharp, no curve too round. By looking carefully the slight swelling of her belly could be seen, but it was the only concession to biological deformity discernable by the unpracticed eye.

She lay down, right by the fire, drew up her legs and closed her eyes.

'A cyclops!' cried Jarrol.

'With green hair, over all but its face.' This from a girl called Hayzel.

'And a forked tail, threshing wildly!' A man named Helix.

'And a cry like a house-spider . . .' Jarrol again.

'And—'

'Enough!' I shouted, smiling to let them see I meant no dis-
respect. 'There may be time for all your tastes.'

We sat back and watched, then. Harmony began to whine
as she directed the forces of her mind and imagination to the
task at hand; her belly writhed as the life within went through
its multifarious changes, and her hands clutched the distorted
flesh to ease the pain and pressure.

Finally – only a few minutes had elapsed– she cried aloud
and seemed to be exerting great effort. Her womb opened and a
single eye regarded us, unblinking, neither hostile nor friendly,
a neutral eye, in a pink bare face. The foetus slipped from its
watery hiding place, green fur sticky and plastered in bizarre
patterns about its eight-inch body. A tail – unforked I noticed –
whipped this way, that way, striking the insides of Harmony's
legs so that she yelled and sat up.

Stricken with panic the homunculus shrieked high and loud
and began to run, ducking under legs and crawling over laps,
pleading with cries and strange sounds as if sensing its im-
pending doom. I touched it as it scampered past, and it turned
and grasped my finger with two little hands, staring up at me
imploringly with its huge single eye. Amused, I poked it away,
trying not to hurt it, and it darted towards Silver who – with a
flick of his hand – sent it reeling back towards the fire. Finally
Harmony snared the tiny being.in a neural web and carried it
back through the air into her clutches.

It struggled in her grasp for a moment, its plaintive cry
bringing sympathetic responses from some of the elite. Then
swiftly she dug her thumb and forefinger into its neck, pinch-
ing until the soft bones parted. The homunculus kicked and
squeaked, scrabbling at Harmony's fingers until its eye glazed
over and it fell limp in her grasp; the monstrous head lolled
as she tossed the pitiful corpse towards Jarrol, who snatched
and scrutinised it, a satisfied expression upon his face.

'Any more ?' begged Hayzel. Harmony shook her head apolo-
getically.

'I'm exhausted. That creation was very difficult.'

There were murmurs of disappointment, but no argument.
Harmony probably had three or four more half-formed em-

bryos in her womb, but would discard them rather than re-incorporate them into her strange germinal tissue. I smiled at her as she sat down beside me, pulling her flimsy robe about her body. Harmony was a true artist! There were no others in the world who could do what she could do, sculpting life itself, moulding the living flesh of her own body. And for that matter, there were few who could compete, with Silver. How lucky I was, a non-artist, to be a part of a triad containing two such truly unique artists.

Time passed, minutes only, as the elite contemplated what they had seen, seated in silence, just the breeze and the river sounds drifting across the camp.

I was about to rise and go to our tent when I heard Harmony's unvoiced puzzlement beside me. I looked at her. She was staring beyond me, round the circle, and as I followed her gaze so there came a murmur of query from all the aesthetes around our fire.

I looked to see what was attracting their attention and my heart raced! Silver was standing, his naked form stretched out in a thin, rigid line with toes digging into the soft earth of the river bank and arms high above his head. His skin flashed as it silvered and a moan of anguish left his lips.

'Silver!' I cried, and ran towards him. In an instant his cry became anger as he opened his eyes and stared at me. 'Leave me alone! Leave me alone, Walker! I don't need you! I don't want you! You're always in the way, Walker. *Go away!*'

Shattered, almost sick, I backed away from him and felt Harmony's arms slip around me, comforting.

'What have I done?' I begged.

Tears in her eyes she shook her head. 'I don't know, Walker. I don't understand . . .'

We both looked back at Silver, still stretched taut and rigid. On his chest a picture began to form, slowly at first, then more and more explicit as the detail filled in. It was a picture of me, facing a Silver who was armed and angry. In my clutches, looking to Silver for help, was a distressed and dishevelled Harmony.

94

'No, Silver!' I shouted, shocked at what he was insinuating 'No . . . she's happy! We're all happy!'

Harmony's hold on me became tighter, her small body transmitting her fear to me.

Silver began to shout. 'None of us are happy, Walker! You've stolen her from me . . . you've come between us from the start! You're an old man and you've stolen her from me. Why don't you *go away*! GO AWAY!'

'Not old, Silver,' I sobbed, unable to keep back tears. 'Not old, just . . . just a passing physical form . . . not old; young! In love with you, with Harmony.' I sat down and hugged my body . . . not old, just the old form I had adopted at the last season of alteration. Silver should know that . . . mature of look, mature of mood. We might reverse everything this coming season. Who knew ? I felt a tremendous depression encompass me. Harmony was crying softly, her face in her hands. Depression. Everywhere depression, as if the prevailing mood of one member of the triad could reach out and infect the others.

Then I noticed, on Silver's chest . . .

'The figures are moving!'

Jarrol's cry convinced me that I was not seeing things, but even so I could hardly believe it. I could hardly believe the evidence of my own eyes!

A great crowd was moving in to watch the display. On Silver's chest my figure was moving towards the figure of Silver, and suddenly – a knife, produced from Silver's imagination, appeared in his hand, and the figure on his chest sent the blade deep into my body, through the heart, deeply through the heart, and there I watched it, my murder, my assassination. And before my body had crumpled to the ground, becoming a shapeless mass of black and silver shadow and light, there was Silver moving into a love lock with Harmony.

The picture faded, but not the atmosphere. *Body mobiles,* the crowds murmured, naming the artform without hesitation. Silver had invented body mobiles.

And, by finally managing to express something he had, perhaps, been unable to express before, he had destroyed our triad!

A gain and a loss in just a few moments of time.

Silver collapsed to the camp floor and his unconscious form was swiftly carried into the security of our tent. I remained seated, bewildered.

A hand on my shoulder, warm lips on my ear. Harmony, tears in her soft, green eyes; she kissed me, caressed me.

'His last alteration was overdone,' she whispered. 'That's all it is, Walker. He opted for depression and they overdid it. In a few weeks he'll want to forget this as much as I do.'

She was right, of course, and yet the wound had gone deep. Too deep. I shook my head. 'He's envious, Harmony. He's jealous of me, and he's broken us up.'

'Not us . . . not you and I, Walker. The three of us, perhaps, but . . .' she trailed off, the words catching in her throat. She no more wanted to break with Silver than she would want to break with me. She was comforting me because of my hurt, but I could detect her concern for Silver. As artists they had always had a special affection for each other, nothing unpermissable, but . . . special.

I kissed her hand. 'Go and see if he's all right,' I said. She smiled and ran towards the tent.

When I returned to the tent both Silver and Harmony were sleeping. I sat for a long while listening to the sound of their breathing, but the exhaustions of the day overtook me eventually.

I woke late in the morning. Harmony was still curled up, but Silver was gone, perhaps out exploring the terrain before the event hit. The day was still and fairly warm, although ominous grey clouds poured across the sky from the hills, and the air was filled with the signs of an approaching storm. But reassuringly the MECH predicted that the weather would be fine all morning, up until the moment when the tiny black hole caught up with the Earth.

I left the tent and indulged myself with a wash in the icy cold waters of the Taim. This high up in the hills the waters were clear and tasteless; I felt as if I was returning to nature.

Drying myself with a palm-dryer I watched the strange shapes and arrows on the MECH; one display, a summary display, showed me the shape of our Earth and the location of the river Taim, and the approach of the black hole. The singularity would penetrate the Earth almost vertically; at that time the planet would be moving away from the approaching event. The final velocity through the Earth would still be more than twenty miles per second. Yet for the instant the black hole was above the river the MECH would vastly slow our time sense so we would observe the passage of the hole across a time span of several seconds. The effect should be marvellous, I thought, as I made my way to the food mash.

The MECH had instructed us to tune our time-space shields to a very high level. The quantum hole, though only one hundred the radius of a small atomic nucleus, would nevertheless exert a gravitational pull of over two gravities at a hundred-foot distance, and we would be sitting a little closer than that!

The depression of the previous evening had lifted but I still felt our triad was doomed. Silver's jealousy, I could accept, was the result of a badly tuned construction during the previous season of alteration. But the emotion had been so powerful that I felt there had to be an underlying rationality. Even without his terribly depressive state, he would still have felt jealousy.

Triads often broke up and reformed, two splitting from one, all splitting from each other – it was no new phenomenon. But I had thought this, my third triad, was stable for life. If it broke again I should have to shrug off my chosen facade of age and maturity and adopt a more youthful persona. This was the way things were done in my home city. I was convinced that any split would be between myself and Silver, with Harmony opting to stay with the youth.

I found Harmony as soon as I had eaten, and we sat by the river as the minutes ticked by. She had recovered her full strength after the exertions of the night before, and now she sat and contemplated the spot indicated by the light focus above the river.

97

'You're very thoughtful, Harmony. Tired?'

'No. Not tired. A little down, that's all. I talked with Silver last night. We talked a lot.'

'About me?'

'Partly. You don't bother him anywhere near as much as he made out last night. That was just anger, and the anger was just . . . frustration.'

'Frustration over what?'

'Over . . .' she searched for the words and the silence was long and strained. Her hand found mine, her head shook, her gaze never left the water. 'I suppose it's what I've felt for a long time, and Silver has felt it too. It's a lack of . . . of significance!'

'Significant art?' I laughed. 'Art is for enjoyment, for relaxation. It was never meant to be significant!'

'Wasn't it? We play a watching game, Walker. We watch each other creating in different ways, we create for others to watch. But we're idle. We lack compassion, too . . . oh we *do* Walker!'

'We do not!' I cried. 'You're taking the myths of Legend Week too seriously. Those times were primitive, irrational. What is shown during that week are the petty attempts of morons to create art – compassion, yes, they had compassion, but what does that mean? Their art was meaningless, compassion or no. Our art is meaningful – even if not all of us have a conception of compassion.'

'You're wrong, Walker,' she said simply. 'Idleness, self centredness, indulgence . . . they've all perverted art in our hands. I'm sure of it. We've lost that very valuable sense of the primitive that just now you held to be something worthless. Without it our art is totally . . . empty!'

I argued no further. If a sense of the past, of the primitive, was really important then it was beyond my ability to see why. But if contact with the past was important then Harmony might find some relevance in the artistic indulgence scheduled for just a few minutes' time – I couldn't believe this particular MECH would advertise a new physical toy unless there was a very real time-contact predicted as well.

Other elite were joining us by the river. I checked the hour and saw no more than ten minutes remained before the arrival of our small event. I ran back to the tent, paged Silver several times without success, and carried the force field generators back to where Harmony was still sitting. Suitably protected in our shells of distorted space-time we were invulnerable to the collision of galaxies.

The MECH was going wild, the Midget frantic.

Where *was* Silver?

We searched the crowds for him, scanned the landscape, the skies. He was nowhere to be seen.

Then:

The wind began to shriek. Above our heads the clouds ceased their graceful flow and became, in an instant, a grey and white confusion of swirling mist . . .

Time slowed.

There was grace in the heavenly motion, the clouds forming a spiral as they spun towards the unexpected gravitational up-set – the wind growled, the river oozed past us, a viscous, sparkling stream.

'Where's Silver?' shrieked Harmony, her voice in my mind filled with panic and unnatural tone; she was communicating at one hundred times her normal rate.

I scoured the raging skies. There was no sign of him. An instant later the cloud patterns changed and great grey and white streamers poured upwards and out of sight; as we watched so the stream of cloud changed direction, lowering focus as the black hole dropped through the atmosphere.

Even the waters of the Taim were violent; the surface broke and jumped, great strands of fluid darting upwards, ten, twenty feet from the main flow before shattering and dispersing under the conflicting forces around them.

Harmony screamed, suddenly and loudly, and I looked from the water to the sky and saw Silver, a small, dark shape, totally at the mercy of the gravitational vacuum. His limbs threshed, his body slowly twisted as he rose and fell, fighting ineffectually with his gravity belt but at the mercy of the upward current. He vanished into cloud, re-appeared to plummet down for a second, up for a second, round and round, tossed and flung – plunging towards the event!

Harmony sobbed, but remained motionless, resigning herself to the inevitable death of her lover. I watched in horror as Silver surged along a streamer of cloud towards . . .

'THERE!' cried a hundred voices. 'SEE – THERE!'

The clouds vanished in the centre of a whirlpool, into an area of distorted imagery and vanishing perspective. And at the very centre flared a brilliant spot of intensely blue-white light.

The quantum black hole itself!

The motionless body of Silver slipped down the gravity gradient followed by a surge of water as the river itself rose in a thrashing sheet and was sucked into the holocaust. Rocks, turf, fragments of mountain followed as the singularity descended toward the dry river bed, sucking water downstream in a miniature *tsurnami*.

At the instant of his death Silver had felt at peace. I had felt it and Harmony had felt it. He had wanted to die, and he had died in a fashion that would never be forgotten. Perhaps he had seen death as the only honourable way to apologise to me; perhaps in some peculiar, unfathomable way he had seen it as an answer to his feelings of futility. Perhaps the act of death itself was creative, and he had forever stolen the field for creative death!

We continued to watch, solemnly, numbly, as the area of distortion passed through the wide, bare river bed. A great cascade of rock and coloured fragments rose slowly, beautifully, up into the air, seeming to rise forever until finally turning to tumble back down to the surrounding countryside, here and there spinning harmlessly away from an onlooker's invulnerable force shield.

At that same moment the time distortions began – in the air, thirty feet above the impacting black hole, I saw the first shape struggling into existence: a huge, black-skinned man, dressed in flowing green and yellow robes – he came into our time only to fall slowly and dreamily into the gaping crater below. But even as he fell, others were bursting out of the past.

Men and women, children of all ages – flaxen haired, black haired, naked, clothed in the most diverse of garments – they came tumbling gracefully out of nowhere, some to die instantly as they hit the ground, others recovering to begin running in exaggerated slowness away from the source of the distortion.

The MECH reverted our time sense to normal.

It was bitterly cold as we came from our protective shields, the howl of the wind mingling with the screams of the time relics and the roars and cries of beasts too, for all manner of animals were also pouring from the rent in space-time. One great grey beast towered above everything else rearing up on hind legs that were huge pillars of flexing muscle; its forearms were tiny and useless, its teeth gleamed in the daylight as the great mouth opened and closed on a fleeing man. After a moment the beast lumbered away from the river, chewing its prey. A large band of the elite set off in hysterical, delighted pursuit.

The time-effect ceased and the outpouring from the past was cut off. Most of the relics were already dead, but a good thirty or forty had survived and were scattering in all directions; men dressed in furs, waving huge metallic weapons (but running just the same), women in brief garments standing and shrieking at the tops of their voices as they were taken by members of the elite ...

The web of a historian reached out from behind me and froze specimen after specimen, and the angry voice of the Collector roared in my ears as he cursed the slaughter of the relics. He managed to secure five of the creatures before they had all dispersed, and set about their examination still grumbling his fury at the waste.

All the rest were in the hills, fleeing, the elite in hot and noisy pursuit.

Harmony ran along the river bank towards a figure that lay writhing and screaming upon a bare rock overhang.

'Walker!' she shouted, by voice and by mind, and I raced

after her, attention half on her and half on the scene of confusion and carnage that was spreading in a widening circle around the crater, itself now beginning to fill with the waters of the Taim.

Harmony was crouched over a woman who was, even to my inexperienced eye, obviously in the final stages of a natural childbirth. Her garments were rough and seemed cut straight from the fur of some shaggy beast. She wore metal bracelets and a necklace of polished stone. Her hair was gathered back in a double plait. Her face was unpainted and contorted with pain as she screamed and sobbed, hands clutching at her swollen belly.

Harmony immersed herself and the woman in a warm-field and tore the garments from the threshing body, exploring the distended belly with its network of blue surface-veins. It was the first time either of us had seen such a sight, except on the medi-grid, and I thought how rich it was in aesthetic qualities.

'Oh Walker!' cried Harmony, delighted with her find. 'What a beautiful sight.'

She pressed her face to the woman's belly and immediately the woman began to fight her, beating futilely with small clenched fists and whimpering in a language as incomprehensible to my ears as the howling of the wind.

'Hold her, Walker!' cried my mate (had she forgotten Silver so soon? Beneath her delight and enthusiasm did there remain any shred of grief for our lost mate?). I entered the warm-field and grasped the arms of the struggling mother-to-be. Again Harmony's head descended to listen to the sound of the unborn child. 'Oh it's so beautiful!' she raved. 'I've never heard anything like it! It's nothing at all like the sounds *I* hear.' She was quiet, then, for a long, long moment, examining with her mind, and then she looked up at me, eyes wide with excited realisation.

'Walker . . . Walker I've got a chance to *really* use my power. Oh Walker what an opportunity, what a moment to be *truly* creative!'

I looked from her to the straining flesh beneath which lay

the unborn child, then to the mother's huge blue eyes that looked up at me, not understanding, but . . . trusting, strangely trusting. Back to Harmony.

'It seems a pity, somehow . . .'

'Oh Walker, silence! You don't understand. I can – I can *really* put my powers to the test. Help me. *Hold her*. Hold her secure and don't argue with me.'

And I obeyed; I held the woman's arms tightly and watched as Harmony placed her hands on the huge belly and closed her eyes to work her mental magic. After a moment the woman began to scream, but my grip only tightened still further. For now Harmony was possessed totally, and as the minutes passed so the sweat began to drip from her face, and her cheeks lost all their colour.

I wondered what was happening in the womb.

Ten minutes went by and still Harmony had not moved. She broke concentration with startling suddenness, stared down at the unsuspecting woman, then at me. 'I did it, Walker. I did it! Walker – *I did it!*'

And there beneath the threatening skies, by the bank of the river Taim, she induced labour in the woman and delivered her of . . . perfect twins!

I stared at them – two perfect and identical boy children, each screeching its head off, each head slick with moist black hair, each tiny face a picture of panic, and Harmony soothed them.

'There's not even a mark.' she said, showing me the backs of each child's head. 'They were joined halfway down their heads and down to mid-spine. Isn't that fantastic? Such things used to happen a lot in the dark ages.'

'Fantastic,' I said, and took a child into my arms, then passed it to the waiting mother who accepted the sobbing infant with great happiness.

I felt humble, and very proud of Harmony. I had failed to comprehend her disillusionment with art when we had talked earlier, but now fully realised what she had been seeking for. I rose and walked to fetch the gyro, passing the celebrating elite and the broken bodies of the time-relics as I did so.

Its function over, the silent mournful shape of the MECH loomed over us and its human operator sullenly regarding the exhibition he had wrought.

BY THE FLICKER OF THE ONE-EYED FLAME

BY WILLIAM F. WU

It sometimes seems to me that life is a quest for one's true identity,. we all seek to prove our individuality in countless ways, conforming or non-conforming to one pattern or other, choosing clothes, patterns of speech, life-style ... yet the accident of skin colour can pre-label an identity, lock a whole people into unbreakable compartments of stereotype and prejudice.

Black, white, red and yellow – there is more than one colour problem.

Bill Wu knows of which he speaks. He is a young American of Chinese descent, third ·generation on one side, second on the other. He was born in Kansas City, Missouri, and is currently doing graduate work at the University of Michigan. Perhaps he is uniquely placed to write this unusually powerful, vivid story. It is his first professional sale.

The flame eternal had become electronic, glaring one-eyed daily and nightly in 12.4 million homes around the City. The Keeper of Images served the 12 million and used the 0.4 to do so, for he was a democrat. This is a story of one of the used rather than one·of the served.

Did I feel the wrench of the chain? The scraping links on white-washed bone? The snap and snarl of freedom's leap? *Believe* it.

Carl Huang sprang tiger-like on to the newsrack, fangs bared and claws flailing. Bystanders drew back, gasped, whistled, screamed. He climbed the shelves with lean limbs in clean motion, angular joints swinging to fend off aproned clerks and an assistant manager with pencils on his ears.

Now, now, they clucked, twiddling their fingers up at him as he ascended the higher slots, flinging magazines to the floor, heaving books and newspapers ceiling-ward, tearing out pages that flew, fell, floated like bloated confetti.

'Which face hides my enemy?' he screamed. He kicked and a chunk of wooden shelf broke like a rifle shot, sending the crowd reeling back. His long fingers with their broken nails pushed into cracks and molding on the wall, and he climbed higher, the leather tool pouch swinging on his belt. 'Paper patsies!' he cried at them. 'Eat staples!' The remnant of chain on the right side of his head was five links long, swinging from its staple just above his ear. The chain on his left side was seven links long, and blood poured from the staple and wound where it had been yanked loose moments before. Uniformed cops poured in below, yelling Get him! Up there . . . this way! Circle around.

Carl Huang kicked away from the wall and flung his arms out for the light fixture in the centre of the ceiling. The crowd withdrew from beneath him with a swelling *whoo!*, staring white-eyed upward like hungry fish at feeding time. He grabbed the light fixture and *swung* through. Twisting in the air, he ducked his head beneath one shoulder and crashed through the top of the plate-glass window. His feet danced in the air and he caught his balance with tippie-toes wiggled imitation-ballet crazily across three mailboxes and a trash can. People on the sidewalk turned to look and the crowd pounded out of the store, led by four cops yelling *Quick! Quick? There he is . . .* and the pencil-waving assistant manager.

'Which face hides my enemy?' he screamed, leaping into the street and bouncing up against bumpers, across hoods, over roofs to the other side, where he disappeared from sight.

The night before, Carl Huang had slept fitfully. He had tossed on his dirty mattress, sweating in the heat of the small room. The sister who shared the room hadn't spoken, but occasionally she, too, would thrash about, flipping her long hair through the darkness, rattling the chain stapled around her head, bumping her knees and elbows on the flimsy wall. Light streamed through the cracks around the door and voices twittered and boomed from around a dining table on the other side.

Dreams scorched Carl Huang's forehead when he dozed. Tall green ovals moved horizontally before him in three lines, targets in a dime gallery, and he with no gun. They shifted into clockwise motion and began to hum We *got* you here, we *keep* you here, ho *ho*. Ho *ho*.

'No, *no*.' His eyes sprang open and he jerked to a sitting position – and the chain tightened on his head. His brain sizzled with bubbling corn oil and his spine ran ice. The chain sank into his brow and he eased into unconsciousness as the staples throbbed in the sides of his skull. The part of the chain on the back of his head, under his hair, loosened slightly and he began to doze again.

A long yellow oval spun upright in front of him, with green shapes floating on its surface like sunspots. The yellow oval grew top heavy, egg-shaped, twirling on its point. Then the colours blurred and ran, adding splashes of red and white, stripes of black, and the scent of sickly-sweet pungents. When the blur shrank, tightened, focused: the face of a man feline, tall and lean; broad-shouldered. The clean, huge brow of a giant intellect covered with a simple black cap. High cheekbones tapered to a narrow jaw; satanic lines and piercing jade-green eyes all on a golden face, a sinister face, the face of Fu.

I keep you here. Enslaved to me. I run your life beyond your chain. You will never touch me. I am your enemy. Your mould, your cast, your mask. Your standard of measure in Their eyes. Your enemy, my meat-cutter.

The face darkened, the shadows ran, oil dripped from the dream-face of Fu Manchu.

In the morning, Carl Huang sat stonily at the table, leaning on the chipped formica. The morning sun slanted over cold bowls of colourless leftovers, smelling mostly of salt. Everyone was gone except the sister, who was tinkering in the oven. His chain was tight, his head swollen.

107

Did I hear the echo of ancient tomes, raising dust with their rampant voices? Did I hear the cashier of literary magnificence, selling the stories of Fu Manchu?

Julie came out of the oven wearing a short white robe and brushing her hair. 'Fixed it,' she said. She adjusted the chain on her head and scratched next to a staple. 'What's wrong, honey? Feel bad on your day off?'

'Faces,' said Carl Huang in a throaty gravel heavy with no sleep. 'Bad dreams again. Lime Quarter dreams. I'm gonna find him today.'

'You're wearing your cleaver.' Julie nodded at the meat-cutter's blade swinging in its leather case from his belt.

'An expert is never without his tools.'

Julie sat down at the table and held her robe closed over crossed knees. 'Where ya gonna look?'

They both turned together to gaze out the window. Across the alley, the black roof of a filthy building mingled broken iron bars, sheets of torn shingle plastic, a pool of fresh red blood. Around the building stood crumbling skyscrapers like their own, dark alley-ways with crowded kitchens, strange dialects, swarming insects. Lime Quarter was waterfront blocks gone putrid, a section of the City turned to urban swamp, a slant-eyed backwater of under-surface tides.

'Books,' muttered Carl Huang. He fingered the staple over his right ear and stroked the stretched links gingerly. 'Magazines. Television. Advertisers. Movies. The face is everywhere, disguised.'

'Disguised?'

'Mandarin collars, meat cleavers, laundries. Slinky moustaches. Phoney accents and "where are you from?" This lousy apartment, that shabby butcher shop, this entire quarter of the City: Lime Quarter, black-topped and amber-skinned. It's him in disguise and today I'm gonna find his face.' He cleared his throat and drank some luke-warm tea.

'It's a big city, Carl. You're leaving Lime Quarter for an uptown search?'

'Yeh – and to most of 'em out there, we're vipers and neuters and whores.'

'That has rhythm, ya know? Vipers and neuters and whores. Lions and tigers and bears.'

'I have a headache,' sighed Carl Huang.

'I'm sorry.'

'I'm going down to the drugstore.'

'I'm going over to the Chens' place; little Jennie is being stapled today. Good luck. If you see his daughter, let me know.'

Carl Huang slunk down the narrow stairs, trailing his long fingers on the stained grey wallpaper. His feet began to trip and skip as the steep stairs grew slippery; down and down, he spun 'round and 'round, leaping and falling and dancing and catching. Then he hit the street and ambled uphill on the crowded sidewalk, ignoring the sunlight glistening on his chain, ignoring the lesser chains on the thousand heads around him. No one of the City escaped a chain, of some type or weight or size. Gold hair, brown hair, cherry hair all sped, slanted, crossed and marched on the hard and polished streets. And they all wore their stapled headbands of roped silver, linked brass, aluminium thread. The smaller the chain, the lesser the limit. But no one wore no chain.

The face of Fu snickered in his mind and his blood pounded. As his pressure rose, the chain shrank, squeezing his cranium. He clenched his teeth in pain as he pushed through the door into the store.

'Which face hides my enemy?' he whispered through his incisors, as he shoved among the customers. He approached the newsrack and then stuttered to a stop, in horror.

Along the comic-book section, row after row of covers sported the face of Fu. A pale green glow suffused his devil lines of smooth and sterling evil. 'Marvel,' said the rows, 'at us.'

Carl Huang's breath leaked out in a sob of rage. His chain vice-tightened and the flesh of his scalp bulged through the centres of the links like putty. Scarlet dots swam the fringe of his vision and his leaden feet melted into the floor. The green face flashed white teeth in the centre of the red haze. The chain pounded in the back of his head, 'Halt! and deliver', but his pulse paced faster and the red faded pink, then grey. Fists trembled and lungs shrieked silent synapses.

I am your mold, your cast. Your standard, your mask...
The face leered.

Did you hear the snap of the chain? The clink and break of that prison sound? The tiger leaped at the face of Fu. You know about that.

Carl Huang ran through alleys from the cops and the crowds and the assistant manager. He pounded behind buildings, down open sidewalks, up fire escapes. At last, free, he sprinted across the loading dock of a department store and leaped headlong into a huge iron bin full of soft, white trash. He sank deep and out of sight, panting. 'I have a headache,' sighed Carl Huang.

The blood ran freely now from his head and he smiled with closed eyes. After a while, he would go out again – when the chase had faded. Of course, by then they would know who he was, and who his friends were – but when the hands of satanic image reached for him, he would be ready.

As the head of Carl Huang began to mend, and stopped bleeding, and began to operate as a whole, the mind of Carl Huang began to whir and spin with an unaccustomed clarity. As he basked peacefully in the sunlit trash, he hatched thoughts in patterns unused since his stapling at the age of six, such as 'Fight! *Resist*. Destroy!'

So that was the chain's function: to imprison standards and funnel priorities into a loop: do not express, but confine. Be as we see you. We have a measure in our literature for your kind, in the adventures of Fu and Chan. And you will be those standards, so that our literature will be right.

But who *was* Fu really? More than a name in pop culture. And who made those staples and chains? Suppose—

And suddenly, Carl Huang thought the worst thought of all. Why did his people dutifully staple their young at the age of six? Why did they chain the priority prison on their kids? Because: they never thought of *not* doing it. Because: their own staples and chains would press them through nightmares and brainfires and thought-scrambles before they could ever think of *not* doing it long enough to remember.

Jennie! Jennie Chen being stapled today? Carl Huang sprang

upward out of the trash and vaulted over the side of the bin. He sprinted back down the loading dock, dodging crates, leaping forklifts, wiggling fingers in playful waves to the laughing, cheering, jeering workers on the dock.

Carl Huang sped spider patterns on the city in search of the Chen place. He tapped and tumbled over concrete steps and iron rails. He twirled and tottered along taut black cables and narrow granite ledges. At last he flew clattering up the firestairs to the ninth level of a broken brick building. Tiger-like, he coiled and jumped for a window ledge to land on all fours. And there, inside, a bedroom had been converted to makeshift antiseptic o.r. for staple-gunning.

The child was resting quietly on a white-sheeted table surrounded by loving Chen parents and a few close friends, including Julie. A curly-haired high-nose surgical mask was inserting acuneedles instead of vibratory anaesthetic, in deference to Jennie's heritage. She smiled sweetly as the last pin punched into her head and the high-nose mask reached for the stapler.

In cold horror, Carl Huang crouched at the window, his staple-wounds throbbing, the bits of chain quivering against his ears. The white-gloved surgeon held the shiny steel gun in a firm hand and casually looped a standard length of psychechain on the loaded staple. Empty vials lay scattered, indicating that the various hallucinogens, depressants, and coagulants had already been injected into the links, soon to course through the staples into Jennie's bloodstream. Sensitive to blood pressure, temperature, and all chemical changes, the formula would limit her perceptions, her reactions, her identity from that time on. Medical check-ups would include formula treatment.

The high-nose mask straightened and raised the gun. A curved staple-remover was on hand in case of small mistakes; larger ones would not require solution. The little crowd began to bow and hum in ritual.

For a moment, Carl Huang felt the links, the missing links, again pressing against his own forehead. He shook his head with a tense whimper and stood up as the high-nose laid the stapler aside Jennie's head and, his curly hair wiggling, pulled the trigger. With a throat-rending scream, Carl Huang smashed through the window toward the stapler. The knot of relatives and friends fell back; concentrating on his work, the high-nose surgical mask plunged the other staple into Jennie's head, locking the tight circle of chain. Carl Huang whipped out his meat cleaver and shoulder-bounced the surgeon into the wall. 'AIIEEE!' With a precision honed years in a no-rise butcher's job, he sliced the hated chain from little Jennie's head with point zero zero four zero one centimeters to spare from little Jennie's scalp. Bits of her hair fluttered in the sunlight.

'Your chain,' screamed the high-nose in horror. '*You're* the one who burst his chain!'

'Carl! Oh, no,' Julie shrank, pressing her chain with her palms.

'Hold it,' ordered the surgical mask, waving the staple-gun. 'You can't hurt me.' Quickly, he went into a western metamorphosed kung-fu cat stance, still holding the stapler. 'Ki-ai,' he added.

Carl Huang snarled, and parted the curly hair to the pharynx. The surgeon crumpled, bright eyes staring startled from separate hemispheres of head. Splattered with blood, Carl Huang turned to Julie and eyed her chain. 'Hold still.'

'N-no, Carl. Please. I'm scared.'

'Hold still. It won't—'

The door to the room burst open.

Two loin-clothed, sun-bronzed Burmans stepped into the room and to one side, folding their arms. The bright light from the window cast a deep shadow behind the door. In the shadow, a tall figure stood motionless in flowing robes. A low, rumbling voice rolled from the silhouette of a massive skull. 'Greetings, Carl Huang. I understand you want me.'

'You found me so soon?' Carl Huang shook his head slightly and the pieces of chain on his head rattled. His fingers rippled up and down the handle of his meat cleaver.

'When you burst your chain – an admirable, unprecedented achievement – your name clicked up in Centercomp. We knew your friends and your Julie and where they would be.'

Carl Huang stood facing the shadow in the doorway. He felt little anger and less fear. Something was wrong with this apparition – he lacked the power, the aura, the emanations of pure evil. He was simply standing there. 'I have a headache,' sighed Carl Huang.

In the sudden dissipation of tension, Jennie wiggled slightly on the sheet, blinking quietly at the ceiling. Julie edged behind Carl Huang and stood near the body of the surgical mask, who lay sprawled with the stapler still in his hand. The Burmans flanking the door stood immobile.

The shadow spoke again: 'You have searched for me. I am Fu Manchu.'

Carl Huang's ears flashed cherry at the name and the wax in his canals began to melt and run. But he felt no grip on his heart, no throb in his temples.

'You aren't Fu Manchu,' muttered Carl Huang. 'Fu Manchu is a mythical beast, created by a pipe-smoking Englishman in 1913.' His voiced hardened. '*Which* face hides my enemy – you?'

The tall black figure remained motionless; in the dreams of Carl Huang this had evoked icicles of fear. But now nothing happened. Quietly, the two Burmans turned and left the room. The tall figure did not move as the bare feet of the Burmans thumped quickly down the hall.

Carl Huang raised his meat cleaver and flicked his wrist. The big knife whirled blade-'round-handle through the air and *thunk!* into the door, opening it wider. Light brightened the standing figure and Carl Huang strode forward, staring.

An aluminium frame stood in the doorway, holding up flowing nycetate gowns, topped with a skull of kiddieputty. Plunged into the putty face was a small wireless microphone. The Burmans were undercover men, then; the voice was the voice of the enemy.

This wasn't just police and it wasn't just Centercomp, who could have sent their uniformed cops or white-coat people. Carl Huang had burst his chain in anger and this unsettling development threatened the entire psychechain system. They couldn't just kill him; they had to find out how he had done it.

Someone was afraid of him. This trick wasn't just anybody's; this was *it.*

Carl Huang squished the putty head in a rocklike fist and squeezed until the putty had oozed out between his fingers and only the mike remained. He dropped it and jerked the robes off the frame with both hands, throwing the aluminium bars to the floor. Baring his teeth, he tore open the robes and fastened his eyes on the label.

Haughton's – a fancy-pants made-to-order whoopie-do clothing shop. A track to the true enemy, and one that could afford high costumery, at that. Carl Huang turned to look at Julie, who was carefully pulling pins out of Jennie's head. The child's parents and friends were all leaning forward in concern and one of them was shyly touching the curved staple-remover. They could learn, if they wanted: if there was time, and more chains broken.

The thunder of pounding feet welled from the stairtube at the end of the corridor outside the room. Only moments had passed since the Burmans/undercovers had padded down the hall; apparently, reserves had been waiting outside. If he could show himself, perhaps in the excitement, they would all follow him and leave the people in the room alone. But no, Center-comp knew all about them anyway. Just run.

Carl Huang led them another jovial scamper. Tremendous anger and maniac fear powered his rubbery legs to incredible speeds, angles, bounces; clumsy cops and a crowded city played him faultless back-up. All the while, *Haughton's* scourged his thoughts, and he zeroed on the massive mid-town offices of the huge company.

The next clues came from the long steel-and-glass records division. They tried the run-around at first, but Carl Huang was better at it: he danced flamenco on balding heads and permacurls, tango'd a coatrack across nine desks, folded an Executive Secretary into reverse lotus position and hung her upside-down from a doorknob. The proper papers were flung at him from several directions. Since someone here, too, called a security squad, he had to escape through another external emergency route, this time a lube slide which left him covered with a fire-resistant synthetic grease. Things were getting easier.

Now Carl Huang knew who was behind the mask – name, no one special; office, unextraordinary; function, supreme. He realized that if it weren't for the residual chemicals from the chain, he might already have known. Who else but the Keeper of Images ? He wagged his street-worn feet to the showdown.

Carl Huang came to a halt in front of City Center. He raised a sweat-drenched face upward along its dizzying heights and took a slow, deep breath for energy. The building looked like a slice of checkerboard, its huge windows alternating with thick, diamond-sculpted ledges at every floor. Drops of golden oil mingled with sweat and slid to the sidewalk under him. As he scanned the towering edifice, people continued to pass him on the street in all directions, jostling, bumping, elbowing. Gradually, he brought his gaze down again. Glass doors.

Through the glass doors, edging among the hard people of a hot city, he passed the magazine shop and reached the bank of elevators. Sixteen elevators. Into one: pushed floor nineteen. Mediatric Control was all of floor nineteen.

The metal door slid open silently. He stepped out, looked in both directions. On his right, the hall ended in a large picture window. To his left, a long, narrow passage stretched empty and quiet. The elevator door closed with a click and he was alone on a river of rich, thick, white carpet, flowing between high walnut panels. He began to walk. His wide and tearing eyes moved from door to closed door – no numbers, no names. He had a headache. Shaking his head slightly, he walked faster down the hall, beginning to sweat again despite the cold, processed air.

And then: one door with a number: One. The knob turned in his hand; he entered. A large, richly furnished office, with more blank doors, lay around him. A pretty secretary sat frozen behind a huge desk. He approached and she cowered, fearful of his dirt, his dried blood, his broken chain, his grease. She glanced at one of the many blank doors and he followed her gaze. The knob turned in his hand again and he stepped inside, pulling the door shut after.

The man behind the desk was large: tall and heavy, like a linebacker gone to seed. His jaw had once been square; now a tendency to jowl rounded the line somewhat. Piercing blue eyes showed pink around the edges. He wore a bright blue suit and leaned back in his black leather chair. Calmly, he raised his eyebrows at Carl Huang over the back of a large viewscreen.

'I was told you might want to see me,' said the media man. 'You look like you've had a rough day.'

'I want you to change the chemical limit in our chains and eliminate the three typecasts from City programming.'

'My, my, so blunt. Well, all right. What three typecasts ?'

'Three types from decades ago – out of a past that no longer exists, types that didn't exist even when the times did: the evil mandarin, the obsequious fat detective, the treacherous, slinky woman.' Carl Huang finished with a sneer.

'Ah, my dear friend. The situation is: types are necessary. They give the many a handle, a recognisable quality to associate with – let's face it, so few of us actually make friends with your sort that we need to have an abbreviated framework—'

'For an abbreviated mentality,' snapped Carl Huang. 'You teach this City that I'm a viper – or else a smiling neuter. That my sister's a whore.'

'Don't talk dirty. Now, then – as you know, the City is a society designed as a four-dimensional grid, each box being both a social and economic unit with projected future development. As it happens, the unit of your people is high, economically, for a minority—'

'Another hunk of garbage! You've been putting out images for so long that you've begun to believe them.' Carl Huang advanced a few steps, shaking with rage.

'As I was *saying*, now, it so happens that the many simply enjoy Sax Rohmer's Fu Manchu and Biggers's Charlie Chan. I serve the many.'

Carl Huang shivered and growled. 'And all their spin-offs and copies, constantly poisoning minds against—'

'The many want to be poisoned,' said the media man. 'They like it.'

Carl Huang sputtered.

The man behind the desk began to write on a notepad. He continued for several minutes, then tore off the sheet and leaned forward to place it on the very edge of his desk nearest Carl Huang. Then he leaned far back in his chair again.

Carl Huang looked passively at the little piece of paper.

'Take it to my secretary,' said the Keeper of Images.

Carl Huang edged forward and took up the note between two fingertips, tagging his eyes on the other man. When he had backed away, he glanced it over:

'Jerri, please flip the following scanfolio into the banks for tomorrow: All networks. Asia documentaries, last six months; Asia feature programming, same period; Asian feature roles, same period. Also, have Political Sensitive draw up abstracts on projected programming for the next year, same categories.'

'Take it to my secretary,' repeated the Keeper of Images.

Carl Huang hesitated, surprised. Without comment, he turned. He opened the door slowly, then looked over his shoulder at the man behind the desk. The man had not moved. Carl Huang stepped out, closed the door, and looked at the secretary, who at once froze in her chair. He extended the note, walking forward. 'Here, I—'

Every door in the room flew open. Carl Huang whirled, dropping the note, to see a horde of white-clad men running at him from every doorway, waving an assortment of nets, bolos, staplers, and chemo-dart guns. 'AIIEEE!' Carl Huang screamed in answer and leaped high, catching one man in the chest with his feet and bowling him over. A chunk of wood hit him on the head as he made for the hall door. A dart stung the back of his right arm and fried him shoulder to fingertip. Someone tried to tackle him low but he squeezed out the doorway as a bolo whipped around his neck, momentarily choking him. The red ball-weights bounced crazily as he raced down the hall, footsteps fluffing a queer silence in the carpet. Behind him, the horde shrieked *Get him! There he goes! There's no elevator waiting! We've got him!*

Carl Huang leaped for the top of the window casing and snagged it with the torn fingers of his left hand. His right arm flapped wildly alongside. He drew up his feet and smashed through the big window. Another dart lit flashfires in his back as he swung out nineteen stories over the pavement, then swung back inside again to imbed a footprint in the forehead of the nearest man. His victim fell back and the pursuers stumbled over each other in a heap. He swung out to the ledge, caught his balance, and dusted away.

Carl Huang never returned home. Several days after he fled the Mediatric Control offices, a squad of white-clads forcibly detained Julie and stapled a much larger chain on her sleek, shiny hair, just in case. Jennie Chen also received a new stapling, this time in a hospital, with armed guards.

No one has heard directly from Carl Huang since, but evenings, a quiet form crouches outside upper story windows near Julie's haunts. Occasionally, residents leave food on the sill before they retire at night. Rumour says that the bolo still hangs from his neck and that the red balls swing back and forth in the City breeze. Young children whisper that he wears pigtails, but the older ones claim that the clink of loose links can be heard from the dangling shadows behind his ears.

Did I stroke the mote in the one-eyed flame ? Cast me out, I'll blink for you.

The flame eternal blazed on, grey and bright and unblinking. A glass torch housing living-room gods, it faithfully maintained. The Keeper of Images maintained.

THREE INTO ONE, RECURRING

BY ROBERT J. M. RICKARD

This is only the second 'space' story so far to have appeared in the ANDROMEDA series and it traces a course far removed from the carefree days when rocketships careered erratically through the cosmos.

Bob Rickard has succeeded admirably in blending together a unique mixture of ingredients into a fully-integrated whole. Beginning from his interest in orthodox SF situations he brings in various items of esoteric lore ranging from occultism and Fortean phenomena through to psycho-analysis and oriental literature. Each contributes to the story and to a growing realisation that Rickard himself is as much of a polymath as his crippled protagonist.

For the past few years our author has edited Fortean Times, *a remarkable journal chronicling inexplicable events in the manner of the late Charles Fort. He has just completed a book (in collaboration with John Mitchell) in the same vein: under the title* PHENOMENA, *it will appear in late 1977. This is his first attempt at writing fiction.*

Ribbons of polychromatic light hissed past the *Kei-lin*, rippling outward to infinity as we fell into the centre of an immense, luminous Frazer spiral, contracting in cosmic peristalsis more majestic than any planetary aurora.

Phantom images of the ship reflected back from this kaleidoscope in a breathtaking version of the terrestrial Brocken Spectre, or Ulloa's Effect. They brought to my mind the

Buddhist vision of the radiant body of Kuanyin, within whose halo were 400 Buddhas, each with 500 followers and countless devas, each fingertip engraved with 84,000 lines, each line with 84,000 hues, and each hue emitting 84,000 rays of soft light, ad infinitum.

In-between is like that.

'Shadow,' I saw the Captain say.

The word was liquid amber, sizzling like fat in a pan. There is only one place you can look in hyperspace – ahead. All around is ahead, only some of it is more ahead than the rest, and that is where the Forerunner sails.

'I see it,' I said in a variegated shimmer that evaporated like mercury vapour.

A dull grey cloud swirled darkly at the centre of our coruscating universe, the shadow-soul of a mass somewhere in normal space, and it was on course for collision. Like separate islands rising out of a common seabed, matter/energy has roots which lie in hyperspace, in the In-between, the reefers call it, a place below the surface of appearances where unknown bulks have their being like drifting icebergs poking their tips into normality.

The reefer's experience of In-between always underlines the bedrock unity of existence. But it has its peculiarities – only things in the forward axis were visible, placed according to their mass, energy and motion. There could be another ship alongside but it might as well be in another universe; you'd never see it.

I was only outside for the view, using the ship's sensors passively without interfering with the Captain's unenviable task of guiding us through this dreamworld. Exact navigation is impossible in an environment that is never twice the same, without stars to steer by and with distance as illusory as time. The Captain would be lying inert in his couch, senses extended through the sensor-instrumentation beyond the narrow confines of his flesh, mind precipitated into a near-mystical clarity by the reefing-drug, playing his intuition against the strange winds and tides like the mariners of old.

My own methods, machines, and drugs were similar so I

had joined with him outside to share the magic of the In-between.

The fleet of images formed a cone about us, a cone whose slope-angle was a function of our velocity. To our eyes the ghost ships lay in concentric circles around us like a Doré illustration of Dante's flights of angels, centred on the front image, the Forerunner. The murky globe of mist had formed in the path of the Forerunner, grey, malignant, and the distance between the two closed rapidly while I heard the far-off voice of the Captain making quick calculations for emergence. Then, just as our leading phantom seemed about to touch the cloud it resolved into a small cluster of spheres, and as suddenly vanished.

We were plunged into the empty, aching blackness of normal space. The wonderful light and wraithlike armada were gone as if they had never been. The shocking wrench from reefer-empathy to cold isolation choked forth a single low sob from the Captain. I thought it was the loneliest sound I had ever heard.

A vacuum of desolation numbed my own being. It had come too swiftly to disengage. Reefers avoid this separation if they can help it but they are uniquely conditioned to bear the transition from the heights into the 'dark night of the soul'. I was not. The psychic paralysis slid over me, and I knew but did not care that my metabolic-monitor was already beginning its chemical rescue, flushing sedatives through my veins.

Dazed, I fumbled to override the programming; stimulants were what I needed most right now.

'What happened?' I asked urgently. 'Did we ram a fogberg?'

'No, we weren't that near. Didn't you see it?'

His voice was attenuated by the effects of his own monitor. 'Four spheres, one brighter than the others. Glowing, a regular pattern, I think.'

'One moment.' I turned to re-run the log on vision. 'Strange ... nothing here. The tapes are wiped!'

'Well, at least we're still on course. I'll continue in normal space. We should have visual contact in about twenty minutes.'

What luck! Even on planned emergence one sometimes

comes out far from the goal. Used though I was to the cruel vicissitudes of fate it would have been too much to bear had we lost this, after planning and waiting so long.

I turned my attention to the other displays in front of me. A screen that normally cycled through the ship's security cameras had stopped on a view of my own library stacks. A book had fallen to the floor. I would have to attend to it later, there was much of greater importance to prepare.

The first sight of the planetoid, adrift in the sunless deep between two galaxies, was worth all previous tribulations. An exquisite certainty of destiny put my stomach into freefall and my breathing became difficult. I had almost forgotten how it felt to be so completely excited.

For a few precious seconds I disconnected the monitor and revelled, before my heart became febrile as asthma resurged. I cancelled the hold and my ever-faithful watchdog raced to compensate, dulling the savour of those unforgettable moments.

The crew knew nothing of our mission, and both Carlos and the Captain would be wondering by now just what it was that their screens were showing. I hardly dared voice my own suspicions.

'Where to park?' the Captain asked.

I ignored him. My fingers pecked and scratcned like demented birds over the consoles around me, recording and analysing. I had had a vague idea of what to expect and had pre-programmed to meet a number of situations. Presently a visual model appeared.

The body was clearly an artifact, nearly spherical, bulging slightly in one quadrant. A regular arrangement of four power-centres showed on the screen as spots of light, three dim and one much brighter. Joined by imaginary lines they made a perfect tetrahedron, the three dim points forming a base and the bright spot the apex of the pyramid. Deep-scanning showed this apex point to be buried directly under the eccentric bulge, and the others located on the surface of the egg-shaped little world below us.

Inspiration came and I put the tetrahedron in elevation so

that it appeared as an equilateral triangle on the diameter of the planetoid, about 770 kilometres. At each point I constructed a tangent to give a larger, inverted triangle enclosing the body. Then I drew a concentric circle to touch each point on this larger triangle. Circle, triangle, circle, triangle – one inside the other like Matryoshka dolls.

In a moment of realisation the geometry of the four-in-one artifact became clear. All the clues, including the major axis of the body, led to the apex of this outer triangle. And somehow its builders had also engineered its mass and rotation so that this was exactly the correct distance out for synchronous orbit.

'X marks the spot, Captain,' I said as I fed the data through to the control room. In my screen I saw his smile.

'Neat!'

Still drugged into keen spatial awareness he had grasped the aesthetic solution immediately – but then, he was one of the best reefers money could buy. The *Shu Ching* records that in the dawn of China, Fu Hsi found order in the universe; 'Looking upwards he contemplated the images in the heavens; looking downwards, he observed the patterns on the Earth.' I could well imagine how he felt.

My quarters on the *Kei-lin* had been fitted out at great expense. I had taken full control of my father's resources after his disappearance and had used his research teams and funds to develop equipment that would free me from dependence on bodily ability. Except for certain undelegatable functions and essential calisthenics to prevent further physical atrophy I need never leave my couch.

Hiring the experts of several worlds as donors, or to programme my libraries and machines I eventually had the knowledge to set myself free; and that knowledge brought greater resources, and both brought immense power. I was one of the richest men in the known worlds, yet I couldn't go to the toilet without bringing myself to the verge of physical collapse. Space suited me more than surface life – ship-G was minimal, and I could move about for greater periods.

I could have sent a proxy but decided to retrieve the fallen book in person. So, uncoupling the umbilicals that linked the monitor to the valve-plate in my abdomen I propelled myself toward the stacks. I was still sufficiently elated not to notice one clumsy collision that in other times would have had me grovelling with fear at the thought of being damaged so far away from the monitor.

Though the book was face down I recognised my travelling-copy of the prose of Han Yu, a ninth-century Confucian essayist, collected into one volume by an ancestor of mine who, eager to beard the literati at their own game, added a scurrilous anti-Confucian commentary. Our family is of course Taoist, in unbroken lineage from the first mortal to earn godhood for his magical services to Heaven and Earth, Chang tao-ling. The same family Chang that the arrogant Christian missionaries sneeringly called 'Taoist popes'.

The book had fallen open at a familiar page and I looked with interest at a passage I had marked years ago. It was about unicorns, and began:

'It is universally admitted that the unicorn is a supernatural being and one of good omen; this is declared in the Odes, in the Annals, in the biographies of illustrious men, and other texts of unquestionable authority.'

I closed the replica and replaced it. I could see no reason why it should have fallen. There had been no jolts on emergence and the shelves were ridged and sprung to prevent such things. My thoughts drifted back to my father, who had given me the original of the Han Yu commentary one birthday. In the excitement I had forgotten the hatred of him that has kept me alive. I would teach him the meaning of pain, if I could. Never would I forgive his demonic treatment of my mother in his laboratories, when he knew that she was carrying me. The revenge that burned in me had allowed me to bear his humiliations, his experiments, and ultimately the most heartless jest of all, his disappearance, my vengeance snatched away, like the Grail, as I reached for it.

He was alive somewhere, laughing. Had he passed this way? Rumour within rumour, bar gossip in the cesspits of a dozen worlds, nothing much to go on, but then I had nothing else worth doing. A hint of something that would have interested him; so at great expense and across countless lightyears I go. How could I not!

Pain began to intrude on my thoughts, and I made it back to the couch and linked up just in time. The monitor flooded me with analgesics. The book was a good omen, I decided. Even Han Yu's beloved Confucius would concur on that. And then I proceeded to lose myself in my work.

On our fourth day the Captain asked to see me, saying that my robotic tricks were having a bad effect upon the crew.

'It even gives me the creeps, dealing with a man I never see. For all I know, Mr Chang, you might be a biomorphic computer on the other side of our screens.'

Sooner or later it always came to this.

'It was clearly stated in your contract, Captain. Call it an obsession if you will but it is as much for the peace of mind of the crew as for myself.'

I owed him no explanations – but I told him enough about the weaknesses that chain me to these cursed machines for him to conjecture the rest. Alas, man's nature has always led him to wonder what lies beyond the walls erected to keep him out; and if he cannot know for sure he will people it with monsters. It would be no comfort to the crew to know they were right; better instead the devil they invented.

I didn't like to show any of my cards, but I had to convince the Captain that despite my condition I was operational and in charge, because in many ways the sailors of space are as superstitious as their ancient counterparts. With my specialized machines and skills I could perform even major surgery on myself without assistance, should the need occur.

While we argued a communicator button lit up. It was Carlos with detailed results of the survey of the three surface locations. They were thick-walled hollow spheres just under a kilometre in diameter, each buried up to their middles in solid rock.

'I'm sending the data through now,' he said, putting several cassettes into the hopper-reader.

I had been delighted when the Captain located Henry Carlos. He had been hired primarily as the ship's medic, of course, but I had been more interested in his auxilary qualifications. As was the practice among those with sufficient ability, Carlos had specialized in another field, as well as holding first-class mate and normal-space pilots' tickets. During planetary stopovers he indulged in ET archeology and so I had known of this tall, balding vulture of a person through his series of monographs, long respected as models of procedure in the field. I had rarely seen anyone remain excited for as long as he had been during the last few days.

All around me the waiting devices sprang into life. Carlos himself had supervised the teams that had visited the nestling structures and he had voiced-over the film compilation of the excavations.

'We found a large circular hole at ground-level on each sphere,' he said, 'and nearby lay a threaded plug. Each one fitted the holes, and they are made of the same material as the spheres themselves. Holroyd has never seen its like and he has been unable to cut or penetrate the stuff.

'Deep-scanning below ground shows three flats on the under-curvature of each sphere, aligning perfectly with each other and with the fourth one, I guess. They remind me of aerial dishes, as though some sort of beam might have connected them to each other, but Holroyd pointed out that the thickness of rock would prevent that.'

'They're obviously not buildings in the occupational sense. Could they have been storehouses, perhaps?' I asked.

'It seems unlikely. There are brackets in one area on the outside which seem to have been used only once, as though the entire building had a single use after which it was abandoned. Everything that could be carried away has been taken. Inside there is nothing, except for a strange deposit coating the entire inner surface of each sphere. Every one is the same.'

The screen dwelt on this grim concave world, the camera viewing from bottom centre. High up on the curve was a lighted hole that indicated the short cylindrical passage to the outside, and from it were marks made by an inner plug which after being unscrewed had slid to rest at the bottom of the sphere.

'No footprints of any kind?' I queried.

'Only ours.'

I thought for a moment. 'If the spheres were linked, as you're suggesting, couldn't the whole group of them constitute some sort of huge machine? But what machine would be built on this scale and then abandoned?'

'An experiment, perhaps – or something that was needed only once,' he said slowly.

'They must have had fantastic resources.' said the Captain.

'Or they were desperate,' Carlos suggested darkly.

'What do you mean?'

'Look at this,' he said. A fine chequered pattern like random video static appeared on the screen. 'Under all that black dust I found a band of raised hexagons. They form a low relief in the same place in each sphere.'

Two more patterns followed on the screen, looking equally as meaningless. 'They're all different, but watch! If you do this . . .' The three designs were superimposed on the same screen. They now formed a very clear, intricate motif.

'Very complex. No sign of a syntactical structure, code or script. It's more like a pictograph, a highly stylised representation of something for which we have no referents.'

'If it's a work of art it's not very well placed for viewing, is it?' I said.

'No. Not in the ordinary way. But why decorate something so elaborately to use only once?' Carlos' hawkish features came closer to the pickup. 'We know little of the builders. They may have had eidetic memories, able to superimpose the three patterns in their minds. Let me venture an opinion. I'm inclined to think there may have been a special viewing occasion, or conditions under which the design could be perceived as a whole. It speaks to me of ritual significance.'

The Captain snorted. 'Every archaeologist says that about things he can't recognise immediately,' he said with mild scorn.

'No, the more I think about this, the more it seems to me the sort of graphic or heraldic trick that Initiates might use,' argued Carlos, his eyes shining like a searchlight. 'If it was a human construction I'd call it a temple or initiation chamber of a secret society.'

'An occult experiment, then!' I suggested.

'Possibly. Look, consider the deliberate geometry of this whole set-up, extending even into hyperspace. Every part neatly integrated into a whole, guiding you step by step like a ritual ground-plan or three-dimensional mandala. There's sufficient degree of co-ordination here to point to a group mind, with a single purpose.'

'To focus attention on what?' asked the Captain. 'The fourth sphere?'

'Yes! The centre of the web!' Carlos said.

I reflected for a moment. 'There are certainly enough analogies in our own past,' I said slowly. 'The common belief that knowing the name of a thing will give you power over it. That's the basis of nearly all systems of magic. Couple that with an elaborate network of taboos and you have the key to any culture at any level, from children's games to power politics.'

'Yes, that's what I mean here,' said Carlos. 'If these builders had the same naming ritual in their psychic make-up . . . Why, I can't imagine any sentient lifeform not having it! Look at the Tetragrammaton of the Cabbala, the four Hebraic initials that substituted for the name of God and could only be pronounced in full by the Sanhedrin, and only then on certain high occasions. By naming something you call it forth.'

'You think we have the name of a God, or a word of power?' I began to ask him.

'Or of horror.' he interrupted.

'. . . so that having been used, or spoken once, it lost its power?'

'Or rendered the place unusable again! Contamination is also a law of magic. Perhaps they achieved their purpose and needed, or hoped, never to repeat the performance again. We can't get much nearer on the present evidence.'

Another button flashed insistently. It was Holroyd, our engineer, and I patched him into the joint circuit. He wiped his jowls in a nervous gesture as he spoke.

'I thought you'd want to hear as soon as possible about that grime in the domes.' He hesitated. 'It's made up of a variety of organic carbon compounds. Animal tissue plus traces of metallic elements.'

'Burnt offerings,' grunted Carlos in satisfaction.

Holroyd looked even more uncomfortable. 'It's burnt all right! Charred to a fine powder and the particles sintered together without any stresses or discontinuities. If it was flesh it must have been subjected suddenly to great heat and pressure. There wasn't time for normal combustion, it must have vapourised instantly.'

'An explosion?' I queried.

'Must have been,' he answered. 'Or some sort of incandescent source at the centre of the spheres. But I don't see how something like that could have been supported, not unless they had anti-gravity too!'

I was struck by the full realisation of what Carlos had said. 'So drastic, for animal sacrifice? The scale of it, Carlos! The scale of it!'

'My god!' he said quietly. 'What's in that fourth sphere?'

Into the silence that followed I said, 'We'll just have to go and see, won't we?'

That same evening the Captain told me of the crew's growing uneasiness. I had been too busy to keep tight check on things and was surprised to hear of a series of odd occurrences which had them in a mild panic. Ordinarily I have no time for their tales, for the sailors of today, as I have said, are a superstitious lot, but perhaps it was this weird place we had come to that made me, too, prey to the ancient stirrings of fear. That, and my growing despondency as it seemed that another slender lead on my father's whereabouts was drawing to a dead-end.

Fights had broken out in the card-schools on the *Kei-lin*, he said, as an unprecedented series of runs and coincidences led to accusations of crooked dealing. Several men swore they were becoming telepathic and Barbari, the mate, voiced his concern to the Captain over the stability of a youth named Dirc, who after a horrible nightmare had woken to find his watch stopped at 17.47 and was proclaiming to the rest of the crew that they would all perish at that hour on the following day.

None of this was entirely unusual, except in degree. Abrupt emergence from hyperspace has been known to mildly enhance mediumistic powers in certain individuals, although the effect has always been considered only temporary and of limited importance.

More disturbing were the physical phenomena. The canteen lights went through a period of switching themselves on or off as they pleased, even with the circuits isolated. Three men had each injured an arm in roughly the same way in three separate accidents on the same day. And then the Captain told me of the stones found in the control room.

He slept in a small cabin adjoining the bridge and, hearing a noise in there, the night before last (our first in orbit here), got up to investigate. The door was secure and when he put his keycard into the lock the noises ceased. As the lights came on the Captain had seen instantly that there were no intruders, but when he noticed the small heap of stones he could not register for a few seconds what precisely they were.

They could not have fallen from a shelf or locker and they certainly had not been there when the door had been locked, a few hours earlier. He had picked one up, and been surprised to find it warm. The Captain showed it to me now, an angular fragment of quartzite, streaks of various browns overlaid on one side by a blackish fusion of the quartz. It had been in contact with something hot enough to melt the rock locally.

The stones seemed to have appeared from thin air, but although the Captain had kept watch for a half-hour or so, no more had fallen. In the end he had picked up the stones, locked up, and taken them to Holroyd for analysis.

'What do you think is happening to us, Captain?' I asked him.

He looked determinedly at the screen. If we had been face to face he would have been seeking out my eyes, weighing up just how direct he should be.

'I think we're being haunted, Mr Chang,' he said.

An involuntary 'Ah!' escaped from my lips. Since the talk with Carlos dark clouds had been gathering on my mental horizon. I had back-tracked on my security camera log to determine how the Han Yu book had fallen. This record had not been wiped. I had clearly seen how it had simply slid out, opening at the page I had found as it turned over in the air, in such a smooth, slow, continuous motion that watching the graceful drift to the deck had made my hair stand on end.

There was something else, too. The quotation from Han Yu began to take on a more ominous colouring. It had continued:

'The unicorn is not always easy to find and does not lend itself to classification. It is not like the horse or bull, the wolf or deer. And therefore we could be in the presence of a unicorn and we would not know for certain that it was one.'

I found the passage profoundly disturbing, not the least because in Chinese the unicorn is called *kei-lin*.

'We have a lot to think about, Captain,' I said. 'First thing tomorrow we must have a meeting with Dr Carlos and Mr Holroyd, if you'd be kind enough to inform them. Good night.'

'There's little doubt this artifact pushed us out of hyperspace as soon as it sensed our Forerunner,' said Holroyd.

'A "Keep Off" notice that means what it says,' laughed Carlos. He was really enjoying this.

Holroyd continued, 'And I have an idea why the Captain saw the shadow-mass of this planetoid as a cluster, In-between. Henry's earlier idea of a beam-link between the flats on the spheres is too crude. They have somehow been engineered to the most sophisticated solution of all – the flats are in direct surface-to-surface contact with each other through hyperspace. Simple when you know how,' he said. 'I just wish I *did* know how!'

Our talk turned to the strange events of the last few days and the feelings of foreboding that I think even Holroyd, the most pragmatic of us, was starting to experience. Carlos suggested there could be connexions between these phenomena and the artifact.

131

'Look at the thousands of well-documented accounts of poltergeists and you'll see time after time the same effects we are witnessing here. And it has to do with that . . . that *thing* out there!'

'What are you talking about!' exclaimed our engineer. 'Ghosts! That's ridiculous.'

'Not ghosts, but what Jung and Pauli, a long time ago, called synchronistic phenomena. Events not necessarily associated with what we usually think of as paranormal situations, but instances where the normal cause-and-effect processes seem to have been suspended, by-passed or even rearranged.'

'But it's absurd,' Holroyd protested. 'It makes a mess of everything we know about science.'

Carlos banged a fist upon his table. 'How can a man who can talk one minute of this massive ship apporting in and out of hyperspace balk in the next at the mere suggestion that poltergeists can do the same?'

'It doesn't necessarily undermine your physics, Holroyd,' I said. 'Our Reality may be only a semantic structure based on a concensus of opinion and entrenched in all of us from birth. Just because it is the only one most of us are likely to perceive shouldn't blind us to other potentials. It may be that under certain conditions the building blocks of our Reality can be rearranged to spell out a different version. It may not be by accident that so much psychic and so-called paranormal activity goes contrary to our expectations of commonsense behaviour.'

Holroyd pulled a face.

'Mr Chang, I'll admit some strange things have gone on recently for which I have no explanation. Logic suggests there must be some connection with that structure below, but why drag in the human mind?'

Carlos spoke up. 'Jung's idea of synchronicity was never meant to explain the workings of chance, it only applies to a class of events that have no apparent causal connection yet are somehow related. Meaningful coincidences, if you like. Let me explain.

'One of Jung's analyses concerned a patient who dreamed

about Egyptian scarabs, and at a critical point in a long and difficult analysis session, just when Jung thought he could unlock the secret of the scarab-symbol, he was disturbed by a tapping at the window. When he opened it, in flew a scarab-beetle, rare and entirely unexpected in the latitudes of Switzerland!

'To Jung synchronicity meant events charged with meaning from their context, in a way chance events are not. What is important to us is his observation that synchronous events often use the language of symbolism. It is an unconscious language of archetypes, closely linked with our primary interactions with whatever Reality is. Poltergeists are often described as 'wilful' and their behaviour is certainly amoral as if they had merely adopted an idea of how to behave without understanding it.'

The Captain looked troubled. 'Are you suggesting we're all going mad, that our mental gibbers are being given shape by some newfound power?'

'No,' answered Carlos, 'but I am beginning to suspect that thing out there is working through us, working through our unconscious Reality – making processes and using our Reality as its pen and paper, as it were.'

'But it doesn't make sense,' Holroyd protested.

'Why should it?' Carlos said. 'For all we know it could be a message on such a vast scale that we are only getting a minute fragment. Or perhaps time itself is being rearranged and our little linear conditioned perceptions simply cannot grasp the greater totality.'

We were silent for a moment then Holroyd voiced what we had all been brought to realise. 'If we are being communicated with, or through, there must be something in the fourth sphere. *And it's alive!*'

'It could be a machine,' said Carlos without enthusiasm. 'A clever machine.'

'But *alive!*' repeated the Captain.

We talked on, but we all knew already that we would have to go down to that buried, waiting sphere. The Captain tried to suggest we should go back to port and return in a few weeks, fully equipped materially and mentally to face this Unknown. Carlos pointed out that a discovery of this magnitude would be impossible to keep secret and by the time we returned the artifact would be swarming with all the newsmen and tourists in this arm of the Galaxy. It took the practical Holroyd to state the real problem.

'If we triggered that defence mechanism on our arrival,' he said grimly, 'it already knows we are here. We may already be running out of time.'

Overwhelmingly, but reluctantly, we voted to begin the new excavations immediately.

The fourth sphere was only marginally more difficult to investigate than its three brothers. Barbari had no problems burning a tunnel down from the surface and in scooping out a working cavern outside the entrance to the sphere. The rock at this depth was a coarse breccia and the lasers cut through it like a knife through cake. Holroyd took great delight in showing the Captain where his mysterious stones had come from.

The circular plug was still in place at the entrance to this sphere. The impervious material rapidly absorbed the energy of the scanner beams so we could not discover if there was a locking mechanism, but we guessed it would be like the others and that the plug rode on a slow thread. We forced it with powerjacks, knowing there was no risk of stripping the thread since it was made of the same nearly indestructible material as the walls themselves.

Harsh blue lights dangled from cables stapled into the rock ceiling, and their cold glare was at odds with the heat in the cavern deep inside the planetoid. The jacks whined as they took the torque, and escaping trickles of hydraulic fluid quickly boiled away in the heat and thin atmosphere. In protective suits the men cursed the crazy Chinese as they broiled alive around the jacks. A muffled far-off thump-thump-thump drifted down the tunnel from the heat-pumps and ventilator on the surface, reminding all of the nervous racing of their hearts.

Slowly the bulky plug spiralled outwards and finally the supporting crane swung aside, almost buckling under its weight.

A whisper of balancing pressures made the men shudder as they looked into the velvet-black darkness. The hole was filled with man's ancient fear of dark places. Only crewman Madoc, from the Celtic resettlement of Mag Mell, did not avoid that cyclopian stare.

In that strange place he recited Gaelic verses about the heroes of the *Mabinogion* standing at the doors of green-domed tombs, for they knew they were entrances to the sidhe-worlds of the fairyfolk. The huge form of Barbari in foreman's red, dwarfed by the buried white giant, walked to my waiting proxy.

And I, Chang hsiao-lung, a latterday Tannhauser, was summoned to my Hörselberg.

Most people cannot imagine or cannot bear to imagine trading their body for a machine – but they do not have my crippling congenital inadequacies to imprison their spirit. My birth had been in pain and pain was the theme of my life. My proxies were my release from that confinement, frustration and suffering. My death, however painful, would make that release permanent.

I had money, and power. So I created semi-robotic and remote-controlled body substitutes, my proxies. My parasympathetic nervous system was tapped at several hundred points and linked via telemetry to the proxies, which after years of patient practice I could manoeuvre more precisely than any normal human body. The price was loss of human flexibility, hence a range of specialised machines, some of which could extend my abilities into realms undreamt of by others. But though I have proxies that can wander under the airless gaze of distant galaxies, crawl on high-gravity planets, or swim in acid seas, I lie in my rooms, weak and vulnerable, chained to the couch by three umbilicals, one for renal waste, one for telemetry, and the monitor.

For long periods of proxy-use the monitor was programmed to take over most of the automatic functions of my body, and to sustain it intravenously. Our family tradition of herbal pharmacology had enabled me to develop yet more sophisicated versions of the reefing-drug, which enlarged my concentration and identification with the proxies, giving me courage to venture far away from my body.

'I'll lead the way,' I said as my proxy came alive in the cavern. I had ordered Barbari to adapt one of my utility designs, fitting a powerjack to tackle the plug at the inner end of the short cylindrical passage. The trolley bristled with telemetry and sensory equipment, and my voice came from a tiny speaker near the back.

'I can see in most ranges of the electromagnetic spectrum, enough to give ample warning of any danger ahead. And I have defences to cover your retreat, should it be necessary, please regard this proxy as dispensable.'

In my haste I'd forgotten the anxieties of the men. Only when I had stopped speaking did I notice the grim faces behind the circle of faceplates.

'It's okay for you,' shouted a voice from the rear. 'We're risking our lives while you're safe back on the ship.'

'Quiet!' ordered Barbari. Then, looking at me, 'but it's true, sir. With all respect we decline to accompany you. I speak for the men here when I say that psychological stress and unspecified danger are not covered under our contractual obligations.'

'Haven't I said I'll take care of any danger? I'll double the pay of any man who comes in with me. All of you.'

'No thank you, sir,' said Barbari firmly. 'Were you here when that door opened? The wind blew then with the scent of death itself. I feel it in my blood and my bones that this is a great mistake, and I ask you, beg you, for us, yourself, for those who sleep inside, not to go in.'

An image touched my mind, the surreality of this place, the tension of the past few days, my trolley starting up like a corpse at a funeral, remonstrating with them. They were frightened and there was no sympathy in my impatience.

'You're as superstitious as savages,' I shouted.

'Perhaps,' said Barbari sadly. 'But we have heard you and Dr Carlos speak of this place and of the wizards who built it. My fears are not nameless, they are very old. My ancestors gave warning to Lord Carnarvon and other avatars of your

136

kind, and when they robbed the secret places of Egypt, retribution followed them down their days. Yes, I'm afraid, and not unmanned to admit it.'

There were rumbles of support from his men.

I was fully drugged for proxy-contact and my own fears battled with my lust to be under way. I was aware of the mounting hysteria in the voice that emerged from the trolley and yet I listened almost helplessly as I heard myself rave.

'And my ancestors were demon-catchers. They roamed China before your people were civilised, imprisoning and killing the devils in the land and sky. For this my ancestors were made gods, and down the centuries we have kept this power. And so I say that curses are rubbish, perpetrated only by credulous peasants.'

'But without the impiety and arrogance of grave-robbers and 'scholars' they would have no need to exist,' Barbari said. 'We stay here.'

I was indignant and angry, partly at myself for the spectacle of arguing in public. Suddenly I realised I didn't really need them all.

'Very well! I go alone.'

My cautious advance down the cylindrical passage was singularly uneventful. The absorbent gloom was quite featureless and closed up behind as if I had never been this way. I proceeded very cautiously until a sudden shift in sonic echoes startled me. It was the plug at the far end of the passage.

I negotiated a good purchase, locked the trolley wheels, and twisted and pushed with the powerjack. The plug unscrewed easily, eventually falling away from me with a booming that rolled around the interior of the sphere like a dire and distant death-knell. To my great surprise, however, it fell not down but sideways, settling like a spun-coin some distance away on the wall to the right. But this detail, curious though it was, was soon forgotten as I faced the scene before me, hunting through the spectrum for the best vision.

I stood at the lip of the passage where it entered the vast, hollow sphere. But unlike the others this one was not empty.

A huge tetrahedral pyramid hung upside-down before me, filling the centre of the volume, touching the sphere-surface with all its points.

'As above; so below,' I whispered.

The beauty of that place was made even more awesome by the different modes of seeing I could employ. I could see, for instance, that the builders had been able to shape gravity itself to their will. Here the force was perpendicular to every surface so that downwards was wherever you stood. This explained the behaviour of the plug. I recalled Dante's reaction to his divine vision:

> 'And so my mind, bedazzled and amazed,
> Stood fixed in wonder, motionless, intent,
> And still my wonder kindled as I gazed,
> How weak are words, and how unfit to frame my concept...'

The clatter of the plug's fall was still echoing, perpetrated disturbingly in the void about that great solid. I fancied I heard many other sounds in that deep belling. I began to retreat – I needed a proxy that could step out of the passage into the sphere, and to abandon the trolley here would effectively block all access. I took a last look at the shifting patterns of colours caused by the overlapping plane and concave energy gradients. The sound had decayed to a smooth throbbing that also pulsed in these patterns, rising and falling like a meditational chant. In a vertiginous flash I could not tell if I was looking down a well at the pyramid or whether it was hanging in space above me. My awareness split between the reversing motion of my trolley, my recumbent body on the *Kei-lin* in which my heart was dangerously pounding, and another place I could not understand. Another wave of vertigo swelled through me with that vibrating sound, roaring and crashing throughout my being.

There came a stinging, crushing pressure and a heat so pure and clean that its glass-edged light shredded me viciously and quickly.

And then I returned to consciousness on the *Kei-lin*, soaked in sweat and trembling at the memory. Ten or fifteen minutes had passed. Once again the monitor had saved my life, efficiently and without any sense of obligation. I thanked it nevertheless.

'Captain, I cannot re-establish contact with my proxy and Barbari is not answering.' He was in his cabin and seemed to be expecting my call.

'Carlos and a crewman called Madoc are dead,' he said, his voice as flat as a reefer's in emergence-shock.

'What!' I was taken aback.

'I am abandoning this venture,' he said. 'Your curiosity has put us all at risk.'

I would not agree. I wanted to return to the sphere once more with a more suitable proxy. Only then would we leave the planetoid.

The Captain gave me formal notice that he had taken his decision in the interests of the shipping company in order to protect their vessel and crewmen.

I revealed my deeds of ownership of that company. As both owner and client I *demanded* he accorded with my instructions. I promised that the ship would return after one more trip that need not involve any member of the crew. I would go alone. My own safety was assured, as my disengagement had proved just a few minutes before.

'Very well,' he finally conceded. 'But there will be an inquest on Carlos and Madoc and my protests are now on record.'

'But what happened down there ?' I demanded.

He turned away to look at his own screens. 'Something took place down there which none of us can understand,' he said. 'Perhaps Carlos could have explained. But he's dead!

'After your mobile went into the passage Barbari thought to occupy his men by having them dismantle and pack the equipment. But almost immediately they began to hear many strange sounds drifting from that brooding hole, the snorts of animals, the clatter of hooves. Sounds so absurd in that context that they knew it was illusion. Like automatons they were drawn nearer and nearer, some taking up shelter behind boxes, waiting . . .

'Carlos arrived just as you went in, and he was as spellbound as the others. And then it emerged.

'No one saw it, but suddenly it was at the top of the ramp as if it had been there all the time. An animal of sorts. Each man seems to have seen something different, an abomination, an embodiment of all their fears. But more than fear, it was a thing of loathing, a thing to be slain. Killing it would cleanse them of the dirt of living, would absolve all sin and guilt.

'Our screens had clouded before the monster appeared. But we heard it trot down the ramp and strut among the men, and we heard their cries and roars of hatred as they picked up lengths of iron, lumps of rock, tools, and began to rain blows upon the beast. They tore it limb from limb, kicking, stabbing, beating, until gradually their frenzy calmed.

'And then a faint radiance began to form around the carnage and as they watched helplessly it grew brighter and more unbearable. Suddenly the animal was whole again, but now a creature of exquisite beauty, with tiny deer-like hooves, irridescent blue-green scales on its flanks, and a head that was an indescribable mixture of lion and dragon.

'The men stood stunned until as sight and sense returned they began to realise the full impact of what had happened. Carlos was lying dead in the wreckage of your trolley, mutilated almost beyond recognition. Many of the men were seriously cut and battered. Madoc had been sliced almost in two by a welding laser.'

I remained silent. Words seemed superfluous.

The Captain continued, 'Barbari is with me in my cabin, he has told me what happened. He tells me there was an eerie silence, as though the universe itself held its breath in shock at the grisly play in that cavern.'

I broke contact and spent a few moments checking through the microfilm index of my library. Soon I found what I was looking for in an ancient bestiary and I patched the image through to the Captain's cabin. 'Ask Barbari if this was the beautiful creature he saw,' I said.

The foreman's face appeared in the screen, drained of colour and sobbing. Then the Captain loomed close and said, 'You're heartless, Mr Chang,' and broke contact.

The men had seen my proxy as a strange beast. How odd. The image was that of a kei-lin, the Chinese unicorn.

Barbari had recovered enough to ferry my new proxy down to the planetoid, refusing to allow any of his men to set foot on the little world again. He spoke only once, just before setting down on the surface, near the entrance to the tunnel leading to the buried sphere.

'Dirc is in shock. He has taken Madoc's death upon himself. He found that Madoc's chronometer had stopped at the instant of his death, at exactly 17.47 as Dirc's nightmare foretold.'

I picked my way down to the lampless cave for a second time, striding now on powerful legs. I passed through the cavern, skirting the bloodstained debris of my earlier trolley, and soon was facing that stupendous sculpture once more. 'The sphering thus begot . . .' The words of Dante came to me again,

'So strove I with that wonder – how to fit
The image to the sphere; so sought to see
How it maintained the point of rest in it.'

This time I was careful to make no sound that could echo so strongly, and as I stepped out on to the inner curvature I reflected on the image within an image theme. Jung himself would have warmed to the three-in-one symbolism and the three-dimensional mandala of this whole enormous edifice would doubtless be interpreted as the sign of complete psychic integration. For a moment I understood the minds of the builders, or thought I did.

Now the passage was a vertical well at my feet, and I strode off to the nearest apex of the huge pyramid above. It was a most peculiar sensation, walking up the wall and across the ceiling, for that is what it felt like. As I walked the solid above me appeared to rotate. I reached the apex upon which the whole monstrous bulk now balanced impossibly. I placed one foot on the nearest steeply-angled triangular face and gave a little jump to carry my weight across. When I straightened up the world swung around crazily, and I was standing on a large smooth triangular field under a dark-domed sky.

In wonder I set off across this new ground – then realised I had lost my bearings. I had reasoned there must be some sort of chamber in the mighty tetrahedroid and that its entrance, if the general plan was followed, would be in the apex diametrically opposite the cylindrical passage. Unless I could locate either entrance I had no orientation. Since there were four apices to the solid I decided to head for the nearest and walk around the edge of one plane. If I did not find the new opening then by elimination it would be at the fourth and last apex. Had I kept my wits about me I could have simply marched around the concave curvature directly to it.

When I reached the edge I looked over. I knew immediately it was another mistake but I could not hold back the shock of vertigo. To steady myself I tried to disengage from the proxy, and found to my horror that I could no longer feel my body in the *Kei-lin*. I tried again, and again nothing happened. I was lost, trapped, and I collapsed into panic. All inquisitiveness fled and I ran to the nearest apex and stepped off onto the inside surface of the sphere.

Immediately my confidence was restored and the confusion in my brain lifted like a mist. I was determined to ride this thing out. Thinking only of my hatred for my father I jumped back and began again to trudge determinedly from corner to corner, trusting the red fire of revenge to burn away my fears.

It took about five minutes to cross the distance between one peak and another, although I couldn't be sure for my vision was dimming and both time and space seemed to be distorting. I realised I had lost count, it was a nightmare that repeated again and again like an endlessly-running loop of film. I changed planes, went across one and descended the next, becoming numbly aware that I should have found the opening by now. Then I did, or maybe I only dreamed I did in reaction to the terror of my autistic universe. I found a hole at one peak and slid down into its depths under the pull of a force that pulled down and I fell forever with nothing to tell the passage of time but the sensation of falling, though I came to no bottom and the feeling became superimposed on that weary and interminable trek along edges and shifting planes.

It seemed that each time I went into that pit I was returned back to the beginning of my journey and yet I could not distinguish beginnings and ends. My being fragmented over and over, like an observer's in Dunne's theory of the infinite regression of Time, living out Zeno's Paradox, always approaching nearer and nearer but never finding an end. The patterns in the texture of the surfaces, the minor irregularities in the perfection of the solid form became my most familiar memories. My thoughts became commentaries upon commentaries as my selves split off, multiplied down the corridors between two facing mirrors.

More than lessons from Borges or Kafka some infinitesimal part of me dwelt on the words of the sufi who drowns in his god:

> 'Pilgrim, Pilgrimage, and Road,
> Was but Myself toward Myself; and your
> Arrival but Myself at my own door;
> Who in your fraction of Myself behold
> Myself within the mirror Myself hold
> To see Myself in, and each part of Me
> That sees himself, though drowned, shall ever see.'

No such unifying peace for me, for my horror has no end. Part of me labours like Sysyphus on that geometric enigma. Another descends to its core, and encounters there, *what*? Another fragment of me has lived the lives of my predecessors in this trap, for now I understand it to be, and we are/will be/ have already been absorbed into one.

Once a people were plagued by a vampire god that fed on their fear. It was wherever fear was, and killed terribly without the relief of death. So they devised a plan to rid themselves of the pestilence. An impenetrable material was formulated, a trap was made, and baited with thousands of beings sacrificed (or executed, the effect is the same) in these three spheres. Thrashing bodies locked together in free-fall, knowing that a hyperspatial hole would open into the heart of a sun. The searing light, a wind of fire, and no death, no end to the lingering compression. Sentient screaming agony in megatons three times over fed into the fourth sphere. *And in the fourth it was a feast for the god.*

When, from out of nowhere the bait was taken, the lid was slammed tight and the prison cast adrift in the thinnest sea of all between the galaxies. For in that moment of terrible gluttony its hunger was abated, and in that moment the god could be trapped. Time did not exist outside the paradox of the eternal instant. It could have lain there unknowing forever, but along came one little meddling human, just one, like a cosmic sperm wriggling across the lightyears to fertilise the thing in the indestructible egg to awareness.

I have exchanged one living death for a more terrible one, for there can be no running away from this cellular version of hellfire. I who have lived in pain shall forever die in pain.

On Earth, many centuries ago in the time of the Sung emperor Ren Chen, there lived a Commander Hung, whose idiocy is enshrined in the prologue of the *Shui Hu Chuan*. One day while passing Lung Hu mountain, the ancient home of our family, he heard a legend of a stone in the grounds of a Taoist temple there, that could only be lifted by one named Hung.

The priests could not dissuade him from performing what he considered his duty, and he lifted the stone and loosed 108 demons upon the Earth. They had been imprisoned there by Chang tao-ling, my ancestor, of whom I had boasted to Barbari.

His work was undone by a fool. Well, my honoured ancestor, have you turned your face from me now? Is my father somewhere laughing at the way Chang tao-ling's descendant has loosed a vampire god upon the Galaxy?

Like a snatch of tune that returns maddeningly to the mind those suggestive lines from Hamlet mock me now:

'I could be bounded in a nutshell,
And count myself a king of infinite space,
Were it not that I have bad dreams.'

144

My bad dream is this. That a fool called Chang hsiao-lung, a speck of dust on the great mirror of the void, eternally blunders into the heart of his destiny.

ACCRETION

BY DAVID LANGFORD

Now here's a promising thought: how often have we all wished for our favourite authors to write more about their imaginary worlds? Another three volumes of the FOUNDATION epic, maybe, or a further half-million words about Niven's 'Known Space'.

And if the writers themselves don't want to do it, why not grant license for others to continue the exploration of their fictional continents? To a limited extent this is already happening; 'Conan' stories are still appearing long after the death of Robert E. Howard.

David Langford takes off from this idea and in a splendid vignette unfolds the awful consequences of this ultimate literary incest. At age twenty-two he is employed professionally in Doing Things with atomic energy; after hours he writes science fiction and fantasy with vast ingenuity and rapidly growing proficiency. This is his fifth sale. He is, as they say, one of those names to watch.

The city's founder was forgotten in all but name, and even that was a matter for conjecture: it was only the popular imagination which deduced that the place must be named for him, for this hypothetical Butor. It was, however, certain that one man had founded the city. As is commonly the way of founders, he had not touched brick or stone, had not himself marked patterns in the Earth. This much is commonplace; the thing which made Butor unique among cities was that no one had yet laid solid foundations, though countless hands had laboured to bring it to perfection.

Butor was a city which was not and had never been; which was not to say that it might never be.

Martin stared across the endless, featureless sea. There were others on the ship, who of course knew the rich history of Butor; but despite the direction of this journey, no one showed excitement or interest, save himself. No one made pilgrimages any more, partly because the logical goal of any pilgrimage was in theory unattainable. He was probably a fool to think otherwise.

The abrasive wind blew steadily from ahead, and gulls cried high in the air. Martin, half-hypnotised by the unchanging vista, thought dreamily of the city, recalling the legend of its founding. There had been a man, long ago, who may or may not have been called Butor; and he had founded his city on paper, setting out the half-crazed dream which drew men to the building. The dream was this: that writers might combine in the creation of a great fictional city which, serving as background for all the world's stories, might imprint itself on the human mind as a vision of remote glory; might one day dream its way into a reality, as architects and engineers were inspired by its multiplex myth . . .

It had never been, but one day it *would* be. Soon, very soon, they had hoped once. Sooner than they thought, Martin felt. He looked again to the West, unchangeably grey. The wind rose and fell, tinged now with salt spray. Rough water ahead. Though his eyes strained, he could see no shore beyond.

The magic of the concept had sparked off pioneers. Without them the legend could never have properly begun, for a dream of foundations and plans is not the stuff of undying myth. But Stephenson came, with the practiced eye of an engineer, and in his, the first stories of Butor, a solid grandeur of form was erected. This early vision was bleak and bare, such as the old Norsemen might have built to defy the giants of fire and frost, could they have enlisted the hill-trolls to work the massive stones. Then before Stephenson's rough-hewn towers and machines of sleek steel could age or mellow, he was joined by other writers who were drawn to the raw young mythos of the city: Reed, for one, who must surely have been a woman, with her tales of subtle curves that mocked planes, planes which masqueraded as curves, deceiving the eye and mind alike. And Rohan set down the tables of the law, and filled Butor with music; while Holdstock painted in decadence and sensuality, and set it about with grotesques.

Already, the stories seemed not so important for their own sake as for the new insights into the city's ways. Scott wrote tales of love lost and regained, but the initiates read him for his telling of Butor's myths. Smith commemorated universal agonies, and the growing cult ferreted from his stories the subtleties of Butor's finance. Though Kilworth might plumb psychological depths, his background of Butor's broad gardens was remembered after every plot-turn had been resolved and forgotten. Morgan spilt the first blood there; and for his pains was praised for writing of sunsets over Butor's spires.

For the city was greater than any of its chroniclers, and would not die, would not even remain in the background. These first writers achieved immortality as the Butor Group, and as such alone; their names were forgotten except in the dustier texts which poked and prodded into those earliest days.

Still the city was not; and had never been. Despite this, it became the best-known city of the world.

The station-wagon lurched painfully along jungle paths. Martin noted the slowness of progress, and decided that it was right. Such a journey should not be too easy.

He had found himself alone in wondering about Butor. The nature of his wonder was this: though Butor was better documented, now, than any city of mere stone, its picture would not come clear in his mind. London, less vast, was grey and sprawling to him, an intricate maze studded with unexpected wonders. New York, thrust fantastically into the sky, symbolised the old, lost spirit of America. Paris – Venice – Moscow – Rome – he had visited them all, and found each with a kind of fading personality, an inner truth which crumbled less quickly than the stones. He had only read of Butor: of course. If he could *see* it, he would know the secret which all the writers groped for still.

He hoped he was heading in the right direction.

The strange urge stemmed, in part, from a habit of reading old books, so old that often they were not set in Butor, and might not even mention it. The experience was strange and disturbing at first; but Martin had found that even in those days, intelligent men had written books, often about real cities. One passage stayed in his mind, from a writer named Chesterton, who had described how one might read a hundred books about a place and be no nearer its essential quality. He spoke of visiting Jerusalem and being struck by a thing so obvious that no one troubled to mention it: the city was set on a hill. This had upset his whole mental picture of the place.

Martin had scarcely heard of Jersualem, but there were other cities, occasionally mentioned in the earlier stories and novels of the Butor cycle. London ... Moscow ... Paris ... New York. ...

He realised how much more a place of wonder Butor must be: an intellectual realisation taken from the books. He knew then that he must visit it, so that he would know.

Surely, when half that world believed so devoutly in Butor, the place must be? After all, London and the rest continued to exist, though half-forgotten, which seemed as great a miracle. The world was running down, and myths spoke of no past glories; only of one city which remained glorious. Any single vision of wonder might be splendid, and in Butor all were combined.

The station-wagon struggled on, unheeding of his thoughts.

After the initial Group had shaped the city, other men came to add its transport, its customs and manners, splashes of colour and smears of grime, a thousand small touches. The city was a pearl which grew and grew, nurtured in successive cerebella. It grew by accretion, a word which is not quite an anagram of 'creation'. It drew everything to itself. The cult grew further, and other works joined the fiction of Butor: street directories, maps, guide-books, sober historical accounts. A uniform-edition publishing house was launched, solely to handle the tales of the 'Butor Cycle'; but soon all the publishers produced them, as writer after writer gravitated to the city which had never been. The commonest tale of murder or first love took strength from that background, and in its turn reinforced Butor's quasi-existence – for even a tarnish can be the patina of reality.

The science-fiction writers laboured high on the bright spires, minting fresh wonders to adorn the eternal city; romantics and mystery-mongers touched it further with romance and mystery; and the writers of the intellectual mainstream lovingly gave it slums. More and more Butor became a city which embodied everything; less and less was written of other, less intensely realised, merely genuine cities.

Who could say that such a well-documented place was not?

Martin's legs were growing tired, as he drove himself up the mountain path. He stopped, and consulted a compass. Unless the path turned soon, he would have to leave it and attempt the rough slope to his right. Looking dourly up to the crags, he allowed himself to be momentarily doubtful; then reassured himself with the remembrance of his own care in calculation.

The stories of the Cycle enshrouded ten thousand thousand facts about Butor, and a man with patience might extract any data whatever about it. Martin had considered the climate at first; had then discarded it as an unreliable guide, suited only for rough confirmation of more sophisticated calculations.

The book that had solved his problem was entitled *Night-Piece*; being a late story of the Cycle, it had no author credit, but this was irrelevant. It described a certain week in the life of Carreras, one of the better-established inhabitants of the city (he had been mentioned in only the forty-third Butor tale), and included descriptions of his vigil on the balcony of the Hotel Splendide while awaiting his mistress. This passage was extended and philosophical, leaping from metaphor to metaphor with startling grace; of interest to Martin was the fact that Carreras had seen Sirius that night, framed in a tiny space between the lesser Cathedral spire and the nearer edge of the Jade Tower. In a train of metaphysical speculation too abstruse for paraphrase, which was provoked by this sight, the exact time was given: subtly, elliptically, but it was given. Butor had revealed itself. From available data, Martin had been able to deduce latitude and longitude.

The path turned; he smiled. It could not be far now. Unpromising though the rocks ahead appeared, this was the place where, if it was at all, the city must be.

Polished by innumerable minds, Butor increased in complexity and wonder. Early stories had used it as a background against which any drama might be played; now, in the ceaseless drive toward perfection, the foreground too was woven into the ever-richer tapestry. Minor characters from one narrative would have secret motives explained only by their appearance in another; the principal of a tale of action, fighting to the death in some lonely street, would reappear as a minor disturbance outside a window, required for the plot of a simultaneous love-story; the marriage of two nonentities might snare characters twenty books away in an unexpected web of consanguinity. The dustiest corner of the market square came gradually alive with associations. Gaps in the history were sought out and carefully filled; nonetheless Butor remained multifarious and enigmatic, the richest source of narrative material in the world, the only source for men of discrimination. The 'oblique' story developed, the story charting mysterious and irrational relations or counterpoints, only explicable by reference to other tales of the Cycle which detailed, in another context, what the protagonists were thinking and the nature of their interactions – or lack of them.

The shadows, entwined into almost unbearable complexity, began to assume a deceptive substance; believed in by the world, chronicled to the last falling of a dust-grain, the tiniest ripple on the lakes of its great parks, the phantom city trembled, nine-tenths alive, *Terra Tenebrosa*, slipping silkily along the slope from the things which *are not*, down, down to earth, through the realm of what *may be* . . .

Martin stumbled, gasped for breath; he paused and panted for a moment. The path led on through a labyrinth of high rocks. It turned to the left, to the right, staggered over hard, broken ground: ended.

The high place was hollowed out, a great bowl of a plateau, the gentle slope leading featurelessly down from Martin's feet, to Butor. The sun was low, now: this was the time when the city's poets were most lyrical, pillaging the ancients for their cadences, as: *Inexplicable splendour of Ionian white and gold* . . . Or *the storied windows richly dight, Casting a dim religious light* –

Martin saw it; took it in; the product of countless literary minds made flesh – no, made marble, made basalt and serpentine, jade and onyx, a medley of stones and styles beneath the setting sun.

He remembered the old joke about the camel: A horse designed by a committee. He saw the secret heart of Butor.

It was ugly; a jumble of clashing modes, ugly and appalling.

Slowly Martin turned and left that place, not pausing, not looking back; not caring whether or not the city continued to be.

ONE IMMORTAL MAN

BY RICHARD E. GEIS

Richard Geis has made his living as a writer for more than twenty years. For much the same length of time he has published a magazine dealing exclusively with review and discussion of science fiction – and in process of so doing has collected no less than six Hugo Awards, our field's most coveted honour.

Yet paradoxically this is his first professional piece of science fiction.

Geis has strong views on what writing is all about. As he says in his own SF Review *: 'fiction's role is not the salvation of mankind and the changing of society. It is precisely what Literary and Artistic writers deplore and dread; story-telling that primarily entertains, distracts, diverts.'*

And so 'One Immortal Man' is rich in speculative detail but doubly stands out through the boldness and sheer driving power of its narrative. It is the first of a projected series; and I'm pleased to welcome the Geis blockbuster to ANDRO-MEDA.

Vik Kunzar winced at the sudden, stabbing, alarm pain in the tip of his middle finger, left hand.

He slid his big black arm away from the naked brown body of the young Empress Punia, automatically damping the nerve response. The pain was intrusive and important. It would flare again in a few seconds, but muted.

He shifted to the edge of the oval, spongy, purplish plant that had been genetically adapted to serve as a bed.

She opened wide dark eyes. 'What's the matter?'

His fingertip pulsed again. It contained a microreceiver, set in bone, connected to a nerve.

He padded, naked, across the golden carpet of fuzzy, intertwined hairlike tendrils that sprouted from the floor. Slipping on his white leafcloth toga he positioned its suckers in his armpits. The living cloth glowed with life.

He said, 'I have something important to do. I'm sorry.'

Punia sat up. 'I arranged to be free until dawn.' She was petulant, feeling cheated. She smiled the small, superior smile of the young and eager. 'Are you feeling your age, Masil?'

Vik reflectively glanced at himself in the nearest mirror. His ebony face was lined. His kinky hair showed many, many coils of white. It was convincing.

'Government business.' He picked up her garments from a gourdchair and took them to her. He leaned over and kissed her. 'Next time I'll wear your yoni smooth.'

He meant it. Punia was his type: young, lean, big-breasted, eager, and he had taught her all there was to know about lovemaking since her twelfth birthday. He had even manoeuvred Emperor Ndola into choosing her as Empress.

Vik smiled down at the girl. Power and sex and danger kept him going. It seemed that more and more of each was necessary as the generations rolled past.

She insisted on another kiss. Her hands caressed his deep, well-muscled chest, his hard belly, his thighs. 'Can't you be First Minister only during the day?' Her featherlight touch trailed the length of his organ under his toga. 'You're so young below the neck.'

Vik controlled the natural surge of blood. He pulled her to her feet. She was small, five feet one, and he was a giant at six feet five. 'Dress. I'll see you down the bole.'

She slipped on her imported orange silk chemise, and then the furred leafcloth robe. She let the suckers hang free of her nipples; she didn't want to glow as she rode her lion through the forest city to the gargantuan palace trees.

She followed him to the curving wall of striped moss drapery that hid the mottled, twenty-foot trunk. 'Masil, is it about the weather? And the northern tribes?'

'No.' He pulled the drapery aside and pressed a spot in the discoloured bark. An oval door appeared and rustled inward.

'Quebo said the ice would drive all the white ones south into our territory in the next few years.'

'He's right.' Vik led the way down a narrow, curved stairway. The rough-walled passageway through the solid, dense pink wood was lit by glowleaves suckered to tiny veins of sap. Vik had to stoop and move slightly sideways.

Punia wanted to probe further. Her pride was hurt by his abrupt change of plans for the night. But she knew enough not to question him too closely; there would emerge a cold ruthlessness of manner, a terrifying *distance* in his dark eyes, that frightened her. She avoided provoking that response.

When they reached the bottom of the passage he asked, 'Has Ndola changed toward you lately?'

She frowned. 'I don't think so.' Her face was sickly in the faint green leaflight. 'He doesn't command me to his bed as often ... but he's really old and he can't penetrate like a younger man – like you! But – he told me you're seventy-three ... and he's only sixty-eight.'

'When did he tell you my age?'

'Two nights ago at dinner.' Punia's eyes dilated slightly with anger. 'He's bringing that yellow girl to the table now. That mouth specialist. I've heard that she can take a man deep into her throat. They teach them that in the East, from when they're five and six years old.'

Vik nodded. 'For hundreds of years now.' He smiled. 'How the Chinese have changed.'

'He said ... when he mentioned your age – are you actually seventy-three, Masil? – that it wasn't natural for a man your age to be so well-preserved ... even if you did come from the Nubian Nile where they grow so big.'

'He's jealous.'

'No, he values you. He said you were the most able of all his ministers because of your knowledge of history. No other man in the Empire knows as much about the world and its people as you.'

Vik opened the secret door and let her out into the groomed

maze of hedges that enclosed most of the base of the massive tree. He led her to his lion pen nearby within the tree grounds. The vast branches swept out and out for hundreds of feet. All land under a tree's branches belonged to the owner of the tree; a large Junto tree was an estate.

Punia joined her waiting lady in the shadows. Vik personally led their saddled lions to them. A moment later the great cats glided away with their riders. The night guards at the gate would let them pass without question. Masil's sexual exploits were known by his servants and a few of his tree force. They did not know the identity of the visitors.

Vik walked quickly back to the secret passageway in his tree. Within, as the outer door rustled shut and seated tightly, he pressed another spot in the curved, axe-hewn wall.

A rectangular section opened. He entered a second passage that sloped down and to the left. He carefully closed that door behind him. His fingertip continued to pulse every few seconds.

The passageway left the root and became a tunnel. He came to a wood-panelled, carpeted room sixty feet below ground. Before entering the doorless room he spoke one word: '*Olympia*'. Unseen automatic laser guns switched back to secondary alert.

Vik went to a silvery console and noted the label under the single glowing ruby light among dozens set in a panel. He switched it off.

The periodic, muted sting in his fingertip ended.

Vik sat in the worn, deep-cushioned silvery console chair and thought for a long moment. His finger idly traced a small manufacturer's plate.

KZAR MICROTRONICS
Denver, U.S.A.
2116

His deep, dark eyes focused on the plate. He smiled and shook his head, murmuring, '*The good old days. . . .*'

He stood and left the panelled room. Sensors in the tunnel 'watched' him leave. The lasers warmed again to primary alert.

Vik went back up to his bedroom. He took off his toga.

Naked, he pulled a corner of the living rug free of the floor. The hundreds of tiny suckers made minute popping sounds, leaving dot-like green marks on the raw boards that had fused together and grown solidly to the joists, which had in turn cemented themselves to the broad limb upon which the bedroom rested . . . or from which it grew.

The tree supported thirty-two parasitical rooms with attendant plant furnishings, glowleafs of various colours, and hollow water and sewage vines.

Vik lifted a small trapdoor in the floor and lifted out an unlocked chest from the two-foot-deep cavity. He opened the chest and reached in for a soft, lion hide holster. He strapped it to the side of his massive left thigh.

He took a chamois-wrapped revolver from the chest. The gun was old but well oiled and cared for. It had been made by hand and ancient machine over two hundred and fifty years before, by the steel guildmen in F'Derick in the north-west Sahara where the last deposits of iron had been jealously guarded and gradually used over a millenium.

Vik armed the gun with hand-loaded ammunition. Guns were rare and expensive. Most were rusted museum pieces – in the few museums remaining. Ammunition was the problem. Shell casings were priceless.

He rarely used this pistol anymore, but tonight it would be good to have in reserve. The revolver slid into the pliant holster and he tied the flap shut with a quick-release knot. He returned the chest to its hiding-place in the floor and took a jewelled, razor-sharp knife with matching sheath from a decorative wooden hook on the wall over the bed, strapping it to his left leg below the knee.

Then he stepped into a loin protector of leather and rubber, adjusting his large genitals in the cup. He slipped a dark-red silk tunic over his head and finally cinched a wide, heavy-buckled belt tight around his waist.

Vik left his tree by way of the secret passageway in the trunk. He exited the grounds by way of a tunnel under the high, poisonous thorn hedge that bordered his treeland and began to run, effortlessly, north, weaving between the huge tree homes in the darkness. His bare feet slapped quietly on the smooth, leaf-cushioned ground.

Pale glowleaf path signs dotted the park-like between-trees areas, patches of colourless moonlight penetrated the acres of overhead foliage. Only a few people were out in the wide, intertwining paths that snaked between the trees, for he lived in the exclusive, upper-class residential area of Kinshasa, the imperial city.

Vik avoided the lion-riders, who were easy to see, as were the white skins of lower caste slaves sent out on unknown midnight errands. He was hard to spot, impossible to follow; a black ghost who loped tirelessly north toward the city's slightly less exclusive Stalee Pool suburb.

Vik ran two miles. He slowed to a walk as he approached his destination, a squat tree home of modest two-hundred-foot spread and ten-foot bole.

The glowleaf sign at the gate of the surrounding living thorn fence read: *Doctor Kiambi*, 742011. All residence and business and government trees in the city were registered by number and the current owner.

The trees dated from the last surge of highly specialized technology five hundred years before, when the Egyptians had flourished yet again. They had concentrated on genetics, had developed the home trees, the parasitic plant furnishings . . . had warped both animal and human genes in a vain attempt to maintain 'civilization' on the face of a planet exhausted of mineral wealth . . . and had broken under the waves of white-skinned barbarians fleeing the long-dying ruins of Europe as the ice, decade by decade, crept inexorably southward. Now the Congo empire of Ndola was the only centre of culture and learning and law on the African continent.

Vik was not surprised to find the gate locked. He walked slowly along the vicious fence, searching for a break. The sensitized thorn vines stirred at his nearness and lashed at his form. He found a ten-foot-wide length of the fence lying limp, paralyzed by a sweet-smelling fluid he knew about. Very few others in Kinshasa had a working knowledge of it.

Vik stepped carefully through the still vines and approached the tree. There was a dayglow of light from the oval, transparent membrane windows of a large room fifty feet up the trunk in a major limb room-cluster.

He ignored the small hydraulic elevator. The cage was up at the cluster, anyway, probably locked. For a moment he paused to study the tree's ramps and stairs, then took the narrow, spiral, servants' staircase that followed upward under the more elaborate, inlaid ramp. He went slowly, pausing often to listen. He freed his knife of its sheath and carried it lightly in his upturned hand, ready to throw or fight.

Emerging onto the wide, main porch that semi-circled the tree trunk he passed several ramps and doors and approached the doctor's office. The windows continued to glow with light.

The porch ended at the office door. The only way to look into a window was to edge out from the railing by hanging free from a slippery gutter vine at the cornice.

If he slipped it would mean a fall of fifty feet to the decorative marble set in the ground around the base of the tree.

And he would be vulnerable if discovered out there, spying.

Vik pressed his ear to the expensive, inlaid office door. The deep squares and wedges of vari-coloured woods had grown together; the door lived, fed sap from the five tough but pliant green plant hinges. He could hear a voice – no distinct words. Another voice, more tenor. And . . . a groan ? Both voices were angry, insistent.

Vik carefully tried the sliding, killed-wood door latch. The door was peg-locked from the inside.

The windows, then. He sheathed his knife.

Standing on the solid, carved railing, he tested the gutter vine with his weight. It bowed slightly but the suckers held. He curled his fingers into the leaf-choked trough and swung out into space. The vine bowed downward even more with his full two hundred and forty pounds. The sucker fibres screamed faintly . . . but held.

Vik hung facing the wall and swiftly slid his gripping hands along the oily rim of the vine. His fingers dug into bird droppings and tiny, rotted corpses as well as the broad, sticky tree leaves.

As he approached the nearest oval window, steadily increasing areas of the office came into view: the desk, a series of bright dayglow leaves slowly burning in a large glass surgery lamp, the killed-wood cabinets of records – one drawer open. *The M drawer.* Shelves of herbs, jars of medicinal roots and bottles of fluids. A man's shadow cast on the blond wood interior panelling from another bright lamp deeper in the office, to the right.

Vik hung silently beside the window and carefully made sure of his right-hand grip on the gutter. He let loose with his left and lowered his arm. This angled his body, allowing him to see almost all the interior of the doctor's office while reducing the risk of being noticed from inside.

Doctor Kiambi was strapped to a treatment table. He lay face down, gagged, naked, his old brown scrawny body writhing in agony. A long, thick eater snake had been inserted into his anus. Two-thirds of it was coiled around his jerking, flailing right leg. The other third was deep into the old man's intestines.

Two men watched Kiambi's thrashings. They wore tunics similar in design to Vik's, but of coarse green cotton. They were of the Lualaba tribe – brownish yellow skin and wide fleshy lips and noses.

Ndola was a Lualaba.

One man knelt beside the table, near Kiambi's head. He had a belly on him, and thick legs. He spoke in a low, wheedling voice. The other man stood with hands on hips, grinning. A long knife in a thin green scabbard swung from his iron-vine belt.

Vik brought his left hand up to grip the gutter vine again. He swiftly edged further out until he was hanging opposite the oval window. He swung his legs up, planted his bare feet on each side of the window, bent his knees, kicked himself outward, closed his feet and ripped through the transparent membrane.

Vik twisted as his big black body cleared the oval frame and

162

he landed on all fours beside the desk. He uncoiled, knife in his left hand, and with terrifying grace and power leaped for the astonished, standing man.

The man was a trained professional, he managed to clear his own long knife in the second it took Vik to reach him. He was too slow. He was only beginning to crouch, to bring his knife into defensive position, when Vik clamped a vice grip on his wrist and slammed the jewelled knife full into his stomach, angling up to spear the keen blade into his thudding heart.

The man grunted with the blow and lurched backward, turning, falling, his wide mouth loose, flared eyes staring with fading amazement. Blood spumed from the wound.

Vik pulled his knife free an instant after the savage thrust, knowing from long experience the man was already dead. The body crumpled heavily to the orange carpet.

The other intruder had almost three seconds. He was older, however, and slower. He was pulling a spring-powered dart gun from a leather bag beside the table when Vik slapped his arm away.

Vik did not waste time. He brought his hand back and across the jowled face. The man's head jerked sharply sideways from the blow. His mouth leaked blood. Vik almost casually pushed him down onto his back and sat crushingly on his chest. His knees pinned the man's flabby arms. '*Who sent you?*'

Without waiting for an answer, knowing there would be no information, not wanting to play games, Vik seized the man's right hand and calmly, viciously, snapped the little finger.

The man gasped. His eyes dilated with pain. He laboured to breathe. His breath wheezed and he swallowed blood. He said nothing.

Beside them, on the table, Doctor Kiambi continued to shudder and moan into his tight gag. The eater snake was following the soft tube of his intestine deeper and deeper, consuming his body's wastes, ever hungry, ravenously seeking more . . . Soon the snake would eat its way through the wall of the narrowing, twisting flesh tunnel and would gorge on liver, kidney. . .

'*Who?*' Vik impatiently twisted the man's broken finger.

The man's plump face rippled with pain. His lips drew back in a grimace. He shook his head as he hissed for air. His chest convulsively fought Vik's crushing weight.

Vik undid the man's belt and strapped his feet together. Then he cut the man's tunic free and with it tied his wrists behind his back.

Then Vik stood, grasped the end of the purple, diamond-back eater snake with his powerful right hand and slowly, calmly, pulled the three-foot length from Kiambi's body. The scaly inches emerged sheened with blood.

When the snake's round, wet, suctioning mouth was free, gleaming with half-hidden rows of shark-like teeth, Vik looked to the bound fat man. 'It's still hungry. You've got a lot to feed it.' He nudged the man's heavy gut.

His prisoner was pale with fear.

'Who sent you here?'

'You'll kill me anyway.'

'No, not if you tell me the truth.'

The man's eyes seemed riveted to the snake's undulating, red-rimmed mouth. Then his gaze darted to the body of his dead companion. He said, '*Quebo.*'

The Emperor's Defence Minister.

At that instant the tip of Vik's middle finger, left hand, came alive with a throb of pain. Automatically he damped the nerves. He said to the agent, 'Why is he investigating me?'

'I wasn't told. He wants your medical records. He wanted me to make the doctor talk about you . . . about your past.'

'And what did Kiambi tell you?'

'Only what the records show.'

Vik glanced at the old doctor. Kiambi lay limply, an occasional spasm wracking his body. He continued to moan into his gag. The snake writhed and twisted in Vik's grasp. Vik said, 'Where else is Quebo sending agents to investigate my past?'

'North . . . where you were first seen.'

'Interesting phrasing. Did he say it that way?'

'Yes.'

Vik stared thoughtfully at the man. 'Do you believe I'm seventy-three years old?'

'No! The way you moved! The way you fought!'

'Yes . . . I've waited too long this time.' Vik drove the point of his knife into the snake's spine, just behind the tubular head. The squirming body went limp. He threw it into a corner. 'Where are the doctor's servants and slaves? They would have heard all this.'

'We locked them in the trunk room.'

'Thank you.' Vik moved around behind the heavy agent, knelt, hooked a powerful arm under the man's fleshy chin, lifted—

The agent's chest pumped with sudden terror. He wheezed, '*You promised. . .*'

Vik squeezed off the voice and drove his jewelled knife cleanly between the man's ribs, into the heart. The body convulsed for an instant, then subsided. Vik said quietly, 'I lie often.'

He moved over and looked into Kiambi's pain-ridden eyes. 'I'm sorry. I warned you fifty years ago this time might come. You've been very well paid. You've had a long, good life. I cannot leave you alive. Quebo would take you . . . and you'd talk. Kunzar must remain a myth, a dream . . . a wish.'

He picked up the dart gun and sent the bolt thudding into the old man's brain.

Vik took a deep breath. He smiled wryly. 'I'm getting too old for this sort of thing.'

He picked up the fat agent's leather bag and took out the sheaf of papers he knew would be inside – his medical history as Masil; a series of medical examinations showing his nearly perfect health through the decades, except for recurring stomach trouble (faked – in the record for credibility).

Vik flipped the pages until he came to one with a tiny brown stain on the lower right corner. He sliced off the corner and slipped the bit of paper into a small plastic envelope he took from a slit in his belt. He returned the envelope to its carrying place.

The 'stain' was a micro transmitter, alarm-keyed to light and motion.

Vik continued to feel the timed throbs of diminished pain in his finger which meant another micro alarm had been set off somewhere ... probably in Abu Hamid where his birth record was planted along with that of the plague deaths of his fictional parents. Was this just a security check – or an investigation into the possibility that he could be the mythical one immortal man on Earth?

Vik put his medical records back into place in the file cabinet and closed the drawer. He went to the torn window and peered cautiously out, listening. He checked the sections of the tree, porch and stairs he could see. With his knife ready, he unpegged the door and opened it a crack. Satisfied, he slipped out and disappeared into the night.

The next day Vik sat in an enormous sea-green sofa-lounge in his palace tree's office, and dictated to a series of Messengers.

Messengers were men of great integrity and astonishing, eidetic memory. They were all members of one widespread family whose 'memory gene' traced back to the work of the Egyptians. They were a guild and a clan; they never married outside the family for fear of losing the gene. The males worked for governments, the females for private business where they could keep a home and raise their children. They often carried a pouch of documents, but most of the empire's provinces and client chiefdoms depended on their total recall and inviolable honesty.

It meant death to harm or seriously interfere with a Messenger whether he was on duty or not. An attempted bribe was instantly reported. The last instance of a Messenger violating his trust had occurred more than a century before, and he had been publicly beheaded by members of his inner family.

Messengers could not be tortured for information; when their pain level reached a certain point they died. They were very cautious people. Accidents and disease killed them easily due to their low pain tolerance.

Vik wore his purple First Minister's robe of office, as usual, and his gold pendant. A male secretary sat cross-legged on the deep amber grass carpet, taking down his words on a square

166

paperleaf with an inkstick. Real paper was available but it was too expensive for casual note-taking.

Vik noticed Caiungo, his first assistant, enter the large room. Caiungo knew he had Vik's eye. He pointed toward the ceiling and jabbed once. Emperor Ndola wanted Masil. Nodding, Vik continued giving the Messenger instructions for the east central provinces. In five minutes he was done.

As the Messenger left, with the secretary, Vik asked Caiungo, 'What does he want?'

'Quebo's alone with him. I don't know. High Policy, I suppose. No staff allowed.'

'No word from the vines?' Vik referred to inter-office rumours, leaks and paid informers. He had people in the staffs of every minister, even that of the Emperor . . . and they had a few in his entourage. Palace intrigue always existed in power centres. The trick was to accept it and play the game well.

'Maybe that Quebo wants to break your monopoly of glowleafs. Empire defence requires—'

Vik nodded sharply. 'He's wanted that for ten years. Tell Dikwa to snoop for special agent activity. Quebo is up to something.'

Vik left his office by its private exit and emerged on to the ornate, high ramp that curved up to the Emperor's throne room and office cluster. This giant-among-giants, centre tree of the five sacred palace trees, soared upward into the sky, a living tower that dominated the empire city.

The palace trees had stood for half a millenium. Long ago their major branches had been spliced together to make the grove into a single, joined entity. Ramps and bridges linked the trees at various branch-cluster levels. Slave-powered, counterweighted elevators rose and descended.

Vik looked up at the clear blue sky . . . at the sun, for an instant. He enjoyed the feel of the afternoon warmth. August, and the temperature high was only about twenty-five degrees. Reports told of the glaciers creeping south of the Alps now, and claiming at least half the Black Sea . . . now called the Ice Sea.

Vik looked out over the masses of green foliage that hid all but occasional spots of ground. There were broad, crowded lanes and paths down there: markets and shops, lion pens, pleasure huts, stone banks encircling bank-owned business trees. . . .

The largest bank, The Congo Trading Company, was controlled by Masil Investments. He turned and walked up the ramp to the next level, slowly, limping, and absentmindedly massaging the fingers of his right hand as if they were arthritic. When he entered the outer offices the clerks and lower officials spread their hands, palms up, and bowed their heads.

The Emperor's Private One, a greying, stolid man in a living toga with gold threads woven between the pale yellow fibres, smiled and said, 'Quebo is with him, eating a little. Would you care for something? Yemena wine? An Indian cake?'

Masil's favourite foods were known and stocked.

'No, nothing now.' Vik was midly surprised when the Private One by-passed the usual private conference rooms and led him through to the Emperor's personal quarters.

The man opened a gold-leafed door for him. Vik limped into a luxurious wedge-shaped study he visited maybe five or six times a year. The multi-windowed outer wall provided a view of a third of the city. The transparent membranes flexed from the breeze outside. At this height the tree swayed very slightly.

Ndola and Quebo sat close together on a curving, purple, living sofa. They were both small men: Ndola wrinkled and skull-like, with sharp, dark fox eyes, his thin old body stick-like in the layers of a red silk toga; Quebo still strong and firm in a green military tunic with gold piping, a woven gold belt, self-important with diamond and jade rings on every finger.

Ndola turned his lean head and smiled. He said, 'Masil.' He spoke a fraction off-tone, a fraction too 'late' for normal, and Vik easily caught it.

The 'investigation' was known and approved by the Emperor.

Ndola gestured. 'Sit on my left. Wine?' A bottle of dark red Yemena sat with other wines, cakes, meats, fruits, sweets, breads and cheeses on the low, wheeled, killed-mahogany cart

168

before the sofa. A deaf-mute servant stood ready to serve. He knew all the ministers' preferences.

Quebo lifted a palm in greeting and casual respect. 'These melon pods are exquisitely ripe, Masil. Try one.'

Vik limped to the sofa. 'No, my stomach is hurting again.' When he sat next to the Emperor he seemed a black giant by comparison. The sofa groaned softly as his weight pressed down on its cushions.

Vik abstractedly flexed his right hand. 'Every few years I have to go to the mineral springs of Tukuyu for a few weeks.' He closed his eyes and smiled with memory. 'Soak in that hot, soothing, bubbling water, and drink it hot, day after day. . . .'

Once away from the empire city, on the way to the Mitumba Mountains, Masil's small entourage and armed escort would be set upon by a ruthless band of cutthroats and Masil, First Minister to Emperor Ndola, would be taken, would disappear . . . would never be seen nor heard of again.

Vik had staged such exits many times.

Ndola and Quebo exchanged glances. The Emperor nodded. 'This body of mine is falling apart, too. Every day I live in pain.' He pressed his lower gut. 'Pain that only hemp and zizu can tame for a while.' He laughed. 'But I don't leave my work. The Empire needs me. You, too, Masil.'

Vik said, 'There is nothing critical. Caiungo and my staff are able to function without me, easily, for two ten-days.'

Ndola didn't argue. He slipped off to another subject. 'Quebo has just given me reports of white tribes coming down off the Jef-Jef Plateau. They're being forced south by waves of savages from still further north.'

Vik nodded. 'All of Europe is virtually uninhabitable now, even in summer. We can't blame them.'

Quebo said in his rough voice, 'We have to stop them. They're tough and hungry and vicious. They're slaughtering our people in the Mourdi.'

Vik looked out of the windows and followed the brown curve of a wide tree limb. 'Give up the fourth cataract and fall back to the Khartoum line. That can be defended with five thousand less men. Send them home to rest to act as part of our reserve, and send five thousand of our present reserve to defend the Mourdi.'

Ndola pursed his thick lips. His keen old eyes shifted to Quebo.

Quebo traced an old scar on his thigh. 'That is the obvious military move. The problem is more than military, however. It is also social, and complicated. The whites are fanatics. They are driven by a new religion.' His eyes lanced at Vik.

Vik continued flexing his right hand. 'The Kun-Zar Quest, I know. I've seen the analysis. It's valid.'

Ndola's eyes widened. 'You admit Kun-Zar exists ?'

Vik smiled. 'No. I mean the whites' religion. They believe one of their ancient rulers, Kun-Zar, was immortal and did not die, but left for the south – Africa – and that they must follow him, seek him, and find him in the promised land. They believe he's here in the warm belt, waiting for them, and when they find him again he'll rule them as before, with infinite wisdom, and peace and plenty will come to their favoured race.'

Quebo nodded. 'Yes, that's what drives them south into our lands. Kun-Zar. Not just the pressure of new migrations from the north, nor the cold. It's not that cold in the Sahara, and there is room in that vastness for all the people in the world. But they know he's not there.'

Ndola said, 'And, Masil, from all your learning and knowledge of ancient times . . . is it possible that this god, this Kun-Zar, *does* exist ?'

'No. He's a convenient myth, a creation of the white priests and chiefs, to move their tribes, to justify their migration and their invasions and slaughters. They must think of themselves as a special people, and therefore all other peoples are lesser, and may be killed without remorse. Dehumanizing your enemy is a common technique . . . and necessity.'

Quebo said sharply, 'The Egyptians have a belief in an immortal man, a superman who lived, disappeared, lived again and again. They believe he founded their great civilization then finally disappeared about four hundred years ago.'

'You've been reading the ancient leaves.'

'A myth is often based—'

Ndola shot a warning glance at Quebo. 'Enough of this. Let's get some work done. I want to spend some time this afternoon with my sweetmouth girl.'

Quebo grinned. Vik smiled.

Ndola smirked. 'Ah, Masil, Quebo can tell you how good she is. I sent her to his tree for a night last week.' He laughed delightedly. He fisted his bony, veined hand. 'My wilted stem grows to a tree between those cunning lips. That dancing tongue of hers. . . .'

Quebo nodded. 'Fantastic skill. I was ten years older by morning.'

Ndola laughed. 'Yes, yes. She can wither any man – even old Kun-Zar!' He fox-glanced at Vik. 'You'll see. I'll send her to you tonight, Masil. She'll swallow your big black pole and you'll live in the Valley of the Sun Goddess for a while.'

Vik smiled widely and inclined his head. He showed his palms. 'Thank you, Highest One. Tomorrow my servants will find me too weak to be of use to the Empire.'

Vik was sure the little Chinese girl would be required to find out certain things about him. It would be a pleasant evening.

Ndola cackled, but his laugh ended as he pressed his right hand to his abdomen. 'She'll be there. Now what about those crystal slabs from the ruins of Nork? They're the key to my tomb.'

Vik said, 'They are at the temple now. Work will begin to-morrow. Caiungo has arranged a triumphant ceremony for this afternoon. The survivors of the expedition will be honoured by your presence and will present you with the twenty slabs they managed to save. Cacola will make a speech recounting his men's adventures crossing the ocean to the Ice Lands of America.'

Quebo growled, 'Incredible that old map was accurate, and the crystal still there.'

Vik replied, 'The older the map the more likely its accuracy. Ancient books in my library tell of a huge structure, five times taller than this tree, constructed almost entirely of blocks and slabs of a kind of crystalline plastic. Impervious to wear and temperature. It isn't a long branch to expect some to still be there. The survivors of the Bio-War weren't capable of—'

Ndola suddenly clutched at his belly and bent over. He gestured sharply at the slave. 'Pipe!'

The slave began swiftly to prepare a pipe of hemp and chalky zizu powder. He mixed in a heavy portion of the addictive, pain-killing drug.

Ndola bent over further. He keened with intense pain. He whispered, '*I don't want to die !*'

Vik said deliberately, 'Every man must die.'

Ndola swivelled narrowed, agony-filled eyes to him, and the wrinkled, bony old face showed naked hate and raw envy for an uncontrolled instant.

Then the slave handed the Emperor the pipe, lit, ready, and the old man sucked in air and smoke greedily. He held the mixture in his lungs and waved away his Private One who had hurriedly entered the room, concerned.

There were eyes and ears in these walls, too.

That did not surprise Vik. The Emperor lived with at least two loyal warriors watching him and whoever he was with, day and night, during sleep, even during his times of passion. Every wall in the palace trees was riddled with peep-holes and listening points.

Now, obviously, Quebo and Ndola strongly suspected him of being Kun-Zar. They were not fools. They had a plan, a sequence, which was in operation. They had to be sure before they acted.

Vik relished the contest, the danger.

He shifted to a more comfortable position on the sofa. The cushions wheezed. His movement caused tilts in other cushions. Ndola swayed and sucked loudly on his pipe, and said, 'Leave me. Tomorrow. . . .' His eyes closed. The Emperor's face was relaxing.

Vik rose and limped to the door. Quebo showed a palm and let him leave first.

Later that afternoon Vik left his offices and took the long elevator to the ground. He was accompanied by his own Private

172

One, a personal secretary, and the president of his shipping company.

Vik had never liked the swaying, creaking, killed-wood cage, the dead rope vines, the pulleys or the six-man gang of white slaves who manned the clacking, ratcheted windlass. It was too easy to have an 'accident'.

But his role and his limp made a long walk down the ramps and stairs out of the question for a man of his proclaimed age.

Vik watched the basketed counterweights rise toward their descending cage. He said, 'Schedule the extension of our docks in Zuccra and here, out to the six-fathom depth at low tide. The ice will claim enough water in the next hundred years to make our present docks unusable.' He automatically scanned the palace grounds as the cage sank below the giant lower branches.

The president asked, 'Why are you concerned about the future of Congo Shipping Company that far ahead?'

'You know I have an heir living in India. It's for him and his son and his son. . . And I'm doing my little bit to ensure trade and civilization will continue. It's a hobby.'

The pattern of people below, most of them going home, seemed normal. His prize lion, Copper Tom, waited with a groom and two of Vik's personal guards.

Vik added, 'Set up an automatic company policy directive: buy all tidal lands as they become available. Buy the continental shelf if you can, now. Put in a formal buy application and I'll see if Ndola will trade worthless sea-covered land for pure gold. One hundred milled emperors per mile.'

The secretary made notes on his pad of white leaves.

Vik's Private One was servant, tree-keeper and friend. He said, 'Borus told me you'll have a lovely one for company tonight. Nimbus soup, water buffalo steak and Iona seeds for dinner?'

Vik nodded. 'Private. You serve.'

The cage bumped down on to its marble platform. A slave opened the door for them.

Three minutes later Vik was astride his huge cat. The golden-maned beast ambled through the crowded lanes and streets of the haphazard ring of shops, huts, buildings of all kinds, tents and cart merchants that encircled the walled grounds of the palace trees.

Vik was in the centre of his small party. He was Masil, First Minister, a magnificent black giant in these times of smaller and smaller men as each generation passed. He enjoyed the awe and respect in most of the faces of the people. He enjoyed the rumours that he was the secret emperor, that Ndola was only a front.

Suddenly the attack began – a sudden clot of men, a braying, maddened donkey, goaded by thorn whips, sent plunging with his loaded fruit cart into the diamond formation of Vik's company.

Vik was the centre. The target.

The lead guard's lion whirled, nearly throwing its rider. The secretary's small female mount hissed and slashed reflexively at the terrified animal. A donkey will never willingly get within ten feet of a lion.

The ass screamed and stumbled, his shaggy brown coat suddenly rippled, running blood. The cart's left wheel came off its axle and the fragrant load of violet werzi grapes was spilled. Someone threw Mongo powder into the muzzle of the rear lion. The cat recoiled and plunged away.

A quick, muscular young man in a tattered jungle tunic raised a dart gun and aimed at Vik from ten feet. He was surrounded by a wedge of other young men dressed as beggars and lower-class labourers.

Vik had only a few seconds in which to try to escape the attack. The wedge of men was surging closer. He shifted to throw himself off to his lion's left side and use Copper Tom as a shield, when his Private One's mount, a dun-coloured female reacting to the stink of fear and excitement and the screaming press of people, closed the space and bumped hard against Vik's left leg. The Private One was as wild-eyed as his cat.

For a precious instant Vik lost his balance and co-ordination. The knot of attackers was within five feet of him. The secretary had fallen from his saddle; the small mount crouched and coiled. The men leaped over it, pushing closer.

Vik wore a ceremonial dagger. But he knew his best course was to get clear.

He bellowed, 'TOM! LEAP!'

But the great cat had no space, took too long to crouch for the spring that would take it over the braying, kicking donkey and the lead guard's lion.

The guard was off his mount and lunging with his precious antique sword to defend Vik – but it would be too late. At the last split second Vik lashed out with his own razor-sharp dagger and laid open the face of an attacker. A grotesque slab of raw cheek flapped away from the jaw bone, but simultaneously the man with the dart gun fired at point-blank range.

Pain exploded in Vik's right thigh. The dart buried itself a hands-width below his hip joint, the red and green feathered shaft protruding from his toga, pinning the heavy purple brocade to his thigh. The material soaked up the rapidly welling blood.

Then Copper Tom's great bunched muscles released and Vik was carried upward by that tremendous surge of animal power . . . soaring for an incredible second . . . barely able to shift his weight to stay in the saddle. During that bound, Vik automatically 'disconnected' the input from the nerves of his damaged thigh. And he realized the trigger man hadn't intended to kill. There had been time and freedom for a shot at stomach or heart, even for a less sure head shot. But the gun had been fired directly at his thigh. There had been no hestitation, no shifting of aim. The dart had travelled less than a foot.

Copper Tom landed, snarling, in the midst of scrambling, howling, terrified people. Vik bent low into the clean, abundant yellow mane. '*Home!*' The mighty lion uncoiled again and bounded through a narrow gap in the dense, hysterical crowd.

Vik felt the grating of the dart's saw-tooth ironwood point against his thigh bone during the ride. Blood flowed down his leg in spite of his constriction of the main vessels.

Copper Tom loped toward the home tree by the direct route, the one usually travelled to and from the palace com-

pound. Vik steered him off into side paths, to avoid possible
secondary ambushes. The giant trees loomed in sunset splendour. He avoided any approach to the gate of his tree ground.
He neared the tree from the opposite side and urged Copper
Tom to a full-speed run at the fifteen-foot-high poisonous
thorn hedge that surrounded his land.

'*Up, Tom!*'

The great cat soared in a fantastic leap. No other lion of
those bred and gene-altered for size and strength and obedi-
ence could have done it with Vik's weight on his back.

The green-tipped rows of thorn spikes stirred as Copper
Tom cleared their highest tips by a foot. The landing was
silken as the cat's muscles and bones absorbed the shock and
transferred speed and mass into continuing forward motion on
the deep, tightly woven grass.

Three gardeners working in a new, oval bed of plump Cabon
ferns looked around in astonishment. Vik motioned them back
to work. He rode to the gloom of the pens and dismounted
carefully.

Dambo, the over-eager assistant to his Private One, came
running down a ramp, his light blue servant tunic flapping,
his gold authority bracelet gleaming as he passed through a
thin shaft of orange sunlight.

Vik impatiently cut off the youth's shocked words. 'Send a
messenger for Doctor Choma. Get the elevator down.'

Taleg, a big, muscular black man in rich dark blue leathers
and gold command necklace sprinted around the corner of the
pens. He was followed by a ten-man troop of estate guards –
five swords, five bowmen. His steady eyes flicked at the pinned,
blood-stained toga, the dart still solidly embedded in Vik's leg,
the small trickle of red that was dampening the hard-packed
earth next to Vik's wet, goldcloth sandal.

Taleg snapped, 'The big yellow cushioned chair!' He pointed
to three of the guards and waved them toward the master
gardener's hut.

Vik said, 'Draw forty men from the Kwa orchards. I want
them here by midnight.' He didn't have to tell Taleg to double
the hedge security and send out undercover scouts. But if the

Emperor was ready to move against his First Minister a company of crack private guards couldn't hold against Quebo's massed regulars.

Vik explained to Taleg: 'We were ambushed in the market ring. Send some men to see about Uvira, Mwanza and Isiro and the two guards. I want Caiundo here. I want Luishia and Gombe here at morning sun.'

Dambo had run off. Vik saw a lean, tan messenger on a fast Walla lion riding toward the arched, killed-wood gate. A guard opened a smaller door within the gate and the rider and his mount squeezed out. Other guards stood ready at the gate's arrow and spear ports.

The large elevator creaked down from Vik's private cluster. From the hut the guards brought the master gardener's pride and only real luxury – his massive, deeply cushioned chair.

Vik sank into it. His thigh was aching.

He was carried into the elevator. Sahara slaves loaded more stones into the counterweight basket and pulled him up. As he was carried into his bedroom he caught glimpses of Mwanza, his Private One, and the others straggling in through the gate. They had not been hurt. Ndola and Quebo did not want to have it appear that an organised attack had been mounted against Masil and his band. They did not want the people to suspect the truth, for Masil was very popular. Their attack had only the effect of confining Vik to his tree for a while. An effective, ingenious house arrest.

Vik was lying naked on his soft, living bed, a thick towel under his leg, the dart still in his thigh, when Mwanza entered the room. 'Singida is here.'

The Emperor's personal physician!

Vik thought a few seconds, then contained a wry smile. 'Naturally. Bring him in and stay to observe. If Doctor Choma arrives while Singida is here, have him sent up.'

Vik knew the purpose of Singida's very prompt visit had to be to examine him as closely as possible, to confirm or rule out the possibility that Masil was immortal . . . was Kun-Zar. The attack in the market ring also served this second purpose. No . . . more likely this was the primary reason. Vik mentally saluted Ndola. The old man was still as cunning and shrewd as ever. And now, dying, totally desperate.

After a few minutes, Singida entered, followed by a slave who carried his heavy leather medicine bags. Singida was a deceptive, placid, fat man whose breasts jiggled with his belly beneath his gold-fringed orange robe. He wore a diamond ear pendant signifying his royal appointment.

His slave was a middle-aged white man with a neatly trimmed beard. Vik spotted the small endless chain design tattoed on his cheek. It was the symbol of the whites' Kun-Zar Quest religion. The man stared intently at Vik.

Singida stopped and looked down at the deep-fibred living carpet. 'Beautiful. A new strain? I've heard about your experimental gardens.'

'I'll gift you with one, for your fee.'

Singida laughed and approached the big, purple bed. His smiling eyes darted and flicked at Vik's large black body. He wheezed slightly. 'Oh, no fee.'

The slave opened the bags.

Singida continued. 'I was with the Emperor when the news reached him. He sent me to you instantly with an escort of a dozen of his inner palace guards. The lions they have! My poor Zingu could barely keep up.'

Singida examined the oozing wound and dart without touching them. 'The paths nowdays! Those damned Egyptians!'

Vik said, 'Those who attacked were of our race.'

'Yes, traitors, hired assassins. Gold will buy anything.' He took Vik's pulse.

Vik had speeded his heartbeats from his normal fifty per minute to eighty-six. He consciously elevated his blood pressure when the physician applied a cuff and poit tube to his upper left arm. The pointer surged up to 190 over 120.

Vik asked, 'Still high?'

'It could be because of your excitement and shock.'

'It's usually high anyway.'

Singida made notes on a pad. 'I hope you can stand pain. I'll have to cut to free the dart.'

'I want you to use Zizu powder.'

'It raises the blood pressure too much. It affects the mind.'

'Not that much.'

'Very well.' Singida personally rummaged in his bags. He brought up small bottles and packets. 'I'll have to test for skin reaction . . . allergies. . . .'

Vik wanted Zizu to dull the pain. He was putting too much concentration and mental energy into manipulating his body processes. If he had to damp nerves and diminish bleeding during the cutting of his thigh he'd be exhausted. An irrisistible need for sleep would overwhelm him. He had been through it before.

And Zizu had some interesting side effects.

Finally, Singida produced from inside his robe his priceless, ancient scalpel. He opened its velvet and leather case.

As Vik watched, amused, Singida swabbed the skin around the wound with a series of acid solutions. He rubbed Vik's left forearm with various substances – powders, oils, pastes. He clucked and hummed as he worked. He said, 'You have a magnificent body, Masil, for your age. It's incredible . . .' His eyes drifted enviously to Vik's heavy male organ, then to the backs of Vik's hands, to the underside of Vik's chin, to Vik's abundant greying hair, to the corners of Vik's eyes. 'I'd like to look at your teeth.'

'My teeth are good. Tend to the dart.'

Singida seemed fascinated, however. 'Remarkable muscle tone and especially youthful skin. No loss of elasticity.' He pinched and prodded.

Vik said impatiently, 'I am of long-lived people. I eat intelligently and I keep my body exercised. But I ache and pain in my joints. That's where my age is.'

He knew Singida was testing his skin for dyes and other artificial colouring – on Ndola's orders. But his pigmentation was natural . . . and had been for over five hundred years. However, Vik would not allow an extremely close examination of his face. There were very tiny signs of the plastic surgery required to alter his lips and nose to full negroid legitimacy. It would take a sharp eye to spot the almost invisible scars, but if Singida knew what to look for. . .

The physician finally opened a packet of Zizu and sprinkled the wound liberally. 'It will be a moment. You'll feel very little when I cut, but . . .' He smiled widely. 'You know Zizu.'

Vik felt the powder dissolving, being absorbed. The ache in his leg dimmed. He began to feel a golden euphoria and a tickling, itching glow in his genitals. Zizu was an aphrodisiac as well as a disinfectant and pain killer. He replied, smiling softly, 'I know its reputation. But I don't envy Ndola's need for it, even if the erotic aspect brings him some pleasures.'

Vik heard the faint creaking of the elevator. Choma was arriving.

Singida made a face. 'Yes, I have to permit him massive doses. The strains of his sex life may kill him before the cancer.'

Vik asked casually, confidentially, 'How long does he have?'

'Not much more than a month. He—' Singida realised he had blundered. 'The Emperor is a tremendously strong-willed man. He will not permit himself to die. I have seen cases where such powerful minds arrest disease and even conquer it. Ndola may outlive us both. My estimate is highly uncertain. I should not have mentioned it. It is of course highly confidential.' He frowned at Mwanza.

Vik said happily to Mwanza, 'You do not hear our words.'

His Private One replied obediently, 'I do not hear your words.'

Singida did not look much relieved. He unwrapped his scalpel, sprinkled its blade with Zizu and heated it above a candle.

Dambo opened the bedroom door. 'Physician Choma is here.'

Singida appeared surprised. He began to speak, stopped, and his normally wide eyes narrowed. 'Isn't Kiambi your physician?'

'Choma is young and quick, skilled and near.'

'Of course. He is of Egyptian ancestry, isn't he?'

Vik shrugged. The Zizu in his blood was filling him with euphoria. He wanted a woman. His desire was becoming obvious.

Vik said, 'A fine doctor is a fine doctor. I sent for him before you arrived.'

Singida shrugged in return. 'Of course.'

Choma entered, a small, thin, intense man in his early thirties. He was followed by a slave, a blonde, blue-eyed youth who carried his bags. The slave was astonished at Vik's size.

Singida greeted Choma warmly. For a moment, the two physicians conferred in a far corner of the bedroom about the cutting that had to be done. Then they returned. They worked together well. Choma deferred to Singida, who did the delicate flesh cutting. Vik watched alertly. His right thigh from the hip to near his knee was dead to sensation.

Singida used his scalpel with skill – slicing deep into muscle to free the dart's head. His hand was steady and knowing. He said, 'Remarkable lack of bleeding.'

Vik said nothing.

Choma stood ready to swab and use small springwood clamps on tiny arteries. He said jokingly, 'That's the Zizu – all his blood is in his pole.'

Within five minutes the dart was removed. Singida dropped the short, bloody shaft into a draw-stringed cotton bag. His slave started to put it away.

Vik said, 'I want that.'

'I was asked to retain it for study. It might lead to those who attacked you.'

'I'll return it to Quebo soon.'

Singida hesitated. He signalled his slave to give the bag to Mwanza. Then he looked sharply at Vik, but said nothing more.

Choma had stitched the wound. His full lips quirked as he sprinkled on more Zizu. He applied a dressing of clean, white cotton and covered everything with a rubbery, porous, adhesive membrane peeled from Jop tree scabs.

One tree, skilfully slashed, would produce enough membrane to cover ten large wounds per day. Vik owned most of the Jop tree orchards in the Empire.

'How long will I be on my back?'

Singida rubbed his wide nose. 'You can take a few steps a day. Nothing violent or you'll rip it open. No riding, no travel for at least a ten-day.'

Choma nodded in agreement.

Vik set special autonomic fast-healing processes in action. He thanked Singida. 'If you will, express my appreciation to Ndola. I'll be back in the palace trees as soon as possible. Until then I will be in constant contact with my able assistants.'

He said to Choma, 'Will you return frequently to check the healing and renew the bandage?'

Choma nodded. His was a large, secret retainer fee. This was the first time he had been called upon in eight years.

'One last thing – provided I stay on my back and stay quiet, is it medically advisable to indulge the Zizu?' It was a mock question, and Vik's lips quirked.

Both doctors laughed. Singida said, 'Yes, enjoy the Emperor's favour tonight!'

The doctors left, followed by their slaves, and Mwanza entered with two girl servants who sponge-bathed Vik. They giggled at his arousal. They patted him dry with thick, soft towels and helped him into a pale green silk robe.

Vik enjoyed himself by caressing their sleek brown bodies. Warm, smooth female flesh always pleased him. One of the two, Feshi, a new girl, all golden brown and velvet-skinned, rounded and buoyant with the juices of puberty, flushed and licked her lips constantly. Her nipples were spectacular little purple fingers. She squirmed when he suckled one for a few seconds. He whispered, '*When I'm well, Feshi. . . .*'

She flushed even more and giggled uncontrollably with the excitement and importance of being wanted by the great Masil.

Twilight was deepening. Glowleaves were uncovered.

Mwanza left with the girls.

Vik lay relaxed. He tuned out the insistent Zizu lust and considered his situation.

He had been careless and he had seriously under-estimated Ndola and Quebo. It had been decades since he had been in any serious personal danger. He'd settled into a rut of power and sex. He'd played the eternally fascinating high finance game again and neglected the little signs of Ndola's illness and personality change. He had ignored Quebo's steady accretion of influence and power.

182

The human element – greed, the fear of death, and the urge to greater power in rulers and would-be rulers – it never changed and it was always deadly.

Vik knew he had to tighten up his economic empire. It was important that the central bank survive and the plan go forward after his disappearance and presumed death. For the ten millionth time, he wished he were not so damned tall! Why had They chosen a six foot five basketball player to become the one immortal man on Earth? Had the alien experimenters expected the average man's size to increase over the generations? Instead, after the horror of the Bio-War had wiped out the world's cows and so many other animals, mankind began to shrink as basic nutrition suffered.

Now he was a giant. His size made hiding after 'dying' and then reappearing with another identity almost impossible. No wonder there was a Kun-Zar myth. No wonder he was always fighting the suspicions and wishes of mortal men and women.

He estimated that Singida would report Masil truly black, merely an exceptional old man. Ndola would have to give up that hope.

But Quebo . . . That man was young enough not to care much about death. He wanted to be Emperor and he wanted to bring down Masil and confiscate the Masil fortune and economic leverage. Quebo was undoubtedly using Ndola's pain and dread of death to manoeuvre the Emperor into constructing a case against Masil – if not as Kun-Zar, then as a traitor, a conspirator with the Indians . . . The northern tribes, even the Allied Amazon States.

Vik knew all about the process of public and private manipulation aimed at destroying a man. So Quebo and Ndola thought they had him vined down while they investigated him, while they made certain arrangements. . . .

No doubt Ndola's favourite love-slave would try to pry in certain areas, and maybe even carry on Singida's experiments in her own way. Vik chuckled. It would be an interesting game; he could use her in more ways than one.

And tomorrow the counter-attack. Stories would spread of Quebo's stealing vast sums of Army gold, cheating the soldiers of their pay as they fought the white barbarians. The bank would delay certain loans and payments. There would be leaf-work problems, hints of corruption in high trees, and the word would go out that Ndola was dying, incapable of rule. Shipments of vital war materials would be delayed. Ships would miss tides, would not arrive on schedule, certain key guilds would walk off government projects.

More important, the east coast tribes would begin to talk again of secession and independence. And there would be plenty of money behind them, many skilled agents, and many army and navy units would declare their sympathy with the movement.

That would show Ndola and Quebo how dangerous it was to strike against Masil. The Emperor had to be reminded of the fragility of his rule and the thinness of his power. He was essentially a figurehead. He held the palace trees because Masil and his banks permitted it. In fact, Vik had had Emperor Pemba assassinated in order to put Ndola into the palace trees. But agony and rapidly approaching extinction had made the man desperate; what had Ndola to lose?

Vik realized Ndola should have been retired years ago. He smiled disgustedly to himself. *Sloppy. Stupid.* He decided to sleep for an hour, or until Mwanza announced the arrival of Chen Li.

It was full dark when his Private One awakened Vik and announced her presence. A few moments later Vik received her.

Chen Li glided regally into the room. Tiny ring-bells decorated her bare toes and tinkled with each step on the golden, living carpet. She wore a violet spidervine gown that clung to her slender, graceful body, rippled free as she moved, then clung briefly again. The gown glowed softly with life. The purple suckers on her nipples were almost as large as her diminutive breasts themselves. Her straight black hair flowed and twisted luxuriously into a smooth knot at the back of her finely modelled head. Jewelled pins sparkled in her hair. Her features were strongly Asian. Her mouth was a delicate rosebud.

She bowed. 'I am proud to be in the presence of the great Masil.'

'I'm happy the news of my injury did not keep you away.'

'The Emperor instructed me to give you pleasure if you wish, or to converse, or to leave . . . if you wish.'

Vik gestured her to his bed. He smiled. 'I'm Zizued to my eyeballs, Li. But we'll eat and talk a bit before we pit you against the drug.'

Chen Li's dark, slanted eyes sparkled. She climbed, child-like, unceremoniously, on to the big purple bed. She was very small beside him.

Mwanza arranged large fluffy pillows behind her and served tall, thin, blue glass drinks of an amber liquor. He served cheese and carved fruit, bread arrows and cinnamon fingers.

Vik joked with her. He noticed she ate carefully and favoured the left side of her jaw. 'Bad tooth?'

Her eyes flickered. 'Yes. But it will not interfere . . .'

'I'm sure it won't.'

After a few minutes, Mwanza entered with a serving cart and two bed trays.

As they ate, Vik asked, 'Are you very recently from the Yaan Temple of Glorious Sun?'

Her eyes widened. 'Yes, only a year. It is not often that any-one this far from my homeland knows of the Temple name.'

'I've known other priestesses of Yaan . . . in my travels.'

Chen Li said proudly, 'I am of the First Order.' But her eyes brimmed with tears. 'I am so far away . . .'

'I know, homesickness.' He knew a special kind of total des-pair, sometimes. Home for him was over a thousand years ago . . . and no way to return.

Chen Li pressed close to him, to his warmth and strength. 'I do not like being a slave. I am not happy. Could the great Masil buy me? . . . and send me home?'

Vik wished she wouldn't beg. But he was used to it; the weak always used their weakness as a weapon against the strong. The problem was there were so many weak and so few strong.

He said, 'Not until the Emperor tires of you. But you know he might die soon.'

'He has given me to Quebo upon his death! That man is

crude and foul. He tried to enter me! He is not interested in my ways.'

'Quebo would never sell you to me. He hates me.'

Li was desperate. 'You are powerful. I have heard that you are more powerful than anyone, even the Emperor. You could acquire me if you wished. I can give you the purest ecstasy. I can. . . .'

She slipped her hand gently, sinuously, into his robe. Her touch was exquisitely light and knowing. She whispered, '*The Zizu will be my ally, not my foe. The great Masil will want me with him forever.*'

Vik signalled Mwanza. He said, 'Take these trays away and you can go to your apartment. Come at dawn.'

Vik was sure Chen Li had no weapon on her body; the loosely woven spidervine material allowed no hiding place. There might be a long, deadly pin in her knotted mass of hair, but Vik intended to check that out very soon. But he didn't believe she had been sent to kill him or further disable him. She was another test, another investigator.

Mwanza retired.

Chen Li left the bed and, facing him, proudly removed her gown. When she eased off the vine's nipple-suckers, the gown faded to a dull lilac. Her body hair had been plucked.

She returned to the bed and curiously, artfully, opened his robe. 'Ahhh . . .'

Vik risked allowing his sexual appetite full satisfaction. He enjoyed her varied techniques, her elaborate sensual preliminaries.

In time he was trembling. Chen Li lay upon him, her slender ivory thighs spread wide on his massive black chest, her warm little hands cupped his sack, her rosebud mouth engulfed him as her head and shoulders rocked to and fro, taking and taking and taking. . .

The hours passed. Chen Li practiced her fantastic skills. She brought him to mind-bending rapture time after time.

It was early morning, before dawn. He was nearly exhausted. Yet the Zizu kept his organ in high erection. He had given her the pleasure of his tongue, delighted her, and had brought her to wracking climaxes. Now she again wept and begged him to save her, to buy her, to free her somehow.

Vik wished he could. He was sleepy, sated, feeling fond of her and sympathetic. But he had to disappear soon. He couldn't take along a pleasure girl, even one as incredibly skilled as Chen Li. Masil had to die and he had to surface, changed, in India. This current period of his immortal life was finished.

Vik said, 'I'm sorry, Li. I can't help you.' He yawned.

She slumped. Her head fell back to his loins. 'Then I am sorry, too. I would have lied for you.' She quickly filled her sweet mouth with his manhood. Her tongue slithered . . . and she suddenly bit down *hard*, using her left molars.

The pain brought him to instant alertness. His big hand crashed against the side of her head. She was knocked aside, senseless.

He was bleeding. He had felt a soft 'give' of one of her teeth and the stab of a hidden sliver of bone. Vik saw bits of hard wax on his flesh. She had injected him with a cunningly hidden hyperdermic syringe. Something was in his bloodstream now, a strange paralysis was spreading in his body. Vik slowed his heartbeat, but it was too late. He cursed and called, 'MWANZA!'.

But his Private One was probably still asleep. No one heard.

Vik couldn't move. In a moment he was barely able to breathe. He knew the drug now: a secretion from a rare vine beetle.

Chen Li stirred, whimpered, and slowly crawled off the bed. She spat several times. She uncovered a bright, white radiance glowleaf lamp, pulled aside the red drapes that covered an oval window, and waved the light before the transparent membrane. Then she sat cross-legged on the carpet and did not look at Vik.

He heard the beginning cries of an all-out assault.

A moment later he heard Mwanza rush in and saw his servant's face appear in his field of vision. He heard Mwanza's anguished questions but could not answer.

The battle outside at the tree's borders and on the grounds was a staccato series of shouts, cries of agony and rage, the throaty roar of disturbed lions.

Mwanza understood after a moment, what Chen Li had done, and the significance of the attack. This was the end. He turned on Chen Li and savagely deflowered her with a long, curved knife. Her shriek seemed to tear out her throat. Then he disembowelled her.

Sobbing, grunting, Mwanza turned Vik on his side so his master could see he had been revenged.

The defenders were quickly overwhelmed. Mwanza and a few servants and tree guards staged a despairing, last-ditch fight outside the high cluster, while Vik lay paralysed, his mind a grim pool of self-recrimination, unable to tell them of the secret passage. He closed his eyes but heard Mwanza's choking, frothy cry as an army spear ripped up through the Private One's lungs. He kept them closed, barely breathing, as triumphant soldiers poured into his bedroom and joked and bragged and pricked his naked body with their spears and swords and bone knives.

He began the process of Slowing. He shut down his body even further, retreating into a kind of half sleep. He was vaguely aware of being moved. He permitted himself marginal hearing and an awareness of body position.

He was taken from his tree. A covered cart. Another room. Lying on his back. A long silence.

He surfaced his awareness: acute hearing first. Footsteps on stone, soldier voices. Grumbling lions. A rat scuttling close by.

Then smell: mustiness . . . straw? A urine-shit smell. The faint, soured aroma of his own body lotion.

Sight: he opened his eyes a crack. Dim . . . a stone ceiling. Rough cut stone walls. A small square gap that leaked daylight. He was in a cell in the palace army prison. He wasn't surprised.

Sensation: the Zizu had worn off, the beetle drug paralysis had almost gone. Pain from his thigh wound, from his bitten organ and from the half dozen or so spear and knife pricks. He damped the injured nerves.

He was naked, lying on a too-short, narrow, vine-latticed wood-frame bed. His bladder was full.

He turned his head slowly to the right and saw the heavy killed-wood counterweighted door. Counterweighted on the outside. The door slid up and down in deep stone grooves. It was locked by wooden bolts that secured the weights and also by bars that sank into slots in the stone.

There was a peephole in the door. He saw a sudden change of light behind the hole as an observer took his face away. Vik knew his own head movement had been noted. The word was on the way to Quebo and Ndola – the prisoner is awake.

The peephole darkened. Another watcher, or the same one returned. Vik lay quiet, thinking. Then he closed his eyes, damped the insistent bladder sensation, and let himself sleep.

He was awakened by voices close to the door to his cell. He recognised Quebo's rough tones. He did not move. Eyes shut.

The bolts and bars were drawn. The door scraped upward. He opened his eyes and watched Quebo enter with three elite army guards, their swords drawn. Singida followed Quebo, and he carried one of his medical bags. No white slaves were permitted in the prison. The door slammed down behind the party.

Quebo met Vik's gaze. He sneered. 'The great Masil.'

Vik began to damp all sensory nerves below the neck. He said laboriously, 'You're clever. But you put too much dungo juice into her tooth. I can only move my head. I can't feel a thing.'

'So much the better, if true.' Quebo ordered Singida, 'Make sure.'

Singida hesitated a second, then came forward. Sweat sheened his fat, round face. He blinked too often. He said, 'There should be sensation . . .' He took a bone needle from a small flat case in his bag and abruptly jabbed Vik's thigh wound through the bandage.

Vik shook his head. His body didn't even quiver. He felt the penetration but no pain. Peripherally, he watched Quebo and studied the tense guards.

Singida jabbed at Vik's sack. No response. Suddenly he stabbed the side of Vik's neck. Vik gasped and violently jerked his head. The rest of his body lay as if dead.

The guards relaxed, as did Quebo. Singida said, 'Yes, she must have gotten in a good solid bite!' He giggled.

Quebo snapped, 'Take your samples.'

Singida took out his priceless scalpel and began to cut off a handful of Vik's greyed, kinky hair.

Vik's fingertip, middle finger, left hand, suddenly throbbed twice, without pain.

He closed his eyes in despair. Quebo's agents had discovered the secret passages. The lasers had fired. The double throb was he signal he had programmed be sent. The minipile that ran the computer and other equipment was now plunging into a swift self-destruct countdown programme. He hadn't wanted it to fall into primitive hands. It, and the other things in that room, was prime evidence of his link to the ancients and their science. It was enough to prove him Kun-Zar the Immortal.

He had thought it better to have the precious computer and allied equipment and lasers destroyed in a mysterious explosion that would kill all witnesses.

Better that Masil be thought a foreign agent or dabbler in the old ways of war. It was out of his hands now. He had no way to stop the automatic countdown. It didn't matter. But he had never thought things would ever get this far out of control. His mouth was dry.

Singida completed cutting free the handful of Vik's dyed, treated hair. He put it into a leather pouch.

Quebo said, 'Ndola is still hoping. He hasn't much time, so he believes in a myth.'

'Where is he ?'

'At the site of his tomb. Supervising its construction. Dying emperors always think of their glory.'

Vik slowly let his bladder go. Urine splashed down between the vine latticework of the crude bed to the straw-littered stone floor.

Singida recoiled. Quebo laughed. The guards relaxed even more. Two of them slid their blades into their scabbards. Vik knew he could kill them all now, in four of five seconds at most. But he wasn't sure it was the best move, there would be other locked doors in the prison building.

His mouth began to taste brassy. He said, 'My associates will take steps to get me out.'

'Your companies and your bank are occupied, under our orders now. They will continue to operate in the Emperor's interest or their officers will be executed.'

Quebo kicked some dirty straw toward the rivulet of urine creeping across the floor. 'Caiundo is under arrest, along with your other assistants in the Ministry. My staff has taken over.'

Vik asked, 'Why did you attack?'

'Doctor Singida found your body amazingly youthful for your age, and so Ndola . . . .'

Singida said quickly, 'Skin . . . body fat. The fingernails. Upper lip. The body hair pattern—'

Quebo cut him off. 'And Chen Li. She knew men, old and young, in special ways. Blindfolded, she could tell an old man's stem and sack from a young man's. We tested her. She was to drug you and signal if she was convinced you were not really an old man.

'The Zizu makes any man young.'

'Zizu aside, she wasn't fooled.'

'I want to see Ndola!'

'You probably will. If you can live forever he naturally wants your secret – and so do I – before killing you.'

In the back of his mind, Vik was counting seconds. He said disgustedly, 'I am not Kun-Zar!'

Quebo shrugged. 'We'll find out. I have men searching your tree, inch by inch. And after Singida—'

The stone floor heaved sharply and settled back, groaning. Dust drifted down from the walls and ceiling.

Singida cringed. There was shouting outside. Lions coughed. Quebo cursed. 'We never have earthquakes!'

A strange, unfamiliar, stomach-rolling terror ruptured Vik's composure for an instant. He felt vulnerable now. He hadn't been in this bad a situation for six hundred years. And this time it could be the end. He desperately wanted to keep on living!

Then the rumbling thunder of a distant explosion filled the cell. The deep reverberation penetrated stone, wood, flesh and bone. A fine rain of grit settled from the ceiling. Quebo, Singida, and the guards were disconcerted. They all glanced up.

One guard, sword unsheathed, alert, stood close by the head of the bed upon which Vik lay. A second guard stood uneasily by the closed door. He was lean and nervous. The third guard, sword sheathed, stood alone in the back corner of the cell, near the tiny window. Singida was unarmed. Quebo wore a ceremonial dagger with his robe of office. It was now or never.

Vik exploded into action!

One powerful, vicious kick sent Singida sprawling into the guard in the far corner.

In a split second Vik was up and turning, reaching for the most dangerous guard whose naked sword was coming up. With a stiff, ruthless, two-fingered jab he put out the man's eyes.

Vik roared terrifyingly for effect as he seized the sword and simultaneously shoved the man at the door off balance. He whipped around and slashed deep into the side of that guard's neck. The severed artery spurted blood toward the ceiling.

Both guards were screaming. Quebo bellowed and struggled with the golden scabbard fastener that retained his dagger.

Vik went for the third elite guard, who was barely on his feet after Singida had crashed into him. Vik's bloody sword pierced his throat. Vik twisted and pulled it free. The man collapsed, gurgling horribly.

Quebo had freed his dagger. Vik expertly hacked, parting the thumb tendon. The dagger fell to the dirty, bloody straw and Quebo went to his knees, clutching his hand.

Vik stood alert among the bodies and the screams. He waited for the heavy, killed-wood door of the cell to rise and for more guards to enter.

It was what he wanted.

But he heard more bolts slide into place. An eye peered at the peephole. Cursing, he lunged and sent the sword point through the hole. It scraped into bone and brought an agonised shriek.

He yanked the sword free and spun. Quebo was still on his knees. Singida simply cowered and mewed with terror.

Vik quickly and precisely killed the writhing, blinded guard. The one with the spurting neck artery had slumped to the floor. His hand uselessly covered the flowing, surging wound. He watched, dull-eyed with shock, as Vik took up Quebo's dagger and plunged the curved blade into his chest beneath the sternum – to his heart.

Quebo watched with fear and hatred.

Vik moved to Quebo, towering over him. 'Order the door up!'

'No. They have orders. If something like this happened – under no circumstances. Even if I try to countermand those orders from inside. Even if you torture us. The door will never go up.'

Vik believed him, but lifted Quebo roughly to his feet and shoved him to the door. 'Try, anyway.' He held Quebo's slashed hand in a tightening vice grip.

Quebo panted with the excruciating pain. He croaked, '*Let us out! I'm wounded. I order the door up!*'

An eye came briefly to the peephole. 'We cannot, sir.'

'*I command it!*'

'We dare not. We have sent word to the Emperor.'

Vik let Quebo stagger to the back wall of the cell. He gathered the swords, sat on the bed, and waited.

He gave permission for Singida to gather the scattered medical tools, retrieve the bag, and attend to Quebo's ruined hand.

Quebo sat with his back to the wall. He glowered. He asked, 'If you're immortal, why do you fight like this? Why do you risk everything? It was you – you personally who killed my agents at old Kiambi's tree, didn't you? *Why?*'

Vik stared, but didn't answer.

It was three hours before there were significant sounds beyond the door. It was still daylight.

Then Ndola's tired, faint voice came. 'Kun-Zar?'

Vik didn't bother denying it. He spoke to the door. 'I want free. How can that be arranged?'

'Come to the peephole.'

Vik gestured Singida and Quebo to the rear of the cell. If they moved he'd hear them in the rustling of the straw. He kept the swords and dagger with him and looked out through the small hole in the thick wood.

Ndola sat wearily in the corridor on a cushioned wooden stool. He was shockingly bent and skeletal in his blue and gold-patterned silk toga. His dark brown skin showed liver spots as spatters of black. Stark veins seemed to crawl in his skull-like temples.

The Emperor was up on Zizu and hemp, but still fighting pain. His gaze was feverishly keen with excitement.

Vik saw no guards, could hear no guards.

Ndola lifted a sticklike arm, pointing. 'You *are* Kun-Zar?'

'Yes.'

Ndola cackled '*Yes, yes, yes!* You *are* immortal?'

'Yes.'

'*HOW?*' The effort and desperation in the question shook the frail body.

Vik didn't know. But he said, 'Free me and I'll tell you. It may not work because of your age and disease, but ... But it might. Free me and I'll give you the secret. I'll leave the empire. I'll never return. There's room on this planet now for two immortal men.'

Ndola licked his lips. He showed teeth in a grimace. He changed the subject. 'What was in the ground beneath your tree? Forty-six men were killed. Steam is still coming from the hole. There is a lot of melted metal down there.'

'I won't tell you.'

'The metal is worth a fortune. It's mine if I let you go free!'

'Agreed.'

Ndola suddenly shuddered and sat very still for a moment. Finally, he asked, 'Will this pain go?'

'Yes, the cancer will die. But you'll stay your present age – forever.'

Ndola's eyes glittered.

Vik said truthfully, as a precaution, 'A long time ago I learned to be absolute master of my body. I can withdraw into my mind and will my body to die, if I have to. I can deaden myself to any pain for any length of time. I can stop all hearing, all sight, all smell, all touch ... all sense contact with the outside world. I am beyond torturing. I can't be *forced* to give what you want.'

Ndola nodded reluctantly. 'I know you were "paralysed" this morning and proved it. The guards watched from the peep-hole. Yet when the explosion came . . .'

From behind Vik, Singida bleated, 'Free us, Great One! This devil will kill us!'

Ndola heard. 'You are not important, Singida. And maybe I am better off without Quebo.' He smiled faintly. He breathed easier. His pain was gone for a while.

Vik said, 'There is no advantage for you in killing me.'

Ndola shrugged. 'There are certain matters to be balanced.' He changed the subject again. 'How did you make yourself into a black man? Kun-Zar is supposed to be white.'

'In Egypt. There used to be drugs that could affect a certain gland which governed skin colour. And there were a few sur-geons in the guild who could change a face – this way. It took five operations.'

'What is the secret of your immortality?'

'Free me.'

'Is it a drug?'

Vik hesitated. 'Yes.'

'You lie! It would be known. The Egyptians would have known of it. The old science . . . They would have known dur-ing the Bio-War. They knew *everything*!'

'Ndola, I lived through the Bio-War. The formula for the drug was given to me long before that war.'

'But their science! They would have discovered it! They knew *everything*!'

'No. Not everything. There were many small corners of knowledge—'

'*How did you become immortal?*'

'It was an accident,' Vik lied. 'There was an immortal man before me. He was fatally wounded in a freak train accident. I was a passenger on a less damaged car. I got to him first. He knew he was dying with only a few moments to live, and he told me the formula.'

'You believed him?'

'No, I thought he was raving. But I remembered the for-mula. And just for fun, because it seemed harmless, I tried it out. I mixed a batch and ate it once a year. After ten years I saw I hadn't aged. After twenty years I was *sure!*'

Ndola was clearly sceptical. 'And what are the ingredients? Are the same things available now, in this empire, as were in ancient times in America?'

'Yes, the elements are in common—'

'What are you telling me, great Kun-Zar? That you wander through the jungle picking this and that, pulling a root here, a root there? Do you take me for that great a fool?'

Vik said nothing for a few seconds. He sighed. 'What do you have to lose? Do you *want* to die?'

Ndola rubbed his bony hand over his eyes. 'No. But I'm a realist. When my men discovered your secret passages below your tree, they sent a man back to the palace trees with the word. He saw a fantastic machine with lights and incredible controls . . . An Ancient's machine . . . pure gleaming metal . . . But then my men must have disturbed the machine. You had it set to explode if the wrong people came close to it.'

Ndola met Vik's eye. 'I ask myself why was it so precious that it could not be allowed to survive in our hands? What secret did it hold? And I answer: It held the secret of your immortality. And now, without that machine you are again mortal. You will die in a few years. Unless . . .'

'You're wrong!'

'Unless there is another machine like it somewhere in the world. The great Kun-Zar would have secreted somewhere a duplicate for emergency use. Hmm?'

Vik shook his head. 'NO!'

'But this second machine would be far away. It would take a healthy man months, perhaps a year to reach. So I must die.'

Vik said desperately, 'It's a formula. The stuff tastes ugly and you must drink it every hour for ten hours—'

'But you just said it had seemed harmless to you when you first tried it.' Ndola shook his head. 'Your lies do not knit well.'

Vik put defeat in his voice. 'The machine is in India. We could reach it in a month.'

'You could. On the way I would probably die. Or your agents would attack . . . You could. . . .'

Ndola bent over, grunting with sudden agony. He whispered, '*It's bad. Worse than . . . before. . . .*' He nearly toppled from the stool.

Vik felt all hope slipping away. Ndola's virulent cancer was eating his life, too.

Ndola looked up. His sneer was distorted, but clear. '*Kun-Zar. Mighty immortal Kun-Zar. Masil! You've been laughing at me for years . . . twenty years . . . playing games with me. Pretending. Ard now I have you! No. I'll die. But in my dying I'll not be made a fool! And I'll have one great satisfaction. I'll be remembered for one great deed.*' He grinned a death grin and gestured weakly. '*Guards!*'

They came and helped him leave.

Vik turned and bleakly regarded Quebo and Singida.

Quebo said mockingly, 'The immortal man is mortal.'

As Vik waited he stared into his mind at his long life. The incredible adventures, triumphs, failures . . . all were a waste . . . because he had been complacent, stupid and careless this time. Beyond any recovery. A blind, smug, arrogant idiot!

It was getting dark in the cell when Vik heard guards approach and begin doing something to the door. A muffled scraping. . .

He left the bed for a close look. They were caulking the cracks and seams. Sealing the cell.

He turned to Quebo. 'Why are they doing this?'

Quebo lowered his head.

The peephole was plugged with cork.

There were sounds outside the tiny window. It was blocked. The cell was plunged into total darkness.

Vik knew then the aliens would let him die. He had long ago decided his immortality was an experiment. Perhaps all mankind was an experiment. Now his part, after a little more than a thousand years, was ending.

Vik heard hissing in the darkness . . . and caught the first whiff of an acrid gas.

He went mad with rage. 'YOU COWARDLY SONS OF DISEASED DOGS! LION FUCKERS! YOU CAN TELL NDOLA . . . HE . . .'

Vik choked as unseen clouds of the gas were pumped into the cell. He heard Singida and Quebo gasping and coughing. He was dizzy. He began slowing his respiration and heartbeat, desperately trying to avoid. . . .

He was abruptly on his back on the cold stone floor. His mind slewed and skidded. He managed to think, *What a shitty way to die.* Then consciousness warped away and he sank into a black whirlpool.

But did not die, did not fully submerge.

Vik's awareness of self returned. His mind swam up from nothingness, captured by a creaking sound. . . . He was lying on his back on softness. . . .

Bright light penetrated his closed eyelids.

Vik opened his eyes slightly. A great slab of sparkling, transparent crystal hung over him, swaying, held in the air by plaited ironvine ropes in a heavy-duty pulley system.

To his right – an on-edge slab of the same clear crystal, only a foot from his shoulder . . . and another slab to his left. Cushioned white velvet under him.

He was lying naked in a tomb of the crystalline plastic from the ice-lands of North America!

As his eyes adjusted to the sunlight and the rainbow glitter from the crystal, Vik saw twenty of the Emperor's Guards spaced on the marble dais around the huge, transparent coffin, facing inward. Their plumed lances were levelled.

The top slab of crystal hung only eighteen inches above the top of the coffin. Another, identical tomb stood a dozen feet away, empty.

A voice said, 'He's awake, Great One.'

Ndola's weak voice came to Vik. 'Good! Be ready at my signal to lower the top.'

Vik considered a quick scramble from the coffin . . . but his first move would bring those deadly, bone lances – Impossible.

Ndola was carried on a cushioned litter close to the giant sarcophagus. Near him, hanging back, was Empress Punia, her lovely brown face a mask of controlled horror.

Ndola wore a golden leaf robe that was only flickeringly alive, with his massive, intricately-worked jewelled Necklace of

Empire. Beside him lay the gold and diamond encrusted staff, while on his sunken-cheeked skull the Empire Crown glittered with hundreds of diamonds, rubies, sapphires, set in gold, silver and platinum.

Ndola stopped five feet from the coffin, just inside the cordon of alert Imperial Guards. He chuckled painfully. 'I've had a gold plaque cast in your honour. It reads, 'Mighty Kun-Zar, the Once Immortal Man, Defeated and Entombed by the Great Ndola.' It will be set in stone – here – and I shall be at your side.'

Vik turned his head to look fully at Ndola, and spotted the amethyst-necklaced commander of the Guards. The commander had taken a lot of money from Masil in exchange for information and secret loyalty.

Vik sat up and put every element of deep, vibrant, baritone power and authority he possessed into his words. He spoke directly to the Guards and their commander.

'*I am Kun-Zar the Immortal. I will reward you all with high command, wealth, and my favour for as long as you live. Disobey me now and my curse will curdle your wives' wombs and you will father monsters! Your stems will wither and you will live in shame and sickness the rest of your lives!*'

His rich, strong voice overrode Ndola's attempt to interrupt. Without pause, without hesitation, Vik commanded, pointing at Ndola, 'SEIZE HIM!' And confidently, calmly, unhurriedly, began to climb from the coffin.

There was an instant of hesitation in the men. A flickering of eyes to see if anyone would obey. The commander was poised – eyes narrowed, body tense, about to act—

Ndola screamed, 'DODOMA!'

And a full company of the elite Palace Trees Defenders rustled into the temple from their secret positions just outside. Every archway was suddenly filled with green and gold clad warriors.

The tension broke and the Imperial Guards prodded Vik back down, inside the rectangular crystal tomb. He closed his eyes in despair. There was almost nothing left, and a terrible dread was claiming him. He opened his eyes and looked around at the guards, at Ndola, at the temple. . .

And noticed an observer in a second-level alcove, a white face peering down. The bearded face of Sinida's slave with the small Kun-Zar Quest religious design tattooed on the cheek.

Ndola had committed a terrible blunder. He had publicly confirmed Kun-Zar's existence in Kinshasa. Word would reach the white barbarian hordes in the north and they would sweep invincibly south to join him, to make him their king again. They did not believe he could be killed, and maybe they were right.

Vik begged. 'I ask of you, Great Ndola, one last request.'

'What do you want ?'

He turned up his palms in supplication, and spoke an old ritual:

'Give me a full belly for my journey into death. Give me meat and let me eat my fill.'

Ndola studied him. A long moment passed. A slow, malicious smile spread the Emperor's lips. 'I can't deny you.'

He pointed to Empress Punia. 'Here is your lover. Eat *her*! Take your fill of her, because if you don't she'll die later to-day for betraying me in your bed.' He gestured to the two nearest Guards. 'Give her to him.'

Punia gasped and shrank away. Her face was pale, her eyes enormous. She screamed as the Guards took her and dragged her to the huge coffin. She disintegrated into hysterical, squalling terror.

Ndola ordered, 'Take her bracelets and crown!'

They obeyed, then lifted her and thrust her into the massive tomb.

The emotionally shattered girl fell on to Vik and blindly clutched at him, sobbing, pressing to him instinctively for warmth and protection. Her pink leafgown had been torn. It flickered softly, one of its suckers hanging loose from her large, exertion-swollen left nipple.

The hanging slab of crystal, its square edges sharp and perfect, swayed ponderously above them in a slow, eccentric arc, disturbed by the Guards and by Punia's flailing body.

Ndola coughed. 'I knew. I knew everything.' He lifted one

thin arm in a brief ritual salute. 'You have your meat, Kun-Zar. Does it matter that it is alive?'

Vik braced himself. He closed off part of his personality, part of his character. *He had to survive!* This was his only chance now. He had to go ahead. His mouth was bone dry.

Mortals mattered to him. He had come to think of them as his property, his pets, his children, his responsibility as a species. He had been guiding and rebuilding civilisation as best he could since the horror of the Bio-War had swept over the world. In another five hundred years or so the few viable monsters inhabiting the icy wastes of what had been the United States and Canada would have bred true and would be spreading south . . . eventually they would cross the oceans.

He had to be alive when that challenge came to mankind.

Vik had not been the perfect steward of his gift. He had indulged himself in every way possible. He had been a ferocious king in the north. And he had been soft and loving for a hundred years in the Pacific. He had been everything and done everything.

And now—

He held Punia and slipped his right hand under her slim neck. He kissed her trembling lips. '*I'm sorry.*' He poured strength into his big hand and made a powerful vice of his thumb and fingers. Her carotid arteries were squeezed shut.

Punia's brain, suddenly deprived of a flow of fresh oxygen and nutrient-rich blood, began to die. Her consciousness winked out. Her body began to convulse.

Vik kept up the pressure until her heart stopped for lack of a proper signal from the dying autonomic system in the lower brain. Other controls stuttered and died. The body voided its wastes with great jerking spasms.

Vik flipped the body to his left side on to its back and tore the leafgown away. He used hooked fingers to rip open its stomach and tear away the muscles. Blood spattered him and welled up in the gaping ragged hole as he plunged his hand into the cavity and found the warm, barely-still heart. He ripped it free and forced himself to eat it in huge rending bites. He barely chewed.

201

Vik was into a kind of trance, a fierce autohypnotic action sequence that forbade most 'human' thought. He heard but did not hear the gasps from the hardened Guards. Even Ndola's shocked, reflexive laughter did not penetrate.

Vik found the liver, clawed it free and wolfed it down. Then both kidneys – biting, swallowing as fast as he could, drawing ragged breaths, snorting against the bloody gobbets he crammed against his working mouth.

He ate only the heart, liver and kidneys. Then he heaved the ruined body out of the crystal coffin.

He lay back on the blood-soaked white velvet. He saw Ndola, face contorted, gesture for the lowering of the massive overhead transparent slab.

The Guardmen closed in to prevent a last-instant attempt at escape. The ironvine cables moved, the pulleys creaked. . . .

Vik closed his eyes and began to slow his metabolism. He had fuel now, rich in the highest quality proteins, fats, vitamins. The interior of the tomb was large enough to provide air for years if he could slow himself enough, and he hoped the lid slab would not be an absolute airtight fit. He hoped the emperor that followed the doomed Ndola would open the coffin. Or that vandals would try to breach the seal . . . or that he could last until the white barbarians heard of Kun-Zar's entombment and came to set him free.

One end of the top slab grated into position. The final ropes were pulled free and the mighty crystal slab thudded down. The sound echoed in the temple.

Vik concentrated on the ancient techniques of body control. His heartbeat quietened and slowed. Forty beats per minute . . . twenty . . . ten . . . five. . . . His oxygen requirement sank to the absolute minimum.

He settled into a deep, murky dream.

Earth's one immortal man waited.